CW01669096

The Padre

Danny Crowe

Grosvenor House
Publishing Limited

This book is published by
Grosvenor House Publishing Ltd
Link House
140 The Broadway, Tolworth, Surrey, KT6 7HT.
www.grosvenorhousepublishing.co.uk

This book is a work of fiction. Any resemblance to people or events, past or present, is purely coincidental.

A CIP record for this book
is available from the British Library

ISBN 978-1-78623-330-1

For Joe and Joan Wicks who made the publication of this book possible

Chapter 1

'Wake up, sir! Wake up.'

Simon Renton fought against the impulse to turn over and ignore the voice whispering insistently in his ear. Instead he reluctantly poked his throbbing head out from beneath his army issue blankets and opened his eyes. Raising himself slowly from his bunk bed he turned his stiff, aching body towards the voice coming from the gloom of the officers' sleeping quarters. As he sat up further, a battered tin mug, its contents steaming, was pressed into his shaking hands.

'It's a cold un' this morning and no mistake, sir. Bit of fog about, too. You asked to be called well before stand-to, remember, sir?'

Collins, the duty orderly, was coming into focus now, squatting on his heels, close to the bed.

'Thank you, Collins! I'm awake now. You can carry on.' His voice was hoarse; the inside of his mouth was dry and his tongue felt as woolly as the blankets wrapped tightly around him. He took a sip of the scalding tea and winced as the hot liquid burnt his lips. He blew on the tea to try and cool it down, his cold breath slow to disperse in the cold damp air.

'It's still dark outside, sir.' Collins was still at his side, seemingly in no hurry to move away. 'Mind you, what with the fog and all, it might keep Fritz quiet for a bit.'

'Yes, yes, I dare say you're right.' Renton, the pounding in his head increasing, was in no mood for conversation. 'Look, I told you, I'm awake now. I won't go back to sleep. Get on with your duties. I'll get up when I finish my tea.'

Through bleary eyes he watched Collins slowly move away and disappear into the gloom. I shouldn't take it out on Collins, he told himself. It's not his fault I have to go around the trenches on Sunday mornings. Morris had ordered it; said it would be good for the men's morale. Renton could understand the boy's reluctance not to move. It must be freezing outside. Still, he thought, he's better off working as an orderly than he would be if he were an infantryman in the trenches. Good looking boy too, underneath all that grime and mud. He took another sip of his rapidly cooling tea and pulled the blankets closer. Even though the air was cold, his nose quickly picked up on the fetid smell that constantly pervaded the dugout. He remembered how much it had repulsed him on his arrival some weeks ago when he first entered the labyrinth of tunnels and underground accommodation that made up that part of the front line. It was more a cocktail of smells really, a mixture of unwashed bodies, decay, mildew and stale tobacco smoke. Had he only been here a few weeks? It seemed more like a year. He could hear no movement from the slumbering figures all around him. Lying in the dark, both hands cupped around his mug of tea, he went back over the chain of events that had led him to such a ghastly place.

His career as a chaplain had begun with good intentions and plenty of religious faith some twelve years previously when England was at peace with most of the world. The son of a clergyman, he had benefited from a good education that had seen him get a First in English and Divinity. He had then gone on to a reputable Clergy College and on completion stunned his father by informing him he wished to be an army chaplain. Both his parents opposed his wanting to join the army. His father, a man of peace, who had strong anti-war views, was particularly against it and his concern for his son was heartfelt and sincere. He had assumed that his son would follow in his footsteps and take up a respectable parish in England: the thought of wasting his talents on a career in the army appalled him.

But Renton was adamant. His application was successful and he was given officer rank on joining the army chaplaincy. The first few years of his career were agreeable enough. He was young, and eager to please his superiors. He spent most of his time going from one army base in England to another deputising for his fellow chaplains whom were either serving abroad on leave. He was by nature a loner, and this combined with a certain arrogance in his dealings with people, did not make him overly popular in the mess with his fellow officers. But his patriotism and his eagerness to serve anywhere impressed everyone who met him. In those early years of his service he confidently believed that his superiors looked upon him as a chaplain of great potential. But, for one reason or another, those early aspirations had had never been fulfilled and now, twelve years later, he was full of bitterness and disillusionment.

Renton put the mug down on the floor and reached into the large ammunition box that served as a locker for his personal possessions. Relief swept over him as he felt the reassuring shape of the bottle in his hand. He shook the bottle quietly to confirm that it was nearly empty and made a mental note to speak to the quartermaster sergeant as soon as possible. Not this morning though, unfortunately. After stand to he would have a service to take: he would try to get it as quickly as possible. When the war started he thought, like many others, that it would be over quickly and that it wouldn't affect him. But as the war dragged on more and more men were needed for the fighting. That in turn meant more chaplains were needed to look after the men's spiritual needs and being a bachelor, he was an obvious choice. He hadn't volunteered for a posting so his arrival in France a few months earlier had come as a shock to him. Once he had been slim and reasonably good looking with delicate, almost feminine, features. But over the years his face had filled out and he had put on weight. He was now thirty-four years old and didn't cut a dashing figure by any means. His uniform that had once fitted him like a glove was now stretched tight over his body and he had become careless about other aspects of his personal appearance.

To his great relief he was initially employed on routine chaplain's duties away from the front line. It was boring but at least he was working in a safe area and was housed in reasonable comfort. But then came the moment he had been dreading. He was ordered to report to Colonel Morris, the senior army chaplain of the area. Morris, a tall, immaculately dressed officer kept the interview brief.

'There's a padre needed in this sector here.' Morris had pointed at a large map pinned up on the wall of his office and stabbed his finger over the name of a village that stood a few miles east of the River Somme. 'General Haig's offensive has finally come to a halt in this area after nearly four months of bitter fighting. The army is consolidating its gains and settling in for the winter. A lot of lives were lost to gain that ground and we don't want to lose it if the Germans counter attack. Your job will be to boost the morale of the men by making them realise that religion can be a great source of comfort and salvation in times of great danger.'

It was obvious to Renton that Morris was a man who believed firmly in his God, his King and his country. He was also a man who liked discipline.

'We must make the men realise that God is on our side and that right will prevail,' he carried on, 'they must put their trust in their officers and the generals that are leading them.' It was imperative, Renton was informed, that all chaplains should get this message over to the troops. Morris concluded the interview by saying that the war had provided the opportunity for the right sort of padre to achieve great things and thus enhance his chances of promotion in the chaplainry.

Renton agreed with the Colonel's point of view about senior officers. He was of the opinion that if the rank and file would only do exactly as ordered then England could not fail to win the war. He had no doubt of the bravery and fighting qualities of the British soldier, but he believed that they had to be led by officers who had an upper class background.

He drank the last of the tea and put the mug down by the side of his bed. It had got lighter in the dugout and he could now make out more clearly the figures of his fellow officers still asleep in their beds. Across from him he could see the sleeping figure of the man who had greeted him on his arrival. Major John Kerr was a wiry, taciturn Scot, who had taken over command of the Westhampton Regiment after the death of their colonel. Kerr was a regular soldier and a twelve-month veteran of the front-line fighting on the Western front. At their first meeting he had told Renton that he was thankful to be still alive after his experiences during the Somme offensive and that he was now under no illusions about a rapid outcome to the war.

'You'd better make yourself as comfortable as you can,' he had told Renton, 'I've a feeling the regiment will be holding on here for quite a while. We're in no position to continue attacking after our losses recently: we lost over half the regiment you know.'

'Yes, so I heard. I'm sorry.' Renton had said. 'Still I understand from General Haig's comments that the casualty rate was considered acceptable for the amount of ground gained.'

Kerr hadn't replied but stared at him in such a contemptuous way that made Renton wish he hadn't spoken. It had not been the most auspicious start in his new posting.

It was time to stop reminiscing and get moving. As he got out of his bed he ran his hand quickly over his chin. Not too much stubble; he would be able to get by without a shave this morning. It really was very annoying not to have an orderly to look after him, especially when, with his officer rank he was entitled to one. In the past he had always had a batman who not only had looked after his personal needs but had also assisted him with his religious services. He had mentioned this to Kerr shortly after his arrival and was told he would be allocated someone in due course. Renton didn't want Kerr to allocate him someone. He already knew whom he wanted. The good looking boy, Collins, would do very nicely. He had noticed the way Collins hung around the officers, happy to run their errands, or clean their equipment. He would do anything it seemed, to keep out of the front line. He felt a tingle of anticipation run through him at the prospect of having Collins as his orderly. He would definitely talk to Kerr about the boy later.

Chapter 2

Renton quickly dressed and put on his cap and greatcoat. Remembering to slip a bible into his pocket he quietly left the officers sleeping quarters. The Westhampton Regiment occupied a part of the front line that was made up chiefly of abandoned German trenches and some additional tunnels and defence positions that had been constructed on Kerr's orders. Coming out of the underground accommodation into the damp fog of early morning he instinctively bent low as he trod on the wet, slimy duckboards that lined the trench floor. It would take him about five minutes to get from the rear area of the Westhampton's position to the front line trenches and visibility in the fog was probably only a few yards but he was taking no chances.

Keeping low while moving about in the trenches was imperative: it could prove fatal to show ones head over the parapet. He had seen for himself what it meant to get careless. Shortly after his arrival a private was shot through the throat by a German sniper. The man had managed to get his hands on some wine that one of his mates had bought back with him after a visit to the nearby town. The wine had made him forgetful about the dangers of war. Renton had watched in horror as frothy, bright red blood spurted out of the Private's throat. He took less than a minute to die. Afterwards a horrified Renton had said a prayer over the body. It was a harsh introduction to life at the front.

In some places the duckboards were submerged up to a depth of six inches under a covering of viscous, foul smelling mud. Huge rats, made brave by the rich pickings of half buried decaying corpses, scurried around his feet as he slowly trudged towards the first fire step position. Suddenly he stopped, a shiver running down his spine, as one rat, bolder than the rest attempted to run up his leg and on to the edge of the parapet. Losing its grip, the rat leapt off, and disappeared into the fog to rejoin its companions. Renton leant heavily against the sandbagged wall of the trench and wiped the sweat from his face with the back of his hand. He was shaking uncontrollably and needed time to compose himself. He would never get used to the rats. They were everywhere in the trenches, some as big as the rabbits that played in the fields near the vicarage where his parents lived when he was a child. But these rats were not cuddly creatures like the rabbits he remembered. The rats terrified him. Nothing could be done to stop them getting in the trenches and the rear areas. In the daytime he saw them scavenging for food. During the night he could hear them scratching in the darkness. He even dreamt of them when he was asleep. He looked up and down the trench to see if anybody had seen his encounter with the rat. It was unlikely given the poor visibility. Recovering his composure as best he could he carried on. The fog was turning to rain now. A steady drizzle was falling. In a few hours it would make the trench floor even more of a quagmire than it was now. It had rained almost constantly since the regiment's arrival with the result that everything that a man wore, or slept in, was either damp, or worse still soaking wet and covered in mud.

He could hear the sounds of heavy guns firing some miles further away. He was getting used to the distinctive Crump-Crump sound they made. At least they were not aimed at the Westhampton's section of the line. It was some other poor devil's turn to take a hammering. At last he arrived at the first fire step, a raised section of the floor of the trench on which men could stand and fire at the enemy: a risky undertaking owing to the deadly accuracy of the German snipers. Only recent arrivals with no previous experience of war in the trenches were foolish enough to try and engage the enemy. Most of the time the men, especially the older hands, took the opportunity to catch up on some sleep, play cards, or clean their weapons.

Two faces, both with expressions of bored indifference, looked up at him through the rain. Renton sat down beside them. Knowing how the guard system worked he knew they must be on the last two hours of the night watch

'Morning men,' he tried to sound cheerful: the image of the rat still with him, 'did you have a reasonably quiet night?'

The eldest looking of the two, wearing Corporal's stripes on his arm, answered. 'Can't complain, Padre, a few Whiz Bangs were lobbed over, and some illuminations sent up, but nothing serious. The fog helped a lot. None of their patrols out, I reckon.'

'Yes, that must have been some relief. You must be very tired after straining your eyes in the dark for the last four hours.' Even as he spoke, he was aware of the stupidity of his remark. In the trenches men were constantly tired.

'You're early, Padre. It's not time for stand- to, yet.'

Renton detected a note of sarcasm in the Corporal's voice.

'Did you have trouble sleeping, sir? Is that what's got you up so early?'

'No. I was woken up early by the duty orderly to do my rounds.' Renton was keen to move the conversation on. He didn't see why he had to justify himself to a mere Corporal.

The younger man, skinny, with a thin sly looking face, joined the conversation. 'Drink's the best thing for a good nights sleep, sir. That is, when you can get it, in this hellhole of a place.'

'Yes. A nice tot of rum, or whisky, I prefer whisky myself,' the Corporal said, nodding his head in agreement with his mate, 'how about you, sir? Do you like a drink or is it forbidden because of your profession, like?'

They were looking directly at him now, awaiting his reply, their faces giving nothing away. On the face of it, it was a seemingly innocent question. Or was it?

Anger and embarrassment welled up inside him as he scanned their faces for any signs of insolence. Their expressions remained impassive. Did they know anything? What had they heard? Had Quartermaster Sergeant Watkins been indiscreet? Then suddenly it occurred to him that perhaps he was being paranoid. His anger subsided a little. Maybe it was an innocent question after all. After all, there seemed to be only two topics of conversation with the lower ranks, sex and drink.

Before he could give an answer the Corporal spoke again. 'Well, sir. Is it, 'verboten' then, as old Fritz might say?' The Corporal laughed, pleased with himself for displaying his knowledge of German.

'Verboten, that's a good one, Corp. Very good.' The young Private joined in with the laughter.

'No, Corporal, it's not 'verboten' as you so eloquently put it.' Renton's voice had a touch of irritability to it. 'For your information, as you both seem so interested, I enjoy a social drink as much as the next man. My chaplain's duties don't preclude me from drinking alcohol. I'm not a Muslim, you know. I am allowed a drink if I want one.' He realised that he had said too much: that he was allowing himself to be dragged down to their level. This wasn't the purpose of his being there at such an early hour. Anyway, he should be dictating the conversation, not them. After all, he was there for a reason. 'I'm taking a service later this morning, about 10 o'clock. Will you two be attending, do you think?'

The Corporal shook his head. 'No. Sorry, Padre. We'll be asleep you see, knackered after the night watch.'

'Yea, we're dog tired, Padre.' The young Private tried to sound disappointed but failed.

'Oh, yes of course.' Renton wasn't going to let them off the hook that easily. He took the bible from his pocket. 'Never mind, perhaps you'd like me to say a few words before stand-to begins. How about saying a prayer together now?'

The two men looked at each other in embarrassment before closing their eyes and bending their heads in an attitude of prayer. Renton smiled as he watched their discomfort and savoured his little moral victory over them. He was used to being underestimated. Because he wore a dog collar and was a non-combatant some of the troops thought they could treat him with less respect than their regular front line officers. They tended to lump him in with the medics, stretcher-bearers, and the other auxiliaries. But he had officer status and he knew that as far as the lower ranks were concerned, a request from him was as good as an order. Of course there was another reason that some of the men didn't object. There were many that didn't expect to survive the war and thought that it wouldn't hurt to have a word put in for them in the afterlife. As he finished the prayer, Renton became aware of more men appearing in the trench. Stand-to had begun. Just before dawn was the most likely time of day for any enemy attack. Helmeted, khaki clad figures, bleary eyed and grumbling, were sluggishly taking up their allocated positions around the defensive perimeter of the regiment's sector. It was common practice on both sides for men to "stand-to" with their weapons until it was fully light and the danger of a surprise attack had passed.

For the next forty minutes or so he made his way around the trenches. He stopped at regular intervals to chat with the men and to offer them prayer and encouragement. He told them exactly what Morris had instructed him to tell them. They had God on their side. They would be victorious in the end. For the most part they listened to him politely but disinterestedly. Only one or two were genuinely pleased to see him and willingly joined him in prayer. He was getting impatient. He took out his watch and checked the time. The watch had been a present from his parents after finishing college. It was an expensive one with a gold case and chain. He realised it was out of place in the trenches. To the men it must represent home and comfort and it didn't do to be reminded of such things here. He quickly put the watch away. The rain was falling harder now and the men, huddled under their gas capes, were getting restless and fed up. The guns, firing far away, sounded like thunder accompanying the downpour. Eventually, soaked through and hungry, the order came down the line for the men to stand down. The fog had lifted now and even though the rain persisted visibility was much improved.

Renton was just as fed up as the men. His greatcoat was wet through and weighed a ton on his shoulders. Water dripped off the back of his cap and ran down his neck. Blast Morris and his stupid ideas! He didn't have to get up at some unearthly hour and stand around in the freezing rain trying to knock religion into the heads of soaking wet, exhausted soldiers. Walking back to his quarters he saw Collins returning from his stand-to post, his rifle slung over his shoulder. The young orderly had taken off his helmet and was scratching his head. His thick black hair, made shiny by the rain, was plastered over his forehead. His boyish face had a mournful expression giving him a waif like appearance. Despite the rain, and the mud that sucked at his boots as he moved along, he walked in an easy, almost graceful manner. Underneath the boy's wet uniform, Renton imagined, would be a slender youthful body.

'Collins, have you got a moment?' His tone was friendly to Collins with no trace of the tetchiness that was present earlier.

The boy stopped and hastily replaced his helmet back on his head. 'Yes, sir, sorry, I only took me helmet off for a minute, sir, cos me head was itching so much.'

Renton gave him a reassuring smile. 'I didn't stop you for that, Collins. Although I wouldn't let the RSM catch you without your helmet on if I were you.'

'No, sir, course not. Thank you, sir,' Collins seemed relieved not to be getting the rollicking he had obviously been expecting. 'I can't stop too long, sir, I've got to help get breakfast for the officers.'

They were standing about three feet apart from each other. It was the first time Renton had studied the boy up close. The face, under the steel helmet, looked ridiculously young and innocent. Collins had brown eyes and long eyelashes just like a girl. His teeth, Renton noted with approval, showed white and even, unstained from any use of tobacco. He stared at the boy's lips: they were wet and glistening from the rain. He had a sudden desire to wipe away the raindrops with his finger. 'How do you like working in the officer's mess, Collins?' Renton asked, his voice steady, giving no indication of what he was thinking.

'I like it a lot, sir, but it's only temporary. I could be back with my section any time.'

'Would you prefer that, to go back to your section?' Renton knew Collins would be wary in his reply to him. He was an officer, not an officer in the usual sense true, but an officer all the same. Men often ended up in trouble for speaking their minds to their superiors. He wanted the boy to confide in him. 'It's all right, you know. You've nothing to worry about. This is a confidential conversation between you and me. It won't go any further I promise you.' He paused. 'Do you know what "confidential" means?'

'Yes sir'. Private, like isn't it?'

'That's right; anything you tell me is strictly between you and me.'

'Yea, that's what I thought, sir,' Collins looked up and down the trench before continuing. 'Well, you being the padre and all, you can perhaps understand how I feel, sir. The fact is, I'm scared out of me wits most of the time. I can't help it, sir. I want to be brave, but I'm just not cut out to be a soldier. I volunteered cos all me mates were joining up and I didn't want to be different. But I never knew it was going to be like this. I don't want to die here, sir. I don't want to be shot, or worse still, blown up, like some I've seen.' The boy stopped, seemingly out of breath from his outburst. He was embarrassed and looked down at his mud-covered boots, avoiding Renton's eyes.

'It's all right, Collins, everybody's scared of dying. You're not the only one. It's only natural to want to survive. We all do.' Renton lowered his voice. 'Look here, I'm not asking you just out of idle curiosity. As it happens, I need an orderly to look after me and also help with the religious services. I've been watching you. You seem to be reliable. I'm going to ask Major Kerr if he'll spare you as my batman. What do think? Would you like to work for me?'

Chapter 3

All through stand-to Davy Collins had been thinking about the time when he would have to return to infantry duties. The prospect of going back to the trenches, after the relative safety and comfort of working in the officers' mess, filled him with dread. And now, out of the blue, here he was, being offered a chance of working as batman to an officer. And not even a combat officer at that. It would mean no more patrols or listening posts to worry about. He could hardly believe his good fortune. So overwhelmed was he by Renton's offer that the words gushed out of his mouth in a torrent. 'I'd like that very much, sir. You wouldn't regret it if I worked for you, sir, I promise. I'm a good worker, honest! Ask anyone who knows me. Ask the mess sergeant, he'll tell you I work hard.'

'Are you very religious, Collins? It doesn't matter if you're not. I'm just interested to know, that's all.'

The question caught Collins off guard. He'd only been to one service since the padre's arrival and he was by no means devoutly religious. He had to be careful with his answer: he didn't want to say anything that might make the padre take back his offer. It was vital to make a good impression but, on the other hand, he didn't want to get caught out lying to him. 'I think I'm as religious as the next man, sir. Of course, with me duties and all, I don't get much chance to attend very often.' The padre would know of course that he wasn't a regular worshipper, but his explanation for his non-attendance was reasonable enough. All the same he'd better not hang about and risk further questioning. 'I'll have to get on, sir. The officers' will be waiting on their breakfast. Will there be anything more, sir?'

Rain was biting into his face and mud was clutching at his feet hindering his every step, but Collins hardly noticed. He could remember saluting the padre and being dismissed; that was real enough. It was what had been said to him that he was having trouble digesting. He kept reliving the conversation over and over again in his mind. Had he heard correctly? Had he really been offered a job that would keep him out of the front line? It seemed like it. What he couldn't understand, though, was why the padre had singled him out and not a more experienced man. Still, never look a gift horse in the mouth, as Dad would say.

Thinking of his father bought on a sudden bout of homesickness. Back at home his parents would still be in bed at this time of day on a Sunday morning. Before the war home had been in a dilapidated tenement block in Whitechapel. He lived there with his parents, two brothers and two sisters, all of whom, including himself, were crammed into two bedrooms, sitting room, and a kitchen. There were no baths in the block and only one communal toilet on each floor. The family might be poor and their home not luxurious but it was infinitely more attractive than serving at the front.

Davy Collins was the eldest child and had been out at work since the age of fourteen. He was working in a market in the East End of London when the war started but with his father as the chief breadwinner in the family, and one of his brothers also at work, he couldn't very well stay at home while other lads of his age were going off to war. He agonised about joining up for weeks until eventually the decision was made for him one morning on his way to work when he was confronted in the street by a young woman who without saying a word to him thrust something in his hand and walked on. When he looked down to see what she had given him, he saw a white feather nestling in the palm of his hand. He went straight to the nearest army recruiting office and within three weeks of enlisting was doing basic infantry training. After training he was sent out to France along with thousands of other young men to make up the losses the army had incurred after weeks of bitter fighting on the Somme.

He was terrified from the moment he joined up with the Westhampton's. Even though it was rough back home in his part of London it was nothing compared to daily life on the western front. Here there was no respite from danger. Shellfire, snipers, mines, the noise during a bombardment; it all terrified him. Now he knew what hell on earth was. He particularly hated having to live underground all the time. What he feared most was being trapped below in an explosion and buried alive. Lots of men had died that way, buried under tons of rubble. It wasn't just the danger either; there was the rain, the mud, the food, and the lice. He detested the lice; tiny mites that infested a man's hair and his clothes and made a body itch all over.

Bad as the conditions were he knew he was lucky to have missed the initial offensive. He had listened horrified to men's stories about withering enemy fire, terrible casualties, mounds of bodies and acts of bravery. It seemed to him that the great push that was going to knock the Germans out of the war had resulted instead in the wholesale slaughter of tens of thousands of British troops. Had he been called up a few weeks earlier he might also be just a name on a casualty list by now.

His thoughts returned to his family and his friends back home. He missed the banter of his workmates and the sights and sounds of the market. He especially missed the fun of Saturday night in the pub with dad and his mates. After closing time they'd stop off on their way home to get fish and chips as a treat for the family. Thinking about food made his mouth water; he could almost taste his mother's cooking. What wouldn't he give for a plate of her beef stew with dumplings? Well, the padre had given him a glimmer of hope now: maybe he would return home safely after all.

After leaving Collins, Renton hurried on through the rain to the officers' quarters. As soon as he pulled aside the gas curtains and entered his eyes began smarting. He stood inside the entrance for a few seconds blinking rapidly to clear them. A blue grey smoky haze, caused partly by the oil from the lamps but mostly from cigarettes, floated about like a malignant cloud. When there was the threat of a gas attack the gas curtain was kept closed and great clouds of tobacco smoke drifted around the dugout looking for avenues of escape. Little natural light found its way into the dugout and so it was necessary always to have a lamp burning to give some illumination. He looked through the gloom towards the small space next to the sleeping area that passed for the officers' lounge. Two small packing cases served for tables and the officers' had the added luxury of a few rickety chairs that had been looted from a nearby farmhouse. Major Kerr, as befitted his status of senior officer was sitting in one of the old threadbare armchairs in the mess, waiting for breakfast. Not given much to conversation at the best of times he was reading an old copy of Picture Post and smoking his beloved briar pipe. The pipe, like Kerr, had so far managed to survive everything the Germans had thrown at it but it was becoming increasingly difficult for Kerr to get supplies of tobacco and this sometimes affected his temperament especially early in the day. This morning, however, he was contentedly puffing away on his favourite brand of tobacco that had been sent to him in a parcel from his wife. Next to him, going through some paperwork was his Adjutant, Captain Freddie Beamish, the most popular officer in the regiment. Beamish had been awarded the Military Cross for his actions on the first morning of the Somme offensive. A lieutenant at the time, he had seen most of his platoon cut to ribbons under the murderous machine gun fire of the enemy. He had managed to rally what remained of his men and lead them successfully in a charge at the German front line. After some fierce hand-to-hand fighting the enemy abandoned their trenches and fled. To the men he was a hero and to his fellow officers he was an inspiration.

The other officers, mostly lieutenants and a couple of younger 2nd lieutenants were lying on their beds. Some had gone back to sleep after stand-to. Those that were awake like Kerr waited for breakfast. Renton hung up his sodden cap and greatcoat and flopped gratefully into a vacant chair next to Beamish. The encounter with

Collins had dispelled his earlier bad mood. He had only the morning prayers to take after breakfast and after that he would be free until evening service.

Beamish lowered his paperwork and looked across at him. 'Morning, Simon, and how were the men today? Did they greet you politely and reverently, or were they their normal heathen selves, half asleep and indifferent?'

Breamish's tone was affable but Renton knew when he was being mocked, albeit in a light hearted manner. 'You can never tell, Freddie. God works in weird and wonderful ways remember. Many out there weren't really listening to me I know but come the next heavy bombardment and we all know who they'll be praying to and it won't be General Haig.'

'Can't argue with you there,' Beamish said, grinning. He took out a packet of cigarettes and offered one to Renton. They were Carlton Superior, a good brand, not the usual Woodbines that Renton had smoked since his arrival. They both lit up and sat for a moment enjoying the calming effects of the tobacco.

'Short church parade today I hope, Simon,' Beamish said, breaking the silence, 'I've got a lot of work for the men to do later on.'

'Not on a Sunday, surely! You can't be sending out patrols on a day like to day. Not in this weather.'

'Not fighting patrols, old boy, just the usual listening patrols. No, we've got to get the men filling more sandbags. The trench walls and parapet are getting in a hell of a state. All this rain dislodges the bags. Then they rot away in no time at all. We can't wait for the rain to stop; it might go on for weeks. What with doing that and bailing out the trenches the men are going to be pretty busy today.'

‘Well, under the circumstances, Freddie, I’ll try and be as quick as possible.’ Things were going Renton’s way. Beamish had given him a good reason to keep his service as short as he could. He turned to Kerr. ‘Providing of course it’s all right with you, Sir.’

Kerr put down his magazine. ‘What’s that you said, Padre? I’m afraid I didn’t hear you.’

‘Freddie was asking me not to make the service too long today, sir, if you don’t mind.’

‘Not at all, make it as short as you like, looks as if it’ll be a wet parade though. Mind you. I still expect a good turnout from the officers. Must set the men an example, you know.’

‘Well don’t expect me, John,’ Beamish said, shuffling his papers into a neat pile. ‘You and Simon know that I don’t go in for that sort of thing.’

‘Don’t worry, Freddie I wasn’t including you,’ Kerr said. ‘We all know where you stand on the subject of religion.’

Just then breakfast was served and further conversation was carried on between mouthfuls of food and mugs of tea. Kerr was in a good mood throughout and chatted easily with his officers’ about various matters. When he had finished Renton decided to tackle him about Collins. Kerr had returned to his chair and was lighting up another pipe when Renton sat down beside him. ‘I wondered if it you’d thought anymore about my request for an orderly, sir. It has been a few weeks now and I really do need someone.’

Kerr got his pipe going before answering him ‘Yes, I suppose it has been a while now, Simon. Well, luckily for you, we’ve had some reinforcements since then. God knows we can certainly do with them. I think it’ll be all right. I’ll get Freddie to detail one of the men to you.’

‘If it’s all the same to you, sir, I’d prefer to choose a man myself.’

‘Well that all depends on who it is. I don’t want a good fighting man taken away from his section. Have you anyone in mind, then?’

‘As a matter of fact, I have, sir. As I understand it, Private Collins is already a temporary orderly in the mess at the moment. Instead of returning him to his section I’d like him assigned to me when he’s finished here.’

‘If Freddie thinks it’s all right, you can have him,’ Kerr paused and called Beamish over. ‘Simon here wants one of the men, Collins for his batman. Can he be spared, Freddie?’

‘Yes, I should think so.’ Beamish said, and then added. ‘To be honest it might be the best thing for the lad. He’s scared senseless most of the time and who can blame him at his age, probably best to get him out of the firing line for a bit.’

Renton couldn’t believe how well things had gone. Sitting back in his chair he accepted another one of Freddie’s superior cigarettes and began planning his day.

Chapter 4

After finishing work in the officers' mess, Collins returned to his own quarters. As mess orderly he had been on call for the past twenty-four hours, a tour of duty that would normally leave him tired and lethargic, but the conversation with the padre earlier had dispelled some of his weariness and he decided to write a letter home before catching up on his sleep. He had never had reason to write a letter to anyone before joining the army and found it difficult now writing to his mother because he had to keep reassuring her about his safety. He knew that however cheerful he made his news she would still worry about him.

He looked around his quarters as he sought inspiration to begin his letter. He shared an underground room with ten other men, all regimental headquarter staff. The room that they occupied had once been part of the old German lines and had been captured intact. He grudgingly admired the Germans for the way they built their underground quarters. They were larger and deeper than the British dugouts and even had wooden bunk beds for privates to sleep in. Looking around him his spirits sank at the thought of returning his old section in a front line trench. It would mean going back to a damp camp bed in a crowded dugout that offered far less protection against enemy shelling than his present quarters. He wondered if the padre had spoken to the CO about him yet. Probably not, after all, it had only been a few hours since their conversation and the padre would doubtless have other matters to attend to. Still, it was possible. Lying down on his bed he got out pencil and paper and started to write a letter to his parents.

He got as far as *'Dear Mum and Dad'* before he was interrupted.

'Writing home are we, Davy boy? Who's being a good lad then, hey?' Billy 'Lofty' Webb sat himself down on the bed next to Collins.

'Christ, you gave me start, Lofty. Where did you spring from?'

'Sorry mate, I didn't mean to startle you. You must've bin too interested in your letter to notice me. Don't forget to give me a mention to your family, will you?'

'Don't I always,' Collins grinned, 'I reckon they know as much about you as they know about me.'

Lofty Webb got his nickname on account of only being five feet four tall and was Davy Collins best mate. It was Webb who had got Collins the temporary job in the mess. Six months older than Collins he had joined the regiment just in time for the opening battle of the Somme offensive. He had been in the thick of the fighting and had undergone a terrible ordeal on the very first day of the attack. Sheltering in a bomb crater from enemy fire with four other members of his section they were hit by their own artillery fire. Lofty Webb, with shrapnel wounds to his leg, was the only survivor. Unable to move without risk of being shot he lay there from early morning until nightfall, surrounded by the dismembered, bloody pieces of his former mates. Finally when darkness fell he crawled for six hours over dead and dying men to get back to his own lines. In hospital they had taken care of his leg but the mental scars had taken longer to heal. When Webb returned to the regiment he was in no condition to go back to a fighting unit and was made assistant to the regimental clerk.

When Collins first met him, Webb was withdrawn and suffered bouts of severe depression. But, over a period of months, Collins gradually gained his confidence. Talking about the horrific events of that day seemed to have a therapeutic effect on Lofty and he became more outgoing. As a result they had struck up a firm friendship. Collins mentioned him in his letters home with the result that Lofty had almost become a member of the family. They had already decided that once the war was over they would stick together .Collins was sure he could get jobs for them both in the Whitechapel Market.

'What's happening with your job in the officers' mess?' Webb asked. 'Are they keeping you on, or what?'

'No, I don't think so. I think Captain Beamish would have mentioned it by now if they were.'

'That's true. He's a decent officer is Beamish. Look, you've got to stay here, Davy. You and me, we're muckers, right? If anything was to happen to you, what would I do for a job back home in Blighty?'

Collins glanced around the dugout. Apart from Webb and himself there were only two other men present and they appeared to be sleeping soundly in their bunks. He lowered his voice almost to a whisper so that Lofty had to lean forward to hear him. 'As it happens there may be chance of me being a batman for one of the officers. But, for God's sakes, keep it to yourself for now cos nothing's settled yet.'

'Christ,' Lofty said. 'When did this happen? You never mentioned it yesterday.'

'Didn't know about it then, did I. I only got asked this morning after stand-to.'

'Well, come on then! What officer asked you?'

'It was the Padre. Right out of nowhere he asked me if I wanted to be his orderly. You could have knocked me down with a feather. I didn't even know he was entitled to have one.'

'Fucking hell,' Webb was clearly taken aback, 'bloody, fucking hell. He's not even a combat officer. What a stroke of luck, Davy. I'll keep me fingers crossed for you.'

'Just don't say anything for now in case nothing comes of it,' Collins paused, 'though why he picked me I'll never know.'

'Probably seen you working in the mess,' Lofty said. 'Must have liked what he saw.'

'Maybe, anyway he's going to ask the CO if I can be spared. Do you know anything about the padre? Heard any trench murmurs?'

'Not really, there's a rumour that he likes a drink, but as far as I know nobody's seen him blotto. Anyway he wouldn't be the only one who likes a drink, would he?'

'He can drink as much as he likes for all I care, it won't affect me.'

'Dead right,' Webb said. He rose to his feet. 'Anyway, I'd better get going, I'll let you know if I hear anything.'

After Webb had gone, Collins suddenly felt very tired and was tempted to turn in to his bunk but decided he must finish his letter home first. After staring at the paper for a few minutes he painstakingly wrote a few lines.

How is everyone at home don't worry about me I am getting on alrite and still very much alive. Things have bin a bit quiet lately thank God and I am still working inside. Got your last parcel alrite and me and Lofty enjoyed the cakes and fags. Don't worry about not sendin more often becos I know how dear it must be for you both. Remember me to all at the Red Lion. Lofty sends his regards as usual and looks forward to meetin everyone when we get some leave. Next time I write I might have some really good news to tell you.
Your loving son Davy.

As he read the letter back a lump came to his throat and he fought back the tears. Removing his damp clothing he got into his bunk but tired as he was he could not get off to sleep. He thought of life back home and tried, even if only for a little while, to forget the war. He imagined himself back in his mother's small but spotlessly clean kitchen with his brothers and sisters. He saw his mother, with her prematurely grey hair, standing over a zinc tub doing the family washing, her thin bare arms immersed in soap lather as she busily scrubbed clothes on a wash board. Collins smiled remembering how fanatical his mother was when it came to cleanliness. The building they lived in might be old and dirty on the outside, but inside the Collins' apartment it was a different story. His mother had been in service to a wealthy family before she met her husband and was no stranger to housework. There would probably be a pot of stew steaming away on the oven range containing whatever unwanted vegetables his father brought back from the market. On a Sunday there would even be meat in the pot. Even in the bad times, when there had been days and even weeks without work for Collins father, the family had never starved. His mother would always keep something back for 'a rainy day' as she called it. Davy knew he was her favourite. She was always telling her neighbours, or any one else for that matter, what a good boy her son Davy was. 'He's never any trouble.' She would say proudly. 'Never gets drunk or goes throwing his money away chasing after women.'

She embarrassed him the way she carried on sometimes. He hadn't even had a regular girlfriend yet. He'd had the odd kiss and cuddle with some of the girls from the market but nothing serious. He'd certainly not met any girl his mother would consider good enough for him. Another image came to his mind: it was the public bar of the '*Lion*'. It was Saturday night and it was packed. He and his father were crammed up against the bar downing pints of beer and joking with their mates. He could hear the sound of pub music, the chink of glasses; even image the wonderful aroma of tobacco and ale. Then, gradually, the sound of the upright piano in the saloon bar faded away as he lost the battle with tiredness and finally drifted off to sleep.

Renton's bloodshot eyes were trying to focus on the fifty odd men drawn up before him for the ten o'clock church parade. The rain was beginning to ease at last, which was good news because he had his church robes on over his uniform and he didn't want them to get soaking wet. His congregation was assembled in an abandoned farmyard a safe distance behind the front line. As if by mutual agreement the guns on both sides had ceased firing leaving an eerie silence hanging over the place. Behind him stood a small barn that he had converted for use as a chapel. It was also used as a meeting place where men could come and confide with him about their problems. He had taken the precaution of fortifying himself from his hip flask beforehand and was feeling a little light headed. In front of large gatherings he always got flustered and tongue-tied. It was something he had never overcome in all his years of taking services. Standing a couple of feet off the ground on an old hay cart, his wet, uncombed hair blowing in the wind, he began his nervous opening address by stumbling over his words. Later, whilst reading the sermon he lost his place several times and twice nearly dropped his bible. It needed a strong physical effort on his part to stop his hands shaking. At last he came to the closing hymn, *'Rock of Ages,'* which the men sang heartily, if not very tunefully. By the time the last notes died away he was sweating profusely and in need of another steadying drink from the flask in his pocket. When the service was over he gratefully handed the parade over to Kerr who dismissed the men.

As he was collecting up the hymnbooks, which had been left in a pile on the hay cart, Beamish approached him. 'What are you doing here? I thought you were an atheist,' he asked. He didn't particularly want to talk to Freddie at the moment. He had to try and find Sergeant Watkins. It couldn't wait until later as he originally planned.

Beamish apparently hadn't noticed his brusque manner, or if he had he chose to overlook it. 'I got here a couple of minutes ago with a message for one of the officers. Are you all right, Simon? You're sweating like mad, you know; and your hands are shaking.'

'I'm fine,' Renton hastened to reassure him. 'Probably a slight chill, nothing more, I could do with a nip of something to keep out the cold and the damp.'

'I think you've probably had a nip or two already, Simon,' Beamish said. Renton flashed him a look but before he could say anything Beamish said. 'Now you're not going to like what I'm about to say and you may think it's none of my business but as Adjutant it's my job to notice things. It's all part of the job.'

Renton sat down on the hay cart and took a cigarette out of a packet of Woodbines. He gave one to Beamish, and they both lit up. To cover the awkward silence between them, he pretended to be studying the cigarette packet. 'You know something,' he said. 'There's a Chaplain over here in France who dishes these things out like sweets. The men have started calling him Woodbine Willie. I hear he's very popular.' He looked up at Beamish and added, quietly. 'So, what have you noticed about me, Freddie?'

'Quite a bit, actually,' Beamish said. 'Mostly how you conduct yourself, who you talk to, what you drink; especially what you drink.'

'Are you trying to tell me something?' Renton asked, his voice was even but he felt uneasy.

Beamish shrugged. 'Look, we all have our own way of coping with this war. Some of the men in this unit have quite literally been through hell and it's only their training and the army discipline that's pulling them through. The officers' have got to set an example by their exemplary conduct, and when I say officers, I include you, Simon.'

'I don't understand what you're getting at, Freddie.' Renton said, angrily. 'I'm here for the men's spiritual needs, that's all! I also listen to their problems and try to reassure them that they'll be safe and their wives and sweethearts back home are being faithful. That's what I'm here for, not to lead them in battle or make life and death decisions, that's your job, you and Kerr.'

'You wear the King's uniform, Simon. The army regards you as a commissioned officer and while I'm the adjutant here, I expect you to behave like one.'

'Are you finding fault with me because of something specific I've done, or do you just think a chaplain's not needed here?'

'My religious opinions are neither here nor there. This isn't a personal thing. In fact I've always thought we got on quite well despite our differences on religion.' Beamish hesitated. 'Look, Simon, I'm going to be blunt with you. I don't know if you've got a problem or not, but at the moment it seems to me that you can't get through a day without a drink and sooner or later Kerr is bound to notice.'

'Is that it, have you finished your lecture, is that what all this is about then, a few drinks?'

'If it were only a few you wouldn't smell so strongly of drink at this time of the morning and I wouldn't be having this conversation with you.' Beamish paused. 'It's just not on, Simon. You're an officer as well as a chaplain. For God's sake, act like one!'

Renton was silent. Beamish had never spoken to him like this before. Previous conversations between them had always been friendly and on equal terms over a cigarette and a drink in the mess. This was the first time he had encountered Beamish in his role as serious adjutant. He wondered how he had found out about his drinking habits. The trouble was it wasn't easy to get alcohol in such a grim place. It was too far, and too dangerous, to walk to the nearest town. In the end it always came down to his reliance on Watkins. The Quartermaster Sergeant had that side of things pretty well sewn up.

'Look, maybe I have been drinking a bit too much, Freddie. It's taking me a while to get used to these conditions. I'm not a soldier like you. Anyway don't worry. I'll watch it from now on. It's good of you to be so concerned.' Renton hoped he sounded contrite.

'Not at all, old boy.' Beamish said, tossing his cigarette end into the mud. 'I know it must be terrible for a man of your vocation to live under these conditions and see such a waste of human life. That's why I don't believe any more, Simon. After all, if God's so compassionate, why does he allow this slaughter to go on? Can you tell me that?'

'God didn't start the war.' Renton said. 'Men start wars, and it's up to men to finish them, not God.' It was his standard response to a question that was regularly asked of him.

'Yes, I thought you might say that,' said Beamish smiling. 'You must get fed up listening to other people's troubles every day. I take it, by the way, that you turn to God whenever you have a problem?'

Renton nodded but said nothing. Beamish had made the same assumption that everyone else made. They all thought that, because he had a cross in the front of his cap instead of a regimental cap badge, that he got special treatment from above. The reality was somewhat different. What heavenly favours had God ever granted him since he became a chaplain?

'All right, we'll consider the matter closed then, old boy.' Beamish turned to leave but suddenly stopped.

'Tell me, Simon, just out of curiosity. Why aren't you married? Most chaplains of your age I know are married with about half a dozen kids.'

'Still looking for the right girl, Freddie,' Renton said. 'Just like you I suppose.'

Renton watched Beamish walk away along the muddy track. As he lit yet another cigarette, he noticed with dismay that his hands were trembling. The talk had unsettled him. He would have to be more careful in the future. He thought he had concealed his drinking well but obviously he had been careless. The elation he had felt before breakfast was now gone. He went off in search of Sergeant Watkins in a sullen mood.

Chapter 5

Quartermaster Sergeant Ron Watkins was a regular soldier with twenty years' service behind him. The army was his life and up until now army life had been pretty good to him. As far as he was concerned nothing was going to change that, not even the inconvenience of war. Early on in his service he'd known rough times but nothing he hadn't been able to handle. Being over six feet in height and weighing seventeen stones helped, but people who thought he was all brawn and no brain underestimated him. His promotion in the army had been steady and finally he had hit the jackpot by achieving the enviable position of Regimental Quartermaster: a prize job that entailed overseeing all the stores, equipment, food and drink needed for the regiment's use.

The job had provided plenty of perks for Watkins in peacetime but since arriving in France he had become indisputably the most powerful man in the regiment. He had hand picked his staff and ensured their loyalty by using a mixture of fear and bribery. As a result of his 'reorganisation' of the Quartermaster stores if anything extra was wanted to ease the discomfort of front line life, such as tobacco, drink, or even fresh food and medicines, then Ron Watkins was your man. And it wasn't only the non-commissioned ranks that came to him. Any officer who couldn't afford to have a hamper from Fortnum and Masons sent out to him knew, that for a price, he could rely on the quartermaster to make life a little more bearable. Even Kerr turned a blind eye to Watkins profitable little enterprises. Provided things didn't get out of control, Kerr was happy for the men to try and live as best as they possibly could under the conditions.

Watkins wasn't content with just dealing in army stores. Rouville was a little French market town lying a few miles behind the Westhampton's front line with an army casualty clearing station nearby. Before the war it had been a prosperous provincial town thanks to the surrounding farmland and fruit orchards, but the destruction of war had changed all that. Watkins found the place on one of his reconnoitring trips and quickly made himself a familiar figure in the town. He was soon on first name terms with the merchants and farmers that frequented the cafes and bars. He had got together a working party from the regiment to help out the town's mayor by rebuilding a part of his hotel that had been damaged by a stray shell. Afterwards Watkins suggested that it might be very profitable for the mayor if a couple of rooms could be set aside on weekends to be used as a brothel for the men, and, if the mayor wanted to show his gratitude, well... Under the perfectly legitimate cover of acquiring fresh supplies to supplement army rations, Watkins became a frequent visitor to the town and watched his little empire flourish.

The rat infested conditions that other men lived in at the front were not for the likes of Ron Watkins. When the regiment had moved into the old German positions he had suggested to Kerr, on the grounds of security, that he be near the stores at all times. The CO had given his approval and his living quarters were duly set up in the underground bunker where the regimental stores were kept. Thanks to his contacts in town he had far and away the most comfortably furnished accommodation in that part of the front line.

He had been inconvenienced by the stand-to earlier but had retired back to his quarters directly afterwards, giving orders to one of his men for his breakfast to be prepared. Breakfast over, he was just contemplating a second cup of coffee when his corporal informed him that the padre was outside and wished to see him. After a quick look around to satisfy himself that there was nothing on display that shouldn't be he went out to greet his visitor. 'Morning, Mr Renton, have a good service, did we? I heard the singing from here. I must say it sounded most uplifting. I was just going to have another cup of decent coffee, come inside and join me.'

Watkins cheerful demeanour annoyed Renton, as did his remark that he was 'going to have another cup of decent coffee'. Genuine coffee, not the awful stuff normally served up by the army, was decidedly hard to come by. However, the wonderful aroma wafting past his nose overcame Renton's annoyance. Despising himself for his weakness he accepted the offer and followed Watkins inside. Watkins waved him towards a chair and then busied himself making the coffee. Renton put down his old faded carpetbag and looked around him with envy. How on earth had a mere sergeant managed to fix himself up in such comfort and not even have to share his accommodation? Even Kerr had to share quarters with his fellow officers. Before he was posted to the Westhampton's, he already knew that the Quartermaster Sergeant was the person he would have to cultivate to supply his needs. Years of army life had taught him it was the same in any regiment. But he had never come across anyone quite like Watkins. The man seemed to have unlimited access to all sorts of goodies. On joining the regiment he had mentioned to Watkins in conversation that he enjoyed the occasional drink. Within a few days Watkins had supplied him with his first bottle and there had been a good many bottles since then. But in the last few weeks Watkins had turned the screw and the price of a bottle was becoming extortionate.

Watkins put two mugs of steaming hot coffee down on the table and disappeared behind an old army blanket that separated his sleeping quarters from the storeroom. He reappeared a few moments later carrying a bottle of whisky in his hand. Pulling up a chair to the table, he sat down opposite Renton. 'Care for a strong coffee, padre?' he asked, 'a little something to warm us up on a miserable morning like this.' Without giving Renton time to think about it he poured a generous measure of whisky into each mug of coffee before replacing the cap on the bottle and setting the bottle down tantalisingly close to Renton.

Renton sipped the hot brew and immediately felt the familiar steadying effects of the whisky coming through the flavour of the coffee.

'Top yourself up, padre,' Watkins said, pushing the bottle towards him, 'I'm not charging you for it: at least not at the moment.'

Despite the temptation Renton declined the offer. He didn't want Watkins to think he was that desperate for a drink. He replaced the mug on the table but couldn't help looking longingly at the bottle.

'Go on, padre. Have another, it won't kill you,' Watkins said.

Renton however, was determined to preserve his dignity and show some willpower. 'No. No more, thank you. That was sufficient, but I will have a bottle to take with me, if you have one?'

Watkins smiled at him. 'Always got a bottle for you, padre, you know that. Mind you, it's getting harder and harder to get hold of. I'm afraid it'll cost you more than last time.'

Renton was unable to control his rage. 'What do you mean, cost more? I'm paying nearly double the price I used to.' He was losing his composure and letting his anger get the better of him. 'You're getting greedy, Watkins, much too greedy. Aren't you making enough out of me already?'

'But, padre, I've already told you that you get it at a cheaper price, being a man of the cloth and all that. It's not me as fixes the price, you know, it's the people I have to deal with.'

'Don't try and tell me you're not making a nice little profit out of it,' Renton said.

'I just about cover me costs, and that's the truth,' Watkins said, replacing the cap on the bottle. 'The other officers pay more than you do, you know, and they don't complain. Anyway, you have a lot more bottles than them. Truth is, I have a fair old job keeping up with your demands.'

'Don't be insolent Sergeant! You seem to forget you're talking to an officer.' Renton could see he would have to remind Watkins whom he was dealing with. 'I'm not some green young subaltern just off the boat.'

'No sir, you're not, but, with all respect, just cos you wear a Sam Browne belt, it don't make you no officer.

You're a priest in uniform, that's what you are, and a mighty thirsty one at that.' Watkins sat back in his chair and looked defiantly across the table at Renton.

'How dare you.' Renton leapt to his feet, his face contorted with rage. He could feel the blood pounding through his veins. 'I'll report you to the CO for your insolence. I'll, I'll, have your stripes removed. You'll be back in the trenches in no time.'

'Calm yourself, padre. You'll break a blood vessel if you keep on like that. Come on, sit down and have another drink.' Watkins picked up the bottle and gestured towards Renton's mug. 'We both know you're not going to report me to Major Kerr, cos if you did, then you'd lose your source of supply.' He poured another measure of whisky into Renton's mug. 'Besides that, think of the consequences for you. If the church ever found out how much you're drinking they'd defrock you, I reckon.'

Renton was fuming. How dare this lout talk to him like this? Had he no respect for his superiors? Did he think he could speak to him like that and get away with it? He had to be put in his place. 'I think your little set up here has gone to your head, Watkins. Don't you know it's a courts martial offence to defraud the British army? I could go to Major Kerr about you and tell him about your little transactions.'

Renton's threat was countered, momentarily, with a chilling stare from Watkins. Then the icy look faded. He shrugged his shoulders and, smiling, calmly picked up Renton's mug. 'You really shouldn't try to threaten me, padre' he said, his voice quiet, but confident. 'Shall I tell you why I've survived this long? It's because I can get certain things for the men. Things like drink, chocolate, cigarettes, women even. Things you find in a real world, not a spiritual one. So just who do you think is more valuable to the officers and men in this place, you or me?' He thrust the mug of whisky into Renton's hand. 'Go on then, you go running off to Kerr with your allegations and see how far you get.'

Renton slumped back down in the chair clutching his drink. He was no match for a hardened soldier like Watkins and he knew it. The man knew every trick in the book and it had been stupid to try and threaten him. As chaplain of the regiment he was in an especially vulnerable position. Trying to rescue his dignity, he sat upright and took a couple of deep breaths. Then, conscious of the whisky in his hand, he raised it to his lips and slowly downed it in one go. He was aware of Watkins watching him with an expression of quiet satisfaction on his face. 'I'm sorry,' Renton said, trying to placate him 'I don't know what got into me. My behaviour was inexcusable, I don't usually fly of the handle for no reason, do forgive me.'

'Think nothing of it, Mr Renton,' Watkins said, 'a little misunderstanding between friends, that's all. It's bound to happen sometimes in a place like this. I take it you still want your bottle?'

Renton nodded miserably and Watkins did his disappearing act behind the blanket again emerging a few seconds later with another bottle. Grabbing Renton's carpetbag he slipped the bottle in amongst some hymn books and put the bag on the table.

Renton got to his feet and thrusting his hand into his trouser pocket took out some money and placed it on the table.

'That's too much,' Watkins said pleasantly. 'Take some back. After all, you were moaning about the price a few minutes ago.'

'No, that's all right. I was wrong. Let's call the extra, *'goodwill money'*, shall we? To ensure our little arrangement continues.'

'I always knew you were an understanding gentleman, padre. And I'm sure you appreciate my position here. I haven't always been a Quartermaster Sergeant, you know. I've done my share of fighting in my time, I can tell you. I was in the Boer War you know, and that was no picnic. Course, I was only a lad then. So the way I see it now, its payback time for all those hard years. It's my time right now don't you see? My time for a few perks in life.'

Renton listened in incredulous silence while Watkins justified his profiteering activities. The man obviously had no morals whatsoever and simply looked upon the war as an excellent opportunity to line his pockets. Renton suspected that much of his profits came from men who had died on the battlefield or had been blown to pieces in their trenches as Watkins wheeled and dealed from the safety of his store. The sound of guns in the distance signalled the end of their conversation. Both men stepped outside and watched the tell tale puffs of smoke on the horizon. Watkins looked up at the grey skies and smiled. 'That's it lads, fire away.' he said cheerily.

Renton had heard enough and stumbled off through the mud. He had only gone a few yards when he heard Watkins say, in a loud voice. 'Yes, fire away my lads. Because while I'm making easy money from drunken sots like that one I hope this profitable old war goes on for a good while longer.'

Chapter 6

On Monday morning, Collins was instructed to report to the Adjutant. With mounting excitement he went in search of Captain Beamish who he found sitting on a fire step briefing some junior officers. He waited patiently for the briefing to finish and then stepped smartly forward and snapped off a salute. Like most of the younger men he was somewhat in awe of Beamish. One order from him and Collins could find himself back with his section in the near future and that might mean going over the top with bayonets fixed into a hail of gunfire.

'The padre has asked for you to be his orderly,' Beamish said, 'and the CO has agreed. As from now, you'll report to him for your duties. Is that clear?'

'Yes, sir, I'm to report to the padre, sir.'

'You're to serve him as you would any other officer in the regiment. In addition you'll be expected to assist him with his religious duties, but you don't have to stay and attend services, unless you want to. Any problems with the padre in that department come and see me, understand?'

'Yes, sir, there won't be any problems, sir.'

'I don't know how long this war will last, Collins. But, if your work is satisfactory, who knows? You might finish it working for Mr Renton.'

‘I was hoping it would be over by Christmas, sir. I thought maybe Fritz might have had enough of fighting by now.’

Beamish dispelled Collins optimism. ‘I’m afraid that’s highly unlikely. The Germans aren’t finished yet, not by a long way. We might still be here next Christmas unless we win a decisive battle. Anyway, don’t worry about that now, off you go and report to the padre.’

In the officers’ mess, Renton sat reading a letter from his mother. She had written to him fairly regularly over the years, but since his arrival in France the volume of letters had increased. As usual her letter was full of news about the family. His sister, Joanna was still working for the Red Cross in a secretarial role. She was six years younger than Simon and married to a doctor, a rather dull and colourless young man called Richard. In addition there was the usual information about the neighbours and the weather. Towards the end of the letter his mother wrote that his father sent his regards. Renton smiled to himself. His father always sent his regards but never wrote letters himself pleading as an excuse a heavy workload in a busy parish. It was for the most part a typical letter from his mother, but something in its contents worried him. In successive letters now his mother had mentioned that she had been unwell and had been forced to take to her bed for short periods of rest. Renton was very close to his mother. When he was a child she had played a major role in his life. His father had always been busy with his church duties and didn’t have the time to oversee his son’s upbringing. His mother, however, had adored him since the day he was born and continued to lavish her love and affection on him all his life. It was her ideals and teachings that influenced him never his father's, who was happy to leave his children's welfare to his wife. It was to his mother that Renton ran for comfort when teased and bullied when he first attended the local school in the small town in Suffolk where his parents still lived. Being the Vicar's son was bad enough but being better dressed and better spoken than most marked him out and he was a regular victim for teasing. He remembered the warmth and security he felt when he would come home from school sobbing. How many times had he had buried himself into her soft comfortable body as she soothed and reassured him?

His attempts at making friends at school had usually ended in failure. He was an intelligent pupil, good in all subjects, and he knew it so it was demeaning for him to have to mix with children who he thought were not his equal. He showed no interest whatsoever in playing games with his classmates and as a result they thought him stuck up and soft. In an effort to get him to make more friends his mother would invite small parties of his classmates to tea on Sundays, but he never enjoyed her little gatherings, and would usually end up on his own ignoring his guests.

In all his time at the local school he met only a handful of children he got on with and only one person that he considered a friend, someone he thought he could talk to and share common interests with. His name was Maurice and his father was a bank manager, a profession that Renton didn't know much about at the time, but thought must be rather grand. His friendship with Maurice was very much an on and off affair with numerous falling's out, mainly due to Renton always wanting to dominate the other boy despite them being the same age. But when they did get on they played happily enough together and needed no other boys around to play with; and certainly no girls. He lit a cigarette and blew smoke rings into the dim atmosphere of the dugout. It must be more than twenty years since those schooldays with Maurice. He wondered what Maurice was doing now. Perhaps he was working as a bank manager like his father, or like himself, serving somewhere in France? It was with Maurice that he had his first inkling of his sexual tendencies. They were thirteen at the time, getting on well and growing closer together. Playing in Renton's room one summer's day they had stripped off and had examined each other's bodies with adolescent curiosity.

A shiver of pleasure ran through his body as he remembered how they had sexually aroused each other. With youthful clumsiness they fondled and embraced one another with mounting erotic delight until both had masturbated and achieved orgasm. After that it became a regular occurrence in their meetings. Their sexual activities continued for about a year without arousing suspicion. But they became careless and they were caught one day embracing in the garden by Renton's mother. Loving her son as dearly as she did, she was content to let the matter pass as a childish infatuation by both boys, and thought it best to say nothing to her husband. Later, when he first went to college, he missed Maurice. But after a while at college he met another boy and Maurice became just a pleasant memory.

His mother's discretion all those years ago brought his thoughts back to her now. Knowing her like he did, he was pretty sure her illness was a lot worse than she was indicating in her letters. It would be typical of her to let him think that life was going on normally back home. He wanted desperately to see her but he knew he hadn't been in France long enough to qualify for home leave, and anyway, it would be Christmas in six weeks time and leave would be out of the question. Immersed in his thoughts about his mother he failed to notice the slim figure in khaki approach him until he heard a discreet cough.

'Collins sir, I was told by the Adjutant to report to you for orderly duties.'

Taken by surprise, Renton dropped his letter and it landed at the boy's feet. Collins picked it up and handed it back to him. He saw the boy looking at him and thought how very dishevelled his appearance must look in comparison with other officers of the regiment. His hair, badly in need of cutting, fell unkemptly over his forehead and he still hadn't got around to having a shave. His uniform had several stains on it and was in need of pressing: in contrast his white dog collar stood clearly out in the gloom of the dugout.

'Sorry sir didn't mean to disturb you. I can come back another time if you like?'

'That's all right Collins, not your fault, I was miles away.' Renton smiled weakly. 'Well now, I'm glad you got the job of looking after me. To tell you the truth, I really do need someone. You shouldn't find the duties too hard, and provided you do what I tell you, we'll get on fine, all right?'

'Yes, sir, like I told you before, I'm not afraid of hard work, sir.'

'I'm glad to hear it, Collins. I'll tell you what your duties are. Later, when I get more time, I'll write them down for you so you won't forget.'

Collins listened without interruption while Renton explained the duties of an officer's batman. He needed someone to clean his kit, including boots, Sam Browne belt, and uniform. Also to serve his meals and in addition be responsible for religious garments and prayer books used during services.

'Do I have to stay for the services, sir?' Collins enquired, when asked if he had any questions.

Renton shook his head. 'No, just help me with getting ready, carrying my books and things, but who knows? If you stay, you might enjoy the services.'

'I'll probably be too busy doing other things to spare the time, sir,' Collins said.

Renton knew a lame excuse when he heard one. 'We should never be too busy to forget God.' He said. 'Still, don't bother about that now. You can start your duties right away by getting me some hot water so I can have a wash and shave. After you've done that, see what you can do about getting the mud off my uniform and then clean my shoes.'

Renton spent part of his day watching Collins going about the tasks he set him. He delighted in the boy's quick, efficient manner of working and his childish eagerness to please. It also gave him a feeling of sensual pleasure that he had not felt for a long time. He was sure it wouldn't be too difficult to gain the boy's confidence. A couple of weeks probably, he calculated. With a bit of praise here and there, a few personal chats, he would have him eating out of his hand. Privacy would be the problem though, getting the boy alone in the cheek by jowl conditions he was living under with the other officers was going to be difficult, personal space being hard to find. He needed a place where he could get the boy to relax; somewhere nobody could find them together. He thought of the makeshift chapel but rejected the idea. It was a house of God, a place for prayer. He lit a cigarette and as an afterthought, offered one to Collins who refused, explaining shyly that he didn't smoke because his mum had told him it was bad for him. Renton was pleased, it was only a small confidence, but it was a start. Once he had opened him up in conversation, the rest would come naturally. The secret was patience: not to rush the boy into anything. He had made that mistake in the past and it had led him into an embarrassing situation that could have resulted in serious consequences for him.

Thinking of that incident gave him a pang of conscience over his intentions towards his new orderly. For a brief moment he considered the risks involved and the penalty he would have to pay if he were caught. When faced with this sort of dilemma early on in his career he had prayed to God to help him resist temptation. But God had not helped him, and his sexual desires always overcame his religious faith. It was a constant source of anguish to him why God had not made him like other men. If it was some sort of test then he knew he had failed. He looked over at Collins who was bent forward polishing a pair of shoes with youthful enthusiasm, his black, floppy hair falling over his face. Collins stopped polishing momentarily and, seeing Renton looking at him, smiled at him briefly before resuming his work. Renton's moment of doubt passed. The boy was worth the risk.

That evening, beneath the black night sky, Collins sat outside his quarters drinking tea. It was a cold night and he had his greatcoat wrapped around him to keep out the chill night air. He often sat outside for a while in the evenings to escape from the damp atmosphere and fuggy smoke of his dugout. Inside his mates were almost certainly talking about women, their favourite topic of conversation. Some of the older men's stories left him feeling embarrassed and aware of just how inexperienced he was of life in general and women in particular. Looking up into the cold inky darkness, he saw a flash from a heavy gun show up clearly and dramatically in the distance. Suddenly, a German flare shot up in the air and burned with fierce intensity flooding the Westhampton trenches with artificial daylight. Almost immediately there followed the sound of machine gun and rifle fire. He pressed himself against the side of the trench in an effort to make himself part of the sandbagged wall. It was an instinctive but futile action and Davy knew it, but couldn't break the habit. He always felt especially vulnerable at night even when protected by the high trench walls. His thoughts turned to the men in the patrol that had gone out earlier. They would be hugging the ground with fear right now, trying to make themselves invisible and hoping the flare would burn itself out before they were spotted. A shudder went through him as he remembered being in a similar situation once in a working party sent out at night to repair the wire defences. A flare had caught them working out in the open making them visible to the Germans looking out from their trenches. It had seemed a lifetime before the flare died out and darkness once again descended. It was a miracle that everyone in the patrol returned alive. After that experience he thought his life expectancy would be just a matter of weeks or at best months until luckily for him, Lofty Webb had got him the temporary job in the officers' mess. Now, thanks to the padre, his luck was continuing.

The flare died away and the firing stopped immediately. He relaxed as the darkness enveloped him once again. Like most of the men he served with he treasured his moments of privacy. Sometimes, when he wanted to be completely alone, he went to his special place, a place that was avoided because of the dangers involved. It was a foul, marshy area where the trench system ended at the end of the Westhampton's sector. When the Germans had been in occupation they had obviously tried to extend their position but had found the ground too wet, and a low ridge, which offered little protection from sniper fire, was all they had been able to accomplish. Water filled hollows, deep enough to drown a man in, added to the dangers of the area. Despite the risks involved, Collins still went there occasionally for a few hours of relative peace and quiet.

As he finished his tea he realised that he was feeling quite optimistic. For the first time since his arrival in France he had some degree of security. It was also dawning on him just how much he owed to the padre for his new confidence. And if today was anything to go by, it wasn't even going to be very arduous working for him. Previously, he had been at the beck and call of numerous officers, so working for only one man was going to be easy. One thing he had noticed however was that the padre had watched him closely while he worked. And twice during the day he had caught the padre staring at him with a strange far away look in his eyes. It gave him the uneasy feeling that the padre was checking up on him. But he'd had no complaints with his work. When he'd finished for the day, the padre had thanked him for his efforts and handed him a written list of weekly duties that he had made out. All in all, it had been a good first day in his new job.

A burst of raucous laughter came from inside the dugout; probably another rude joke, or story, being told by one of the older men. Davy Collins heard Lofty Webb's voice amongst the laughter. It was higher pitched than the rest and easily recognisable. It was good to hear him laughing and enjoying himself; a stark contrast to the way he used to be. Collins shivered and drew the greatcoat closer to him for warmth. Winter would soon be on them and the old hands in the regiment were saying that conditions would get really bad. It was time to go back inside and join the others. He might even sit with Lofty and listen to the men's stories for a while. He was feeling pleased with himself and didn't want the day to end just yet. Standing up to enter the dugout he heard the sound of a mouth organ being played further along the trench. Listening to the music and hearing the men's laughter from below made Collins forget the war, albeit it if only for a brief few seconds. He threw away the now cold dregs of his tea and went inside to join his mates.

Chapter 7

In the following weeks it seemed to Renton that both sides were too preoccupied with the approach of Christmas to bother about pursuing the war with any great effort. Apart from the obligatory artillery exchanges, only the snipers continued to pursue their deadly occupation with any enthusiasm. The weather had turned bitterly cold and the only concern for men now, apart from staying alive, was keeping warm. To boost morale and break the monotony of trench life, Captain Beamish was instructed to work out a rota for the men so they could each have some time off. Those who wished too, and had the money to spend, could have a day in Rouville if they wished; the town being near enough for them to be brought back quickly if needed. Those wishing to avail themselves of the town's pleasures received a warning talk about drunkenness, fighting and the danger of venereal diseases. Renton knew that despite the warnings there would be a steady trickle of offenders falling foul of army regulations and after the horrific fighting of a few months ago it was only to be expected. Rumour had it that the New Year would bring a fresh offensive but for now the men could relax a little and look forward to Christmas.

It wasn't just the fighting troops who were feeling more relaxed. Since Collins had become his orderly,

Renton had undergone a personality transformation that had not gone unnoticed by his fellow officers. There was a smartness and cleanliness about him that they hadn't seen before and his manner when dealing with people had also changed. He was more approachable and friendly than before. He knew that Beamish would assume that it was solely down to the fact that he had stopped drinking. In reality he hadn't stopped drinking altogether, but had cut down on his intake, and it was having a beneficial effect on his health and appearance. In just a couple of weeks his face had lost it's flushed, bloated look. His eyes were brighter too, and no longer permanently bloodshot. His hair had been cut to a reasonable length and he was shaving regularly. He was even told by Kerr one morning over breakfast that he looked years younger. Nobody was more aware of the changes and the reasons for them, than himself. It had always happened in the past when somebody entered his life that he desired. He wanted to make a good impression with Collins and knew from past encounters that it was essential to get Collins too really like him if they were to get on intimate terms. Being admired and respected wouldn't be enough. He would have to be physically and personably presentable to him, and that meant less drinking. It was already worth the effort as far as he was concerned.

Collins was pleasing to look at and have around. He was also turning out to be everything he wanted in an orderly and more besides, so winning the boy over to him completely was a simple affair. If Collins was an obedient servant, he would act the kind and grateful master and make a point of asking, never ordering a job done. Furthermore, he went out of his way to compliment him even for the most minor chores performed. The strategy was already paying off. Collins was obviously so relieved to be in a safe posting that anything he was asked to do was done promptly and well. There were positive little signs that Collins liked working for him. Mugs of tea appeared without being asked for, hot water ready for shaving, even the occasional egg for breakfast. Anything extra that could be scrounged from the cookhouse was put before him cheerfully and with the minimum of fuss. The way Collins went happily about his duties was proof enough to Renton that the first part of his scheme was working. Soon Collins would be completely dependent on him and would do anything he asked of him.

One afternoon, Renton was sitting in the officers' dugout. He had just finished his notes for his next Sunday sermon and was wondering what to do next to pass the time. Collins was working nearby, quietly whistling to himself as he went about his duties. Watching the youthful figure at work, Renton decided that now was as good a time as any to start encouraging closer relations between the two of them. He looked at his watch. Hostilities permitting, it had become an established routine for him to have tea at around four o'clock. Seeing it was almost time for Collins to depart for the cookhouse, he called the boy over to him. In a casual voice he told Collins to bring two mugs of tea back. They would have tea together, he said; he wished to talk to him.

Collins departed, a worried look etched on his face. Renton knew the boy would be wondering what sort of talk he was in for and was probably racking his brains to think of anything that he might have done wrong.

He was elated to see Collins' insecurity. It merited a little reward. Going to his locker, he took out the whisky bottle and took a generous swallow. It was the first drink he had taken in two days and it felt good, very good. The familiar sensations of warmth, confidence, and exhilaration came flooding back to him; it was like the return of an old friend. He thought about a second drink but decided against it and replaced the bottle back in the locker.

Collins returned with the tea, placed it down, and stood to attention waiting further instructions. Renton, conscious of the fact that Collins must be nervous at the idea of having tea with an officer, took a cigarette from the packet in front of him and lit up. 'Pull up a chair and sit down, Collins,' he said, 'you can drink your tea while we talk.'

Collins sat down looking uneasy and making no attempt to drink his tea.

'You're probably wondering why I want to talk to you.'

Collins nodded apprehensively. 'What's a matter, sir? Have I done something wrong?'

Renton smiled reassuringly at him. 'No, Collins, I'm not going to give you a ticking off, if that's what you're expecting. In fact, quite the contrary, I'm very pleased with your work so far.'

An expression of relief came over the boy's face and Renton noticed him relax a little. 'I thought that as you've proved satisfactory we might have a little chat. After all, if you're going to carry on working for me, I think I ought to know a bit more about you.'

'What sort of things, sir? I haven't bin in any trouble, if that's what you want to know.' Collins said quickly.

'I'm sure you haven't. From what I've seen of you, I'd say you come from a decent enough home; did you live with your parents before coming out here?'

'Yes sir. I live with me mum and dad.'

'What about brothers and sisters, or are you an only child?'

'No, I got two bruvvers and two sisters too.'

'I've got a sister.' Renton said. 'She's younger than me and married. When we were young we were always arguing.' He winked knowingly at Collins. 'Sisters can be hard work at times, can't they?'

'Not arf. Always crying about nothing at all, or else going on about dresses and dolls, and other daft things.'

'Yes, you're so right, I couldn't put it better myself. Don't forget your tea, Collins.' Renton picked up his mug and indicated to Collins to do the same. He could see the boy was bursting with pride as he picked up his mug. He probably couldn't wait to write home and tell his parents that he had drunk tea with an officer. Would they believe him, he wondered? 'I hope you write home regularly?' he said.

Collins took a gulp of tea before answering. 'Oh yeah, mum would worry if I didn't.'

'My mother's the same. In fact, between you and me, she gives me a good ticking off if I don't write home often enough. Do you write to anyone else at home? A good looking chap like you must have a girlfriend to write to.'

The boy reddened before answering. 'No sir, I haven't got no girlfriend. I don't write to anyone except me mum.'

'And have you told her you're my orderly?'

'Yes, sir, she's very pleased about it.'

Renton smiled at Collins. 'It must be a great weight off her mind knowing that you're working for me and not doing anything dangerous. Is she very relieved?'

'Oh yes, sir. She's ever so thankful, and so am I.'

'Well, I try my best for people that need a helping hand. It's my job you know to help lads like you overcome their fears in this awful place. I try to help everybody, but, naturally I have a special interest in the safety of my friends, and I've got a feeling you're going to be a good friend as well as a good orderly.'

'Wot me, sir? You'd like me to be your friend?' The boy was clearly taken aback at the suggestion.

'You seem surprised at the idea. Wouldn't you like us to be friends?' Renton said, stubbing out his cigarette.

'Yes, sir, I'd be real honoured, sir. It's just that, well, to be honest, I didn't think the likes of me mixed with officers.'

Renton leant forward. 'That just applies to the regular officers. As a chaplain I don't have to worry about that sort of thing, although obviously I'm still ranked as an officer and you must treat me as such in front of other people.'

'Oh yes, course I would, sir.'

'And you don't have to keep calling me sir, either. At least, not when we're alone, understood?'

Collins nodded, obviously lost for words. It was probably the longest conversation he'd had with an officer and, Renton imagined, certainly the friendliest.

'I believe your Christian name is David?'

'Yes, but me mates call me, Davy.'

'Well then, Davy Collins, what do you do in your off duty hours, apart from writing letters?'

'Not much really, I sit with the men sometimes, talking about the war and wot's happening at home. But mostly I talk with me mate, Lofty.'

'Do you read at all? Decent books, I mean, not those lurid penny sheets that seem to be so popular.'

'I'm not very good at reading books. I'd like to read more but I can't make out all them long complicated words.'

'Well, I could help you with your reading, your writing too. Would you like that? Would you like to be able to read and write properly?'

'Oh yes, I've always wanted to read and write proper like.'

'You could write really interesting letters home to your mother, then, Davy. I'm sure she'd like that, wouldn't she?'

'If she could read all the long words, she would!'

'I expect she'd manage. Mothers do, you know.'

'Yeah, I think you're right.' The boy thought for a second and then said. 'When could I start lessons, sir?'

'As soon as you like, shall we say an hour a day in the afternoons, starting from tomorrow?'

'That'd be great.'

'Good, that's settled then, we'll begin tomorrow,' Renton said, smiling at Collins. In a more serious tone, he added, 'I've enjoyed our little chat but if we're to be friends it had better be our little secret. The other officers wouldn't approve of such familiarity between us. Now if you've finished your tea you'd better run along.'

After the boy had gone, Renton contemplated having another drink. He deserved one after the way he had conducted himself during his chat with Collins. It had been an exercise in self- restraint. Enchanting was the only way to describe the boy: everything about him was simply enchanting. His face was so beautifully shaped that Renton had been tempted to stretch out his hand and stroke the smooth, young, white skin. Collins, girlish lips had mesmerised Renton and made him want to lean forward and kiss them. And, under long, dark lashes, deep, brown eyes. Eyes that had opened wide with amazement at times as the boy sat and listened with mounting incredulity to every word spoken to him. He had some rough edges in his manner of course, that was only to be expected from a boy of that class and background. But he was not unintelligent and even showed signs of sensitivity. It had been a stroke of genius to think of the reading classes. What better way to meet regularly without arousing undue suspicion? In furthering his education, Collins would put himself deeper in Renton's debt. It was all coming together nicely.

A faint high pitched, whistling noise brought his speculations to an abrupt end. The whistling became louder and more intense. Renton knew the sound well enough by now. He threw himself to the floor and covered his head in his hands. Through the walls of the dugout he heard the deafening crump of the shell as it exploded nearby. The building shook violently from the shock waves. Dirt and stones, loosened by the blast, rained down on Renton from the roof. An eerie silence followed the explosion. Renton, white faced and shaken, got to his feet and ran a hand through his hair dislodging dust and earth. He was trembling with fright but otherwise uninjured and the dugout appeared to have suffered no serious structural damage. But he knew the shell must have detonated in the midst of their lines and grabbing his bible he hurried outside. He didn't have to look far to see where the stray shell had landed. Some seventy yards away to his left, in front of the cookhouse, a pall of grey smoke rose into the sky. From inside the cloud of smoke he could hear the cries of the wounded. From all directions men were hurrying to the scene to help. He saw Kerr emerge, running, from his underground command post and heard his voice, loudly but calmly, issuing orders and calling for medics. As he got nearer, and the smoke thinned, Renton saw the extent of the carnage that the blast had caused. A shallow crater had been made in the ground and strewn all around were the partially naked corpses of men who, only seconds previously, had been sitting outside the cookhouse taking advantage of a bit of warmth and enjoying an afternoon brew up. Most of them had disappeared, blown to pieces by the force of the blast. Renton stopped at the edge of the crater and looked down. A few yards away from his feet lay the bloody remains of a human torso. It was covered in a shred of khaki uniform that flapped obscenely in the chilly afternoon air. Renton felt the gorge rise to his throat and beads of sweat formed on his brow.

Stretcher bearers went quickly among the bodies and took away those that showed any signs of life. After all the injured had been removed, Kerr asked Renton to say a prayer for the deceased. He walked hesitantly forward and, bowing his head prayed aloud for the souls of the dead soldiers. Afterwards, Kerr ordered that the crater be filled in immediately. A sombre Renton stood and watched as the hole was hastily filled with a macabre mixture of earth, rocks and human flesh. Barely thirty minutes after the shell had landed nothing remained to mark the spot where men had died such a horrible death except a small mound of fresh earth. Suddenly, a terrible thought came to him that made his blood run cold. *Collins!* In the confusion and panic he had completely forgotten that the boy had left him only minutes before the explosion. In all probability he would have been heading back to the cookhouse. His heart filled with despair. The boy must have been blown to pieces in the blast.

Chapter 8

Ron Watkins was in his storeroom when the artillery shell landed and was nearly knocked off his feet by the blast. Now he had been summoned to the regimental command post and was curious to know why he had been called away from his quartermaster's duties. On entering the heavily reinforced command post, Watkins found Major Kerr sitting at an old oak dining table speaking on the field telephone. Next to him sat the Adjutant, sifting through a heap of paperwork.

At length Major Kerr finished his phone call. 'Damn it!' he exclaimed loudly, fiddling with his ever present pipe, 'I hate it when men die like that. I know it sounds a stupid thing to say in a war where so many men have already died, but I can't help it. The poor buggers never knew what hit them.'

Watkins had never before heard such an outburst from his normally placid CO. He had been about to ask why he had been summoned but thought better of it and remained silent.

'I know what you mean,' Captain Beamish said, pushing his pile of papers to one side. 'It's so totally unexpected. The ironic part about is, we don't even know whether it was German shell or one of our own.'

'Judging by its bloody efficiency, I'd say it was German,' Kerr said.

The irony of Kerr's remark wasn't lost on Watkins. Many British shells were badly packed and failed to explode on impact; German ammunition was generally more reliable.

'What did HQ have to say?' Beamish asked.

'Not a lot! Claimed it wasn't one of ours, of course. Wants the casualty list as soon as possible; usual drill.'

Watkins saw the Adjutant grimace. Most of the 'usual drill' would fall to him later on when the identities of the dead soldiers were confirmed.

'Just when morale was getting better, too,' Kerr said, trying to force more tobacco into the bowl of his pipe than it was made to accommodate.

Watkins decided he'd heard enough; it was time to get back to his storeroom. He could only trust his subordinates up to a point. Things had a habit of going missing when he wasn't around. 'The men will probably forget about it in a couple of days, sir' he said, reminding Kerr of his presence. 'At least, the older hands will. They've seen it all before. I believe you wanted me, sir?'

'Ah, Watkins,' Kerr said, swinging around to face his quartermaster. 'Sorry, didn't mean to ignore you. I sent for you because I want you to see that a tot of rum is issued with the evening meal. It'll help take the men's minds off things. Have we got enough rum to go round?'

'Yes, sir, I think so. I'll see to it straight away' Watkins said. Then, as an afterthought, asked. 'How many do you think we lost in the blast, sir?'

It was Beamish who answered his question. 'We won't know until the roll call. Not as many as it would have been if the shell had hit the cookhouse, though. Just imagine if that lot had gone up!'

Major Kerr, having managed to fill his pipe, paused in his attempt to light the tightly packed contents. 'Yes, by God! That really would have been a disaster. Were there any casualties in there, Freddie? I didn't have time to look inside.'

'Only minor injuries, I checked while you were dealing with the clearing up operation outside.' Beamish picked up his cap. 'If you don't need me for anything else then, sir—'

Kerr shook his head. 'No, you carry on, Freddie.'

Watkins waited until Beamish had gone and then said, 'It was just bad luck sir, nothing else. Nothing anybody could've done about it.'

'I know,' Kerr said, 'but a stray shell seems such an unlucky way to die.'

'You mean there's a lucky way, sir?' Watkins asked, displaying his morbid sense of humour developed after twenty years of soldiering. He hurriedly threw up a salute and left before his commanding officer had a chance to reply.

Scarcely five minutes after Watkins's departure Renton entered the command post. He had remained at the scene of the bomb tragedy long after all the others had left, his mind in a state of turmoil, not knowing what to do, or where to go. Eventually, he started to think rationally again. He badly needed a drink but knew he had to remain sober; he had to see Kerr and tell him about Collins.

Kerr looked up and nodded a greeting to Renton who went over and sat down beside him. 'Nasty business,' Kerr said to him, 'terrible way for men to die. Thanks for saying a few words back there. Much appreciated.' He drew hard on his pipe. 'Hope it didn't upset you too much, Simon. At least the poor buggers are out of all this misery now.'

Renton wasn't listening. 'I've lost Collins,' he said quietly. 'In the blast, I mean. He was killed in the blast.' He took out a packet of cigarettes and lighting one up with shaking hands, began taking quick nervous puffs.

'I'm sorry, that's really bad luck,' Kerr said without looking up from the papers he was studying, 'from what I saw of his work in the mess, he seemed to have the makings of a good orderly.'

Renton was staggered by Kerr's lack of reaction to Collins death. 'What do you mean? Didn't you hear what I said?' he cried, 'my orderly, Collins, is dead. Doesn't that mean anything more to you than just 'bad luck'?' As he finished his outburst, Beamish returned unexpectedly. Renton was relieved to see him. At least Freddie would understand the extent of the tragedy.

'Renton's got some bad news,' Kerr said, before he had a chance to speak, 'seems his orderly, Collins, was killed in the blast.'

'What! Are you sure, Simon?' Beamish asked.

'Yes, of course I'm sure.'

'Why are you so certain?'

'Because I am.'

'But the RSM hasn't done a roll call yet.'

'It doesn't matter, he's dead I tell you!'

'Did you see him die?'

'No.'

'Then I say again. How do you know he's dead?'

'How many more times do I have to say it? He's dead! He died in the blast! Haven't you got it yet?'

'But how can you know for certain that he was outside the cookhouse?' Beamish said.

'Of course he was,' Renton shouted. 'That's where he was going when he left me.' Renton was amazed at their stupidity. What was the matter with them? Hadn't they heard what he'd been saying?

Kerr pushed his chair back and stood up. 'Look, it's a rotten business losing Collins, Simon, but he wasn't the only casualty, you know. We lost other men today besides him. Some of them were front line troops, men I could ill afford to lose, and that's my main concern, not you're orderly. You'll get a replacement if that's what's worrying you.'

The last sentence was too much for Renton to take. Ever since his arrival he had harboured a suspicion that Kerr despised him because he hadn't been with the regiment when the really heavy fighting had taken place. Kerr's implication that he was only concerned about Collins death because it would mean not having an orderly to look after him made him furious. He leapt to his feet to protest but before he could utter a word, Beamish stepped in between him and Kerr.

'I know it might seem hard to you, Simon, but we can't allow ourselves the luxury of emotions here. We've learnt the hard way not to value one person's life more than another's. The CO is just being realistic about Collins. He's a casualty of war just like the others are.'

'He was my orderly and a decent human being, or doesn't that bother you,' Renton said angrily.

'Look, why don't you wait until the roll call,' Beamish said calmly. 'Until then there's always a chance.'

Renton strode to the door. He was beside himself with rage. He had come in search of sympathy and understanding, and found neither. 'How can the pair of you be so indifferent to death?' he shouted at them. Turning on his heel, he rushed out the door.

The daylight was fading and a chilly wind cut into Renton's body as he made his way through the mud to his quarters. His face was contorted with rage and his fists were clenched so tightly that the knuckles showed white. He couldn't get Kerr and Beamish out of his mind. They had treated him badly, especially Kerr. Why did he always have to make him feel so inadequate?

Entering his dugout he grabbed the bottle of whisky out of his locker and sat on his bed. Raising the bottle to his mouth he drank greedily, shuddering as the fiery liquid ran down his throat. Several drinks later the feeling of bitterness and anger was still with him as the thought of an existence without Collins repeatedly came back to him. As he drank he tried desperately to hold on to the boy's image in his mind. The thought of never again seeing his beautiful face filled him with anguish. He wanted to hit out at someone, anyone, who was in any way responsible for his loss, but there was nothing he could do. Fuelled by his acute sense of loss his mood of anger was followed by a mood of black despair. Wallowing in self- pity, only a state of oblivion would bring relief to his tormented mind. The remaining contents of the bottle were insufficient to drown his sorrows. More drink was needed; he would have to go and see Sergeant Watkins again. Pride, dignity, and common sense had abandoned him. They had all disappeared as rapidly as the whisky that he had poured down his throat.

‘Well, look who it is? I haven’t seen you here for a while, padre.’ Watkins’s voice sounded as if it were coming from somewhere far away and his face kept swimming in and out of focus. In fact everything around Renton kept swimming in and out of focus. Finding the Quartermasters billet had been a minor miracle considering his condition. But getting another bottle from Watkins was all that mattered to him. He waved an arm erratically in the rough direction of Watkins’s face. ‘Bottle of whisky, I need a bottle, *NOW!*’ he shouted. He lurched aggressively forward to reinforce his demand and fell against Watkins who grabbed hold of him to prevent him falling to the ground.

Watkins glanced about him; it was early evening, darkness had fallen. He couldn’t see anyone standing about watching the padre’s drunken antics; grabbing Renton around the waist he hauled him upright and pushed him into his quarters. The padre was roaring drunk; that much was obvious. Watkins was puzzled though; he’d never have taken Renton for a belligerent drunk. Something seriously upsetting must have happened to get him in such a state. ‘Coffee’s what you need, not whisky,’ he said, sitting Renton down in a chair.

Renton seemed to be incapable of coordinating his body movements and started sliding off his chair but somehow managed to stop himself and regain his seat. ‘No coffee! Not yet! Let’s have a drink first,’ he said, thumping the table with his fist. He began searching his pockets and located a packet of Woodbines. Pulling out the packet, he attempted to take out a cigarette but only succeeded in dropping half the contents of the packet on the floor. Muttering to himself, he went down on his hands and knees crawling about on the floor picking up what cigarettes he could find. When he was satisfied that he'd found enough, he hauled himself back into his chair and after a few fumbled efforts, managed to put a cigarette to his lips and light it.

Watkins watched in silent amusement. He'd seen more than a few drunks in his time and knew that the best way to handle Renton was to humour him. 'All right, padre, I'll get you a drink, just try and stay in your chair.' He fetched a bottle and glass and set them down in front of Renton. By the time he had pulled up a chair for himself, Renton had already poured a measure of whisky and was raising the glass to his lips. 'Blimey! What's the hurry? The bottle won't go away, you know.' Renton, having drained his glass, ignored him and reached for the bottle again. 'What's brought all this on, then?' Watkins asked, like a father talking to an upset child.

Renton poured himself another drink before answering. 'You don't understand, Sergeant!' he said in a voice so slurred that Watkins had to lean forward to make out what he was saying, 'nobody here does, that's the problem.'

'Try me.' Watkins didn't mind listening to the padre's drunken ramblings for a little while. It could turn out to be quite entertaining. He might even pick up some gossip about the officers that would be useful to him. He was curious about Renton, too. It had been three weeks since the padre had visited him and he'd heard whispers from various sources that the priest was on the wagon. Looking at the drunken wreck opposite, Watkins came to the conclusion that the whispers were a bit premature.

‘Heartless,’ Renton mumbled, ‘that’s what they are, Sergeant, heartless.’ He stared at Watkins through eyes that were bloodshot, and downed another glass of whisky.

‘No need to be so formal, padre, call me, Ron.’ Watkins put the tips of his fingers together and leaned back in his chair. ‘So tell me then, who’s so bleeding heartless?’ Watkins listened patiently to Renton’s rambling, almost incoherent, account of what had befallen him earlier. It cost him the best part of a bottle, and a lot of prompting and interrupting before he got the whole story out of the padre. What he heard wasn’t greatly to his advantage, but he was curious as to why Renton was taking the death of his orderly so badly. The priest had seen many deaths since his arrival. Why was this one affecting him so much? ‘Fond of him were you, padre?’ he enquired casually, as if Collins had been no more than a pet dog that had had to be put down.

Renton’s eyes were doing their best to focus on Watkins. He was hopelessly drunk now and very near to sleep. ‘Don’t keep saying, padre. It’s Simon, to you, Ron, Ronald, or whatever your name is... what was the question?’

‘I asked if you were fond of him.’ Watkins said loudly.

Renton’s reaction was startling. ‘Fond of him, was I fond of him?’ he cried out, his eyes suddenly brimming with tears. ‘He was a wonderful boy, wonderful.’ Leaning his head back, Renton looked desperately up at the roof as if expecting some divine intervention to come and relieve him from his misery. Then, letting out a low moan, he shut his eyes and allowed his head to fall forward on to his arms that were stretched out on the table. Burying his face into the sleeves of his jacket he began sobbing quietly.

Watkins looked at Renton, started to speak and then changed his mind as suspicion about the chaplain dawned in his mind. Twenty years of army life had taken him many places and he'd seen some strange things. Although married with children, he'd always lived the life of a single man to the full when posted abroad. Free from the constraints of domestic life, the attractions of the bars, clubs and bordellos of the red light districts of the world, had drawn him like a moth to a flame. There were a good many sexual practices he'd seen, and taken part in, and they hadn't all involved women. The result was that he had become a pretty good judge of men's likes when it came to sex. Renton was a drunk, or at least as good as, and in Watkins experience there was usually only two reasons men became drunks; sex or money! He didn't think the padre had money troubles, but the fact that Renton was a priest didn't necessarily mean that he wasn't interested in sex. He had once asked an elderly Roman Catholic army chaplain how he had coped without women. The priest had winked at him and said, 'son, celibacy might make you religiously stronger, but it won't stop your dick growing longer.' Watkins liked that and understood exactly what the old priest was getting at. Maybe Renton liked sex in one particular form and perhaps Collins was more than just his orderly.

He was eager to find out more but unfortunately for him the sobbing had ceased and been replaced by the sounds of heavy rhythmic snoring. Renton had finally succumbed to the effects of the whisky and fallen into a drunken sleep. Watkins didn't want him remaining where he was, but on the other hand, he couldn't very well take the padre back to the officers' quarters in the state he was in. He had to try and get him to the chapel somehow. It was the best place to let him sleep off his drinking session. The only trouble was how to get him there? He was strong, but the padre looked as if he would be no lightweight to lift.

Just as he was resigning himself to the fact that Renton would have to stay the night, he heard a knock on his door. Opening it a fraction, he peered out and saw the answer to his dilemma standing there in the unlikely forms of Cpl Brown and Pte Leggett. Watkins had completely forgotten he'd given them the job of issuing the rum ration. They'd finished their task and now stood before him confidently expecting to be dismissed; but their confidence was misplaced. He quickly ushered them in and shut the door behind them. They stared open mouthed for a second at the comatose figure of Renton slumped across the table before both broke into peals of laughter.

'Yeah, yeah, I know it's very funny but just don't go telling anybody about this, or you'll find yourselves back on patrol in no time, understood?' Watkins' words had the desired effect and the two men fell silent. 'All right then; this what I want you to do—'

The two soldiers lay Renton on a stretcher and Watkins placed a couple of blankets under his head. They were all ready to carry him to the chapel when it occurred to Watkins that it had been a costly night in whisky for him. He knelt down and went through Renton's pockets until he found what he was looking for. Pulling out a handful of banknotes, he peeled off five, and stuffed the rest back. Then he stood up, looked at his helpers, and tapped the side of his nose with his index finger. 'Mum's the word,' he said, handing Cpl Brown one of the banknotes. Then he told him to get Renton out of his sight.

The freezing night air easily found its way into the small timbered barn that served as Renton's chapel. It stole in under the ill fitted door and through the gaps in the old wooden shutters hanging at the windows. In the middle of the floor, Renton lay sleeping on the stretcher provided by Watkins. The soldiers had covered him with one of the blankets to give him some protection from the elements, but the amount of whisky he had drunk earlier made him oblivious to the cold or any other discomforts. As the night went on however, the sedative benefits of the whisky wore off, and his sleep became less heavy and more fitful. The alcohol worked its way into his sub-conscious and made his mind hyper active. The result was a terrifying nightmare. In it, he was wandering, lost and alone, through a dark and bleak landscape. A thick mist hung over the place making it impossible to see further than an a few yards in front of him. Suddenly the mist cleared and the area ahead of him was bathed in a bright ethereal light. Coming towards the light were a group of naked male figures dancing, their bodies swaying sensuously to the sound of exotic music. Behind the dancers came a second group of naked men who were dragging a struggling youth along behind them. To his amazement, Renton recognised the naked figures in the second group as men he had encountered in his past. But the handsome features they had once possessed were gone, and their faces looked old and ugly. The unreal procession stopped a little distance in front of him. Laying the youth down on the ground they formed a circle and began stroking and caressing his prone body in an erotic manner.

With mounting horror Renton saw that it was Collins who was the object of their lust. The boy's face was haggard and drawn and he appeared to be in great agony. He lifted his head and on seeing Renton, his eyes opened wide with hope and expectation. Renton's blood ran cold with fear and a sense of evil foreboding overtook him. He tried to stop them fondling Collins body but found he couldn't move. He tried to scream at them, but no sound came from his mouth. They laughed mockingly at his despair. Then, like a pack of wild animals, they bared their teeth and fell upon the boy's body. Renton stood, powerless to help, as they pulled and ripped frenziedly at Collin's pale, defenceless flesh until it came apart in their hands. When they had dismembered the body they pranced around carrying their bloody trophies in their hands and waving their gruesome spoils at him. He attempted to pursue one who taunted him with Collin's head but fast as he tried to run he remained firmly rooted to the spot. Then the mist closed in again and the figures faded away until finally only Collin's head remained in view. Renton watched helplessly as a pair of dark brown eyes stared back at him through the gloom. The eyes were pleading with him for help, but he could do nothing. After what seemed an eternity, they disappeared into the mist and he was alone again. He screamed and shouted after them to come back.

His terrified shouts woke him from his nightmare. Struggling into a sitting position, he gulped in great mouthfuls of air. He could feel his heart pounding under his clothing, and, despite the cold he was sweating profusely. Beads of perspiration dripped off his forehead and on to the blankets stretched over him. He had no idea where he was or how he had got there but with great relief he realised that what had just taken place had been nothing more than a bad dream. He was exhausted and had a splitting headache. Pulling the blankets closer around him he closed his eyes and tried to go back to sleep but the nightmare kept returning and he awoke several times with the image of Collin's eyes staring at him. At last his mind seemed finally to free itself from torment and he slipped into a shallow sleep.

Suddenly he became aware of a new dream. He was in bed and someone was shaking him by the shoulder and calling his name. He couldn't respond, he was desperately tired and his limbs felt as heavy as lead. But the person wouldn't give up and kept repeating his name. The voice sounded more real than the voices he had heard earlier in the other dream. He tried to open his eyes and make the dream go away, but his eyelids felt like they'd been glued together. His shoulder was being shaken again, but more forcibly this time. With great effort he forced his eyelids apart. To his horror a face came into view. He blinked rapidly to help focus his eyes. It wasn't possible. He must be back in the nightmare.

'Mr Renton, sir, wake up,' the voice was insistent, 'Mr Renton, its late, please get up.' He shook his head from side to side to make sure he was truly awake and with a mounting sense of trepidation looked again at the features of the person kneeling beside him. Stifling a cry, he sat bolt upright and stared open mouthed in disbelief.

Chapter 9

The chat with the padre had left Collins feeling happy for almost the first time since enlisting in the army. Up until now nobody in the regiment, other than Lofty, had shown any interest in his personal life or welfare; certainly no officer had taken him aside and talked with him like the padre had. Collins thought all officers were aloof and unapproachable. Senior officers were by far the worst of all. He'd seen enough Generals giving out their orders in posh voices to form an opinion of them. The war was just a big game to them; an opportunity to gain promotion and pin some extra medals on their chests. Living in safety and comfort behind the front lines, they never gave a thought about the awful conditions the poor buggers doing the fighting had to put up with. At least the padre had shown some concern for him, which was far more than any other officer had ever done, and what's more he'd used language that a fellow could understand. Collins started for the cookhouse happily but after only going a few yards, he stopped. It was no good; his news couldn't wait. He was simply bursting to tell Lofty about his talk with the padre. Turning around, he hurried off in the opposite direction towards his quarters.

He was just about to enter his accommodation when he heard the whistle of an approaching artillery shell.

Throwing the mugs to the ground he hurled himself down the steps into his dugout and hit the bottom on all fours. His momentum carried him along and he crashed headlong into a group of men sitting on the floor playing cards. Winded by the fall, he landed breathless on his back in their midst. Cards, money and men were scattered all over the floor. The group, which he noted included Lofty Webb, lay spread-eagled on the ground looking at him with amazement and annoyance, but before they could open their mouths to protest, the blast of the exploding shell shook the dugout. When the shock wave had passed everybody froze and remained motionless on the floor. After a few tense minutes no more shells could be heard exploding and they realised that it was just a stray and not the beginning of a barrage. The men leapt to their feet and dashed out to see what help they could give if needed. Collins started after them but only got as far as the doorway before noticing that Lofty Webb hadn't joined them. Looking back he saw him sitting on the floor with his legs drawn up to his chest and his arms tightly wound around his knees. His chin was resting on his knees and he was staring down at the floor. Webb's face was deathly pale and the dark veins on his forehead stood out clearly.

Collins went over and sat down beside him. 'What's up, Lofty,' he said, trying to make light of the situation, 'did I knock the breath out of you?'

'I don't want to go out there,' Webb said in a dull voice. He continued to stare at the floor.

'That's all right. Don't worry about it. They'll be plenty of help. They won't miss us.' Collins could understand Webb's reluctance to leave the safety of the dugout after his recent experience.

‘I know what it’ll be like out there, you see.’ Webb’s voice grew louder and his body trembled as he spoke. Suddenly he turned and gripped Collins by the shoulders, an expression of grim determination on his face. ‘I’ve seen it before,’ he shouted, ‘and I don’t ever want to see it again, understand?’

‘Course I do,’ Collins said sympathetically. ‘We’ll just sit here quiet like, for a minute, all right?’ Webb didn’t answer. Pain and misery were etched on his face and Collins could imagine what awful memories the explosion must be invoking in his friend’s mind

‘They’ll never make me go through that again, do you hear me, never!’ As he spoke, Webb’s fingers dug hard into Collins shoulders and made him wince in pain. Suddenly he relaxed his fingers and let his hands drop limply into his lap. ‘Sorry,’ he mumbled, ‘I didn’t mean to grip you so tightly.’ Webb’s face was red with embarrassment and he looked as if he would burst into tears any minute.

‘It’s all right. You didn’t hurt me.’ Collins lied. It suddenly occurred to him that telling Webb about his chat with the padre might snap him out of his mood of depression. ‘Hey listen, do you wanna hear my latest bit of news?’ he said. Without giving Webb time to think about it, he went into an account of his conversation with the padre. Webb appeared apathetic at first, but soon got interested until finally he was listening avidly to every word. By the time Collins got to the part about learning to read and write properly he could see that Webb’s **dark mood had vanished and the old Lofty was re-emerging**

He had just finished talking when one of the men returned and told them about the explosion outside the cookhouse. The colour drained from Webb's face as he heard about the casualties. 'Bloody hell,' he said in a quiet voice, 'I was supposed to go there! If I hadn't ave been so keen to tell you me news, Lofty, I'd ave been outside there when the shell hit.'

Webb's eyes opened wide. 'Christ! You lucky sod, Davy! There might be something in this religious lark after all. Who knows? You might have one of them guardian angels watching over you.'

'Yeah,' Collins said, awestruck, 'you could be right at that. Just think, me very own guardian angel looking out for me.'

'Well, don't forget to put in a word for me, will you. You're not the only one who wants to get through this war alive, you know.'

Collins started to laugh but stopped abruptly as a sudden thought came into his head. 'Christ, Lofty! It's just occurred to me. The padre thought I was going to the cookhouse. He might think I'm dead. Should I go and see him and let him know I'm all right?'

Lofty Webb shook his head. 'I wouldn't bother if I were you. You're gonna see him when you take his meal to him later, anyway.'

'True enough. Besides, he'll probably know by now who'd died in the blast because he'd have to go there and say some prayers or something.' Collins decided Lofty was right, it wasn't worth worrying about; after all, he'd be seeing the padre at supper. By now the remainder of the dugout's occupants had trickled back in groups of two's and three's. The corporal in charge took a head count and then went off to report to the

RSM. Afterwards the explosion was the only topic of conversation among the men. When the talk dried up a depressing silence hung over the dugout. No one seemed interested in resuming the game of cards that had been so dramatically interrupted. The majority went and lay on top of their beds, lost in their thoughts. Collins thought about the men who had died in the blast; it was a reminder to him that it could be anybody next, himself included.

On his arrival at the cookhouse in the evening Collins found things were pretty much back to normal again after the disruption of the explosion earlier. He knew the padre's eating habits well enough to know that he never took very long over his meals. Perfectly understandable since evening meals nearly always consisted of an unappetising mess of stew heaped on a tin plate with two slices of hard bread slapped on top. The padre would normally finish his meal in about twenty minutes, sometimes leaving half his meal untouched. But when Collins arrived, the padre wasn't in the mess which wasn't unusual. The padre was often late for supper and when that happened, Collins simply left the meal and came back later to clear the remains away. Placing the tray on the padre's bed, he returned to the cookhouse to pick up his own supper. Later that evening he returned to the officer's mess. It was more crowded and a lot noisier than it had been earlier. Groups of officers sat together drinking and talking while others whiled away the time playing cards. Collins looked around the mess but couldn't see the padre. The tray and its contents hadn't been touched; they were still on the bed, just as he had left them. It was nine o'clock now and Collins knew there was no chance of the padre eating the cold revolting mess that had congealed on the plate. He picked up the tray and was about to depart when the Adjutant came up to him.

'Well, Collins,' he said. 'What's it like to be resurrected from the dead?'

A puzzled look came over Davy's face. 'Pardon, sir, resurr... what? I don't understand what you're saying, sir.'

'Never mind,' Beamish said. 'You're alive and kicking, that's the main thing. Mr Renton must be very relieved.'

Collins didn't understand what the Adjutant was saying. Had the padre thought him dead after all? If he had, then surely by now he knew otherwise. He wondered if the Adjutant knew of the chaplain's whereabouts. 'Have you seen, Mr Renton, sir? Only I haven't seen him since before the explosion, what's more, he ain't touched his supper neither.'

'You mean he hasn't seen you yet? He doesn't know you're alive?' The Adjutant had a look of amazement on his face.

Collins was worried, but tried not to show it. He acted as if he was surprised by the Adjutant's remarks. 'Sorry sir, do you mean that the padre thinks I'm dead?'

'That's right, Collins, that's exactly what I mean.'

Collins listened in stunned silence as he was told of the padre's visit to the command post earlier. Finally the Adjutant dismissed him with the advice that he seek the padre out as soon as possible and let him see that he was alive and well. Davy Collins wondered where the padre could possibly have gone and whether or not he'd been told yet that his orderly was alive. It sickened him now that he hadn't gone and seen the padre earlier.

Disposing of the padre's untouched meal, he set out towards the only place he could think where the padre might be, the chapel.

It was a cold moonlit night, and from the West came the distant rumble of artillery fire. To get to the chapel, Collins had to pass the Quartermasters accommodation. As he approached he saw the burly figure of Sergeant Watkins standing outside his billet smoking a cheroot. Drawing level with the sergeant, Collins was about to pass him by when he felt a hand on his arm.

'Wait a minute, lad! Not so fast. Aren't you Collins, the chaplain's new orderly?'

He was in a hurry. He didn't want to stop but he had to obey the Quartermaster's order. 'Yes, that's right Sergeant. Why do you ask?'

'Because, my son, according to Mr Renton, you're supposed to be dead.'

Collins sighed heavily. Not the Quartermaster as well! How many people had the padre been speaking to, he wondered? 'Well I'm not, Sarge. In fact, I'm trying to find him now and sort this out,' he looked hopefully at Watkins, 'do you know where he is then?'

'Might do,' Watkins said, removing his hand. He eyed Collins up and down slowly and took a long drag on his cheroot.

In the silvery light of the bright December moon, the end of Watkins' cheroot glowed fiery red and Collins got a fleeting glimpse of the Quartermaster's face. He was grinning from ear to ear. He waited patiently but Watkins didn't elaborate on his remark. 'I'm going to the chapel. It's the only place I can think of,' He said, finally. It was getting late and he didn't want to waste any more time. He turned to move off, but felt Watkins's hand go back on his arm.

'No need to.' Watkins said. 'He's there all right, and he's not going anyplace with the amount of whisky he's got inside him. He was pretty cut up over you, lad. Must think a lot of you, I reckon.'

Collins remained silent. He was relieved to have found out the padre's whereabouts but was worried to think that he was the cause of so much trouble and misery.

Watkins, looking at him intently, seemed to read his mind. 'Not your fault, boy! He shouldn't jump to conclusions, should he?' He gave Davy Collins arm a gentle squeeze.

He's right, Collins thought, it's not my fault. He'd see the padre in the morning and explain everything. They'd probably have a good laugh together about it.

'Good to work for, is he?'

Watkins's hand was still on Collins arm, preventing him from moving off.

'You know something, lad? We had quiet a long chat about you. You'd be surprised what the chaplain tells me.'

Collins had no idea what the Sergeant was talking about. What could the padre possibly have said about him that would be of any interest to the Quartermaster?

'You see, the thing is, Davy boy, and, I don't expect for one minute that the padre has ever mentioned it to you, but we're good mates, him and me, see.' Watkins glanced about him and lowered his voice. 'He talks to me a lot you know, on account of him not getting on with most of the officer's. They look down on him cos he's not a fighting officer, see.'

That made sense to Collins. He'd heard some of the officers' making fun of the padre, sometimes gently to his face, other times more harshly behind his back. He had never seen the padre get annoyed but knew it must irritate him. The Quartermaster wasn't a commissioned officer but he was a respected figure in the regiment. The sort of person the padre might well find it easier to talk to than the young snobbish Lieutenants he had to put up with in the mess.

'Do you think he'll be all right, Sarge?' Collins asked. He was worried that Renton might catch pneumonia sleeping in the freezing chapel.

Sergeant Watkins blew a series of smoke rings into the night sky before answering. 'Your concern does you credit, Davy boy, but no need to fret. I had a couple of my men tuck him up nice and cosy on a stretcher under a couple of blankets. Believe me; he'll sleep like a bug in a rug until morning.' Watkins let go of Colins arm and taking a last drag on his cheroot, flicked the butt into the air. 'I reckon you two must get on pretty well together to be so considerate of each others welfare,' he said looking hard into the boy's face.

Collins sensed that Watkins was looking for a reaction from him. Perhaps he meant well but he doubted it, anyway, he felt uncomfortable with the sergeant's easy familiarity towards him. Now that he knew the padre was all right there was no reason to stay here talking. Bidding Watkins goodnight, Collins turned to leave. He had only taken one step when he heard the Quartermasters voice ring out behind him.

'Just a minute, Private, I haven't dismissed you yet,' Watkins tone was firm and authorative and without hesitation Collins turned about and stood to attention facing Watkins. The smug look was gone from the Sergeant's face and been replaced by a sterner expression.

'That's better. You're still in the army, lad and don't you ever forget that.'

'Yes, Sergeant, I mean no, Sergeant.' Davy's face blushed in the cold night air.

'Just because the padre's taken a shine to you and you've got a cushy job it doesn't mean you can be a sloppy soldier, understand?'

'Yes, Sergeant, sorry.'

'Right, well, we'll say no more about it, then. Private Collins, you're dismissed, off you go'

As he made his way back to his accommodation, Collins cheeks were still burning from Watkins's rebuke. But it wasn't just the rebuke that had stung him. His meeting with Watkins had disturbed him. Throughout their encounter, he had the feeling that the Quartermaster was toying with him. Watkins had said he was a friend of the padre and he had looked after him so he should be grateful to him for that. But the fact that the he seemed to know so much about him still unnerved him.

In bed later that night, he lay awake for some time thinking about his meeting with Watkins. Before he finally went to asleep he had made a decision; in future he would try and steer clear of Quartermaster Sergeant Watkins.

The next morning after stand-to, Collins went to the officer's mess. The padre still hadn't put in an appearance so he figured he must still be sleeping off his hangover and decided to have his own breakfast before waking him. Since working for the padre he had seen little evidence so far of his reputed heavy drinking but he knew that the padre liked a drink occasionally because he had seen a bottle in his locker. Collins ate quickly and without much appetite; he was thinking about the padre's reaction to seeing him alive. Would he be overjoyed that he was uninjured, or would he be angry with him for putting him through such anxiety? Best to get it over with, he thought to himself. Carrying a mug of tea, he walked the short distance to the chapel. When he arrived he stopped outside for a moment and listened. Apart from the sound of a scurrying rat, no noise came from inside. He opened the barn door cautiously and looked into the dim interior. The padre was asleep in the centre of the chapel, just as Watkins had said he would be. Taking a deep breath, Davy Collins went over and knelt by his side.

Chapter 10

Renton's hand trembled as he scraped the razor over his chin. His head throbbed and he felt nauseous. He was still recovering from the shock of seeing Collins kneeling down beside him in the chapel. The boy had awoken him as if nothing out of the ordinary had occurred. Renton, however, had been unable to hide his joy at seeing him alive and had run his hands through the boy's hair to make sure he wasn't still dreaming. It was clear that Collins was taken aback by this display of affection. He looked embarrassed and kept apologising for not seeking him out earlier and explained why he hadn't done so. But Renton was so overjoyed at Collin's miraculous escape from death that he scarcely heard a word.

As he continued shaving, he began to reflect more soberly on the events of the previous afternoon and evening. The little he could remember made his euphoric mood disappear fast. His aching head and the taste of stale tobacco in his mouth was testament to the amount of whisky he'd consumed. What troubled him most was that he could remember his heated conversation with Kerr and Beamish in the afternoon but what had happened after that was all a bit hazy. Kerr had given him a cool reception when he returned to the mess and he knew he'd have some fences to mend where the CO and Beamish were concerned but that didn't worry him too much. It was what happened after leaving them that troubled him most! He had a vague recollection of meeting Sergeant Watkins and drinking whisky with him, but no idea of what he'd said or done while in his company. Looking into his shaving mirror he studied the red eyed, puffed up face staring back at him. It was the first time in weeks that he'd woken up looking such a mess. The first time, he told himself, since Collins had come to work for him. The importance of Collins to him suddenly aroused a moment of irritation and anger in him. He had been so happy to see the boy alive and unharmed that that any thought of tearing into him for putting him through such terrible mental anguish had never occurred to him. The significance of failing to rebuke Collins was not lost on him. If it was mere lust he felt for the boy, why had he got himself into such an emotional state when he believed him dead? As well as his confused feelings about Collins, there was also the nagging belief that he had made a drunken fool of himself in front of Sergeant Watkins. By the time he had finished shaving, Renton's thoughts towards Collins had changed completely.

Collins was thoroughly confused by the padre's sudden changes in attitude towards him. One minute, the padre would be polite and courteous, and the next minute short tempered and ill mannered. The following morning was even more miserable with the padre finding fault with everything that was done for him. In the afternoon, the writing lessons that had been promised to him, never took place. The padre said he was too busy with his religious duties to have time for anything else. Collins was disappointed and resigned himself to the fact that there would be no lessons ever. But after two days, the padre's mood suddenly improved. He became his old self again and Collins was informed that lessons would commence again if he were still interested. It was two weeks before Christmas and he was taken completely by surprise. He'd given up all hope of the padre sticking by his promise and wondered what had brought on the change of mind.

Unknown to Collins, Renton had made his peace with Kerr and Beamish. Apologising to Kerr had been galling to him but there was no alternative; he couldn't afford to get on the wrong side of the CO. Kerr heard him out in silence and then told him to forget the matter. He never mentioned his absence from the mess that evening or gave any indication of knowing about his drinking spree. As in all his previous conversations with Kerr, Renton got the impression that his CO hadn't got much time for him. Freddie Beamish however was a different matter. Renton liked Beamish and was closer to him than anyone else in the regiment; he didn't want to lose his friendship. As it was, Beamish listened to him with good humour and showed concern for him.

'I thought your drinking wasn't a problem,' Beamish said in reply to his apology. 'But it seems to me that if you're going to hit the bottle every time someone close to you is killed, then you're not going to be much good as a padre.'

Renton conceded Beamish's point and did his best to reassure him that there would be no repetition of the Collins' incident. Beamish didn't dwell on the subject and they were soon talking about other matters. Beamish shared a love of classical music and they both had a particular fondness for Bach. They began reminiscing about concerts they had attended before the war. Their conversation made Renton long to be back in England and he told Beamish so.

'What you want is a day off, Simon,' Beamish told him. 'Get away from the trenches for a bit. This coming Saturday is HQ Company's turn for a day off in Rouville. All the fighting companies have had a go, now it's our turn. Why don't you come along with me and take in the sights? I hear they've got a fine old church that's managed to stay intact. Who knows? We might even get some decent food in town.'

Renton accepted Beamish's offer without hesitation. It would do him good to get out of the awful conditions they were living in and relax for a few hours. It would also strengthen his friendship with Freddie who might be a useful ally in any further run-ins with Kerr. That only left Watkins to deal with. Renton hadn't spoken to him since the night he's got drunk, and he couldn't put his mind at ease until he knew whether he'd said or done anything to disgrace himself in front of the Quartermaster. The trouble was he couldn't remember what had been said between them during the course of that evening. One thing was for certain; if he had run off at the mouth too much, Watkins would exploit it. He decided to compromise; he would go and see Watkins on the pretext of paying him for the whisky. With any luck the money would put the Quartermaster in a good humour, good enough, Renton hoped, to tell him what had taken place that evening. But he was still apprehensive and decided that it could wait until after his day out on Saturday.

In fact Watkins was in no hurry to see Renton. He knew the padre's curiosity would eventually get the better of him. He would definitely be getting a visit sometime soon and when he did, he would hold all the cards. He visualised the scene in his mind. He would receive the padre with friendship, but confident in his ability to dominate. He would say little and give nothing away. By contrast Renton would squirm before him, desperate to find out if he'd said anything indiscreet. Watkins was going over the events of that night again in his mind when an idea came to him; an idea that might just solve a little problem he had concerning a bit of business he had in town. Pierre Chaval, the Mayor of Rouville was turning out to be a good provider and, despite the ravages of war, all sorts of foodstuffs and drink were being offered to him to sell on to the men of the regiment. For soldiers existing on bully beef, hard biscuits, and tea sweetened with tinned milk, any type of fresh meat or vegetables were welcome. It mattered little that the meat was usually horsemeat, or even squirrel, and the vegetables were often hard and unripe. If it was edible and didn't come in a tin men would pay for it. But it was the drink that was really profitable and old Pierre seemed to be able to lay his hands on a constant supply of wine, cider, and brandy. It wasn't of the greatest quality, in fact most of it was pretty rough, but Watkins knew the lower ranks would drink anything to make life more bearable in the trenches. It wouldn't do for the officers of course; they always had to have the good stuff. The goods were arriving so fast and in such quantities that for some weeks now Watkins had been wondering where he could hide all his extra merchandise safely in the event of a visit by the Army Quartermasters' Dept. Now he thought he had the answer.

Renton wasn't the only one looking forward to the trip to Rouville. Collins and Webb, along with others from their dugout had also been given permission to go into town for the day and enjoy themselves. Expectations were high, especially from Lofty who told Davy that there would be all sorts of delights on offer.

'They've got plenty of women there,' he told an excited Davy, 'high class tarts from Paris. Really beautiful looking girls, they are. A mate of mine told me they're yours for only a few francs.'

Collins was looking forward to the prospect of meeting such exotic creatures but at the same time he couldn't help feeling uneasy. He was aware of his shyness with girls, especially if they were the forward type, and he didn't want to make a fool of himself in front of his mates. Then there was the other problem; how do you talk to a girl when you can't speak her language? Lofty and the others roared with laughter when Davy voiced his worries.

'Don't worry you won't be doing much talking.' Lofty told him. 'Just stick with me. I'll see you all right.'

The padre was less enthusiastic when Collins told him he was going into town and did his best to deter him from going by lecturing him on the dangers of being led astray by the twin evils of women and drink. 'I'm going into town myself and I'd take you with me if I could,' he said, 'but it wouldn't look right. All the same I don't like you being in the company of older men who might lead you into trouble so stick with a couple of lads you can trust and don't drink too much.'

Saturday morning was crisp and frosty, the rain that had plagued them for the last few days had ceased and the skies were cold but clear. After breakfast and morning service, Renton found himself in the company of Beamish and four other officers waiting for transport to take them into Rouville. At 10am they crowded into a motorcar and set off on the forty-minute drive to town. A lorry would leave an hour later carrying the rest of the HQ staff. The reason for the non- commissioned men setting off after the officers soon became clear to Renton. At the outskirts of town they stopped near a casualty clearing station and were informed that they were to have the rare treat of a hot bath and their clothing would be deloused. Nobody, Beamish told him, was allowed in town without first being cleaned up. The ruling applied to officers and men alike and was strictly enforced to try and avoid passing on lice and other undesirable bugs to the French civilians.

The officers had first use of the baths, which had been set up in a derelict farmhouse. Renton wasn't worried about sharing a bath with his fellow officers, even though it meant being surrounded by naked male bodies. It was a frequent occurrence for Renton, and a part of army life that he had got used to. In such situations he had developed a successful method of dealing with the problem. By concentrating his mind on long difficult texts from the Bible he could stop his thoughts from wandering elsewhere. A combination of the Bible, and closing his eyes and pretending to nod off, would save him any embarrassment.

If the facilities were a bit primitive, at least they were going to be the first that day to use them. That meant plenty of clean hot water to wallow in. For twenty minutes they soaped and disinfected their bodies getting rid of grime and lice. After they finished they got out and stood in a little huddle with their bodies wrapped in itchy woollen army blankets to keep themselves warm while they waited for the return of their deloused clothing. Renton noticed that the dirty water they had just used was now being reheated for the non-commissioned ranks coming along behind them. He was getting dressed when the lorry containing the rest of the HQ party arrived. Less restrained than the officers, the men let out yells of delight at the sight of the baths. Not having washed properly in months it wouldn't have mattered to them if a thousand bodies had splashed about in the water before them. In no time at all they had peeled off their lice ridden uniforms and under garments and piled them in a heap.

As he finished dressing, Renton caught sight of Collins waiting in a line of men for a bath. He tried hard not to stare, but his orderly's naked body, with its slender build and flawless white skin, seemed to stand out from the rest. For one brief moment, Renton was seized by a mad impulse to rush over to him and take him in his arms, but the moment passed and he came to his senses. He blushed as he became conscious of a stirring in his loins and was worried that he might draw attention to himself. To his great relief, the transport returned at that moment to pick up his group. Lowering his eyes, he quickly fumbled to do up the last buttons on his tunic before joining Beamish and the others for the short drive into town.

Collins waited patiently in line for his bath. Amongst the men comparisons of physical anatomy, accompanied by a lot of good-natured banter, was taking place. Some of the older men were giving lurid accounts of what they hoped to do when they got to town. As the youngest in the group, Collins was content just to listen and join in with the laughter. He didn't always understand some of the cruder comments that were made but he laughed along with the rest anyway. As if to compensate for his silence, Lofty Webb was doing enough talking for both of them. In a voice loud enough to be heard by everyone in the vicinity, he told the man standing next to him what he had planned. 'Davy and me are gonna have something to eat and drink and afterwards we're gonna find two French girls. Ain't that right, Davy?'

Collins nodded and smiled sheepishly as the attention of the men was momentarily directed towards him. Lofty's words had provoked some choice advice from the naked bodies gathered around them. 'Keep it in yer trousers, Davy, lad… Mind you don't catch anything… Gaw'n, bet you two don't even know what to do with it'…

Collins was saved further embarrassment by a bath in front of him becoming vacant. Sinking gratefully into the warm, scummy water until only his head was visible, he luxuriated in his first bath in months. Afterwards, in a damp, but relatively lice free uniform, he checked that his jacket pocket was securely buttoned up remembering the paying officer's advice about keeping their money safe. When everybody was ready they clambered back on to the lorry and headed for town.

Renton and his fellow officers were deposited at noon in the main square at Rouville with instructions from Beamish for the transport to return at 11.30pm to take them back to their lines. As the weak rays of the winter sun shone down from the cloudless skies, Renton surveyed the town of Rouville and its inhabitants. He knew the Germans had swept through the town during their victorious advance in late August 1914 but they had been in too much of a hurry to get to Paris to worry about occupying much a sleepy little hamlet. Then, after being stopped on the river Marne, almost in sight of the French capital, the Germans had retreated back through the town in early September of the same year pursued by the Allies. As a result of the speed of movement during those opening stages of the war, Rouville had received little damage and appeared to Renton to be relatively untouched by the ravages of war. The main square, he noticed, was cobbled and small but surprisingly neat and tidy. At one end was a small kiosk, which was closed, and shuttered up with a sign hanging on it in French that read '*au dejeurer*'. A few unoccupied wooden tables and chairs stood on a grassy area in front of the kiosk. At the other end of the square was a circular shaped public urinal and next to it a stone horse trough containing muddy water. Surrounding the square were several tall lime trees with rose bushes spaced in between them and on the opposite side of the square stood a variety of shops and cafes. Leading off the southern end of the square was the main street which housed the town's hotel, bank and other notable establishments. At the northern end the main road led up to the church.

Beamish suggested that they have a leisurely lunch and then visit the church in the afternoon. Since it was some four and half hours since he had eaten, Renton readily agreed. Walking around the town looking for a place to eat, he found it hard to believe that it was wartime. The only signs there were that a war was going on was the number of uniformed figures strolling about or sitting at café tables. He mentioned it to Beamish who then pointed out to him something he had missed. All the civilians were old men and women. The young lads of the town had gone off to fight, Beamish told him, and most of the girls were either working in the fields, or in munitions factories.

'Still, got to look on the bright side,' Beamish said, smiling, 'there's probably some off duty British nurses in town.'

Eventually they stopped at a little restaurant with cheerful yellow painted shutters at the windows and a menu board propped up outside the entrance. For the next couple of hours they indulged themselves in the first decent food and drink they'd had in months. Afterwards, lethargic from their heavy meal, which had been washed down with the best wine the amiable owner of the restaurant could find, they wandered towards the town church.

The Cure of Rouville's church made them both very welcome. He insisted on giving them a lengthy guided tour of the church and spoke proudly of its history. Later, in his study, they were served hot chocolate and cakes. By now it was almost five o'clock, and the combination of the study's warmth, and the rich food and drink, was taking its toll on their senses. Both men were having a job to stay awake listening to their host. The Cure, realising how tired his guests were, invited them to stay and take a nap in his study. Within five minutes of his offer, both men had dropped off to sleep in the Cure's comfortable armchairs.

When Renton awoke it was dark outside. The thoughtful Cure had left a lighted candle lantern on the desk and by its flickering light Renton could see the face of the old long case clock in the corner. It showed the time as being nearly eight o'clock. He reached across and woke the sleeping figure of Beamish who was stretched out in the chair next to him. The Cure was in the church finishing Mass and had left two basins of water for them to refresh themselves in before they left. After a hasty toilet, Renton and Beamish stepped out to take in Rouville's nightlife.

Chapter 11

Lofty Webb was drunk. Not falling over or troublesome drunk; just happy drunk. Collins watched in amazement and not a little concern as yet another bottle of red wine was placed on the table in front of them. Wine was something Collins had never experienced until his arrival in France. He had drunk his first glass in a French railway station buffet on route to the front and hadn't been very impressed. He preferred good old British beer to French wine anytime. But Lofty obviously found the local wine to his liking. Davy reckoned that his friend had drunk about three glassfuls to every one of his own! They were in a little bar in the main street of town, not far from Le Grande Rouville Hotel, an establishment they planned to visit later in the evening. They'd been in the bar since their arrival in town. It was Webb who had spotted it as soon as they arrived. He jumped out the back of the lorry so quickly that Collins had to run to catch up with him. As it turned out it was just as well that Webb was quick off the mark. The bar had filled up rapidly and was now full of British soldiers who were enjoying themselves and making plenty of noise with it.

They sat at a large table around which were grouped six other soldiers. Dirty plates and empty wine bottles littered the table top. The bar was thick with tobacco smoke and from the direction of the kitchen came a strong smell of garlic that lingered under their noses. They had finished their meal sometime ago and Webb had dismissed Collins suggestion that they have a stroll around the town looking in shop windows to see if there was anything Collins could send home to his parents.

'It'll never get home, Davy, believe me!' Lofty told him. 'Whatever you buy will never get there, or if by a miracle it does, it's sure to be broken by the time it arrives. No! I like it here; we can have a laugh and fill in time before a bit of *'you know what'*, later on.'

Collins thought Lofty Webb knew what he was doing in matters of worldly affairs and was content to go along with his wishes. But that was two hours ago when Webb had been reasonably sober. It had been daylight when they first entered the bar, but now candles burnt at every table. Four lanterns, hanging on hooks from a low ceiling, illuminated the premises with a dim yellow light. As Collins looked across the table through the clouds of tobacco smoke, he began to think that perhaps Webb was not so experienced with women as he made out and was getting drunk to get up courage for the brothel.

'Drink up, Davy, boy! Whass' a matter? Don't yer like wine?' Webb's cheeks were flushed and the pupils of his eyes looked like huge black marbles.

'I'd sooner have a beer to be honest.' Collins said. He was feeling a bit light headed from the wine, but to please Webb he took another sip from his glass.

'Frog beer's too bloody dear for the likes of us! It's weak as piss anyway. No, we're better off with this stuff.' Lofty picked up his glass and, polishing off the contents in one mouthful, reached across the table intending to refill his glass from the bottle in front of him but he was clumsy and knocked the bottle over. He grabbed wildly at it but missed and the bottle rolled along the table spilling out wine and knocking over several glasses. Unfortunately the glasses belonged to a group of soldiers that were not from the Westhampton Regiment and they did not take kindly to having their drink spilt. A burly soldier grabbed hold of the bottle just in time to prevent it rolling into his lap but couldn't stop some of the wine splashing on to his trousers. With a thunderous look on his face he got to his feet. Picking up the bottle he walked over to Lofty Webb. Towering above them he glowered at Collins before transferring his attention back to Webb.

'What's your game, Laddie? Looking for trouble, are yurr?' he growled in a heavy Scottish accent.

Collins could see the soldier was spoiling for a fight. He'd seen his type many a time on a Saturday night in the *'Red Lion'* when having a drink with his dad. Webb, a drunken grin on his face, seemed oblivious to the possible consequences of his drunken clumsiness.

'It was an accident mate. He didn't mean it. We'll buy you another bottle, all right?' Collins said hastily. He didn't risk standing up; it might give the Scotsman the impression he was looking for a fight.

'Damn right we'll have another bottle, Laddie, and he's gonna fucking well pay for it, not you!' The Scot glared menacingly at Webb who half turned in his seat to get a better look at the owner of the angry voice.

'Whass' a matter, Jock? It's only a drop of wine, not blood.' Lofty Webb shouted. His voice was loud enough to carry over several tables.

Silence fell over the bar and all eyes turned towards their table but before the burly Scotsman had chance to react to such defiant words, Collins leant forward and grabbed hold of Webb's collar. He pulled his friend towards him until their faces were almost touching. 'For God's sake,' he implored, 'shut up and buy the man another bottle quick, before you get us both beaten up.' Ignoring his friends plea, Webb attempted to rise out of his seat but Collins held on to his jacket and forced him back down.

Suddenly, the owner of the bar appeared at the table. 'Non! No trouble please, Tommy,' he said. He turned and signalled frantically towards a frightened looking waitress standing behind the bar. 'Une bouteille rouge, Maria,' he called out, a note of urgency in his voice. He turned and held his hands up in a gesture of appeasement to the angry Scotsman. 'Do not worry about a little drop of wine, soldier! I give you bottle, free. Come, you sit down and enjoy, oui?'

The bar owner looked anxiously at the Scotsman whose attention suddenly switched from Webb to the waitress who was making her way towards the table with a bottle of wine in her hand. He hesitated for a moment, as if deliberating what to do but was saved the bother by one of his mates who made the decision for him.

'Och, away with you, Jock! Leave the wee lad alone, here's the lassie with another bottle to keep us going. Get back here a'fore we drink it all.'

A relieved Collins watched as the big Scotsman, with a last glare at the grinning Webb, grudgingly resumed his seat amongst his laughing mates.

The bar owner looked at Webb with an irate expression on his face and then turned to Collins. 'If Monsieur cannot behave,' he said, indicating Webb, 'he must go. I give him one last chance, comprendez?'

'It's all right. It was an accident, it won't happen again,' Collins said.

'S'right just a little drop of wine spilled. No reason to get upset, garcon,' Webb said cheerfully. 'Tell you what? Let's have another bottle and all be good friends.'

'You want another bottle?' The Frenchman looked anxiously at Collins and then shrugged his shoulders. 'All right, all right! but only the one. You must see your friend causes no more trouble, yes?'

The pair nodded their assent. The proprietor left them and returned a few minutes later with a bottle of wine which he deliberately placed on the table in front of Collins who looked accusingly at Webb. The latter stared back with a hurt expression on his face.

'Lotta trouble over nufink, Davy,' he said carrying on drinking as if nothing had happened.

Collins sat for a little while in angry silence but gradually his anger melted away. He couldn't stay mad at his friend for long despite the fact that Webb had so nearly got them into a fight and thrown out of the bar. To his relief the burly Scotsman and his mates left after finishing their free bottle of wine and they had the table to themselves. At his request Collins went easy on the wine and his behaviour gave no further cause for concern. The light was very dim now in the bar and the candles on the tables were almost burnt down. The time on the old brass clock over the bar showed that it was after seven o'clock and the place was almost empty. Collins pointed this out to Webb who quickly gave him an explanation for the almost deserted bar.

'They've all gone to the hotel. The girls must have started doing business.' He got unsteadily to his feet.

'C'mon Davy, we don't want to miss out on the best ones.' He caught the eye of the bar owner who was hovering nearby. 'Landlord! The bill, quickly please, we're in a hurry.'

The owner of the bar did some rapid mental arithmetic and scribbled down the amount owed on a piece of paper. With a flourish he handed the bill to Webb who took a quick glance at it and passed it on to Collins. 'I s'pose it's right,' he mumbled, 'I can't make head or tail of it me self, but the total seems reasonable, don't it? We'll go halves, all right?'

Collins agreed even though his friend had drunk three times as much as he had. They paid up and left the smoky atmosphere of the bar to head for the delights of Le Grande Rouville Hotel.

After the sleepy warmth of the Cure's study, Renton initially found the night air cold, but the brisk walk to the main square soon warmed him up and cleared the sleepiness from their heads. Drunken British soldiers were to be seen everywhere. Some were gathered together in noisy small groups on street corners, others staggered along the cobbled streets in pairs, presumably looking for yet another bar to spend their pay in. Beamish paused for a moment outside one particular bar and motioned for Renton to listen to the singing coming from within. The tune as a popular favourite with the men; *'Keep the home fires burning'*. They walked on, negotiating their way around two drunken soldiers who gave a hasty salute to Beamish.

'They seem happy enough.' Renton said, laughing. 'Are we going anywhere in particular, Freddie, or just taking in the cold night air for the good of our health?'

The wine he had drunk with his meal earlier on had whetted Renton's appetite. He felt the old familiar craving for something stronger but knew it would be better if any suggestion for the evening's entertainment came from Beamish.

'I thought we might go to the Rouville Hotel,' Beamish said offering Renton a cigarette.

Renton gave him a look of surprise as they lit their cigarettes. He'd heard rumours about what went on in some of the hotel's bedrooms.

'Don't look so alarmed, Simon. I'm talking about the lounge bar in the hotel. It's for officers only and off limits to other ranks. I believe its quite comfortable inside and even frequented by nursing officers occasionally.'

Renton tried to sound enthusiastic. 'I don't mind, Freddie. If you say it's all right, that's fine by me.'

'Oh yes, all the officers go there. It'll be a jolly evening, you'll see.'

Renton was glad he was in his 'walking out' uniform with a regulation army officer's shirt and tie as opposed to his clerical dog collar. It made it a lot easier for him to fit in and not be taken for some stuff shirted padre. As they approached the front of the hotel Renton heard the sound of raised voices and laughter coming from the right hand side of the building. Drawing nearer, he saw that there was an alleyway that led off the main street to an annexe at the rear of the hotel. To his amazement the alley was packed with British soldiers. They had formed themselves into an orderly queue, which ran all the way down the side of the hotel and continued around the back. He was about to move forward for a closer look when he felt a hand on his shoulder.

'Come on, Simon,' Beamish said quietly. 'I don't think we really want to stay here, do you?'

But Renton was too fascinated to move away. Close to where he was standing on the pavement an ornate street lamp shone down illuminating part of the alley. There was enough light coming from the lamp for him to see the features of several men standing near the rear of the queue. To his dismay there was one face that stood out from the rest. A face that was fresher, younger, and more delicate than all the others; Collins! An acute sense of betrayal overwhelmed him. A few streets away, the chimes of the town clock struck the hour and each chime seemed to add to the agony Renton was enduring. He knew that Collins hadn't noticed him; the boy was too busy laughing and talking with the other men in the queue. Renton thought how childish and vulnerable the boy looked compared with the other coarse louts surrounding him. For one, mad moment, he considered dashing forward and dragging Collins away from his companions, but the weight of Beamish's hand on his shoulder stopped him. It flashed through his mind that the scene being played out in front of him was reminiscent of his nightmare in the Chapel. It certainly tormented him in the same way. He turned away and tried to calm his thoughts, praying that his face had not betrayed too much of his feelings. Beamish removed his hand from Renton's shoulder and fell into step with him as they walked in silence towards the hotel.

The smell of alcohol and cigarette smoke wafted towards Renton as soon as they entered the lounge of the hotel. The room was large and had an aura of bygone grandeur. Faded red curtains of heavy velvet hung from the windows and well worn patterned carpet ran around the outside of a polished parquet floor. Lots of elegantly styled easy chairs and several comfortable looking sofas filled up most of the spacious interior. Opposite the entrance at the far end of the lounge was a bar made of carved wood. Affixed to the wall behind the bar was a large decorated mirror that created the impression that the lounge was even bigger than it actually was. Looking around the room, Renton saw that about two thirds of the seats were occupied. There were a few men in civilian clothes but the majority of the men were British officers. Beamish had been right about the nurses frequenting the hotel. They were greatly outnumbered by men and obviously very popular. Judging by the number of drinks some of them had in front of them, they didn't lack for admirers among the younger officers.

Beamish pointed towards a vacant table and they went over and sat down. An aged waiter dressed in a black suit and bow tie appeared and took their order for a whisky and soda apiece with a stiff little bow. After a few drinks, Renton began to relax. The ambience of the hotel's lounge, together with the whisky and Beamish's light hearted conversation, all served to brighten his mood.

In the alleyway, Collins was getting restless. The clock had just chimed eight o'clock so it was still early evening. Having no previous experience in sexual matters he thought that making love was something men and women did after retiring to bed at night so it seemed strange to be queuing to have sex this early in the evening. He mentioned it to Webb who was standing alongside him in the queue.

'We're in France, Davy', come the reply, 'anything goes with the Froggies where love is concerned.'

The queue shuffled slowly forward and Collins wondered what sort of girl he was going to get. He tried to imagine what she would look like, but was unable to form any sort of mental picture in his mind that lasted for more than a couple of seconds. The long wait was wearing away his confidence and twice he had been on the point of suggesting that they should call the whole thing off. But even as he contemplated the idea, he knew deep down, that he'd left it too late. Lofty Webb would never let him forget it if he tried to pull out at this stage. He was beginning to envy Lofty's inebriated state and wished he'd drunk more in the bar earlier. It would have helped to overcome his shyness.

Looking up at the cold night sky he was awed by the wonderful display of stars that shone brightly out of the inky darkness. He wondered if the same stars were shining back at home. Thinking about home made him think of his mother; it brought on a spasm of guilt. What would she say if she knew he was about to pay money to a woman to have sex with him? A brief feeling of shame overcame him, but he consoled himself with the thought that his father would understand his need to lose his virginity and prove himself the equal of his mates. The queue moved forward once again and his heart beat faster as the line of men in front of him decreased to a mere handful.

Chapter 12

Ron Watkins had been told about the history of the Rouville Hotel by Pierre Chaval. The old man had informed him that annexe at the rear of the hotel had been built during the hotel's prosperous years, just after the turn of the century, when Northern France was a very popular destination for wealthy English tourists. But when rumours of war started, the guests dwindled to a trickle and only the rooms in the main building were ever used. It was a waste of money to pay maids to clean and tidy rooms that were never slept in and Chaval, as he often told Watkins, was a man who never wasted money. He closed the rooms in the unused annexe and the windows were shuttered up. As the Germans advanced through the village during the early part of the war an artillery shell struck the hotel annexe and some of the rooms became unusable. Chaval had done nothing to repair the damage but that all changed when Watkins made him a proposition that was guaranteed to make old Pierre a lot of money without any risk to his pocket.

Watkins had seen the need for a brothel to serve the men but could not be involved directly in setting one up. He was looking for someone with a suitable property to set up as a front man and Chaval was the ideal man. His hotel annexe, tucked out of sight behind the main building, afforded plenty of privacy. There was even space to accommodate the waiting clients in the alleyway that ran down the side of the hotel. It meant the front entrance wouldn't have to be used and the rest of the hotel could function as normal, or at least as normal as the war would allow. It was the perfect set up and Watkins had no trouble talking Chaval into agreeing to his idea. He even provided Chaval with most of the labour to do the repairs. Afterwards, he ensured that there were plenty of customers for the women that Chaval installed in the rooms.

In return for his efforts he received a weekly share of the brothel's takings and was allowed the freedom of the hotel whenever he chose to visit. It was the first in a series of mutually profitable transactions between the two men. Watkins was shrewd enough to know the regiment wouldn't be in the area forever and intended to make as much profit as he could while his cosy little arrangement lasted.

At present he was sitting in Chaval's office smoking a cigar and drinking the hotelier's best brandy. He would take a stroll around the premises later on and keep a discreet eye on his investment; he might even pop into the lounge bar for a quick drink. Watkins was the only non-commissioned soldier exempt from the 'officers only' rule and he smiled with satisfaction at the thought of rubbing shoulders with officers. He knew that some of them disapproved of him but they were in the minority. Finishing his brandy he stubbed out his cigar and stood up. After checking his inside pocket to make sure he had the money that Chaval had given him earlier, he left the office to wander around the hotel.

Collins and Webb had made it to the top of the stairs at last. They were at the head of the queue now and waiting outside the partially open door of a brightly lit reception room. An old man sporting a greasy old beret on his head stood guard at the door ready to usher the waiting soldiers in when it was their turn. Looking over the old man's shoulder, Collins peered into the room. He could see a meagre fire burning in a large fireplace directly opposite him. Next to the fire a very fat woman was sitting behind a desk. She wore an old French army greatcoat buttoned up at the front and a pair of wire spectacles perched precariously on the end of a bulbous nose. In front of her on the desk, lay an open metal box and a notebook. Next to the box stood a large earthenware flagon and a wooden platter on which sat some ripe cheese and the remains of a loaf of bread. Taking a pencil from one of the pockets in her coat she wetted the tip in her mouth before painstakingly writing something down in the notebook. When she finished writing she put the notebook and pencil down. Picking up the flagon with one hand she raised it to her lips and took a long swallow.

Collins craned his head forward to look further around the room and noticed a set of double doors that presumably led to the other rooms in the annexe. From beyond the wall behind the fat woman came the muffled sounds of voices and doors slamming. Though it was cold on the stairs, Collins felt beads of sweat forming on his brow and his legs felt decidedly shaky. He licked his lips and glanced over at his pal who looked to be just as nervous. Webb hadn't spoken a word in the last five minutes, which was something of a record for him. Collins was about to say something to break the tension when he heard two loud knocks on the wall behind the fat women. It was obviously a familiar method of communicating with her because she immediately lifted her head and looked across to the old man in the doorway.

'Deux,' she bellowed out to him. Raising her arm, the woman beckoned Collins and Webb towards her.

The old man mumbled something under his breath and let them into the room. As they approached the woman opened her mouth to reveal a set of tobacco stained teeth. 'Bonsoir, Tommy! Four francs. *Each!*'

She thrust out a hand as the two English soldiers fumbled in their pockets for the money. It was more than Collins had expected. Four francs was half a week's pay; pay that he should be sending home to his mother. He looked at Webb who had already handed over his money and was waiting for him to do the same. Webb shot him a look that seemed to say 'don't you dare let me down now.' Collins put his mother out of his mind and counted out four francs. He was about to hand over the notes when he heard Lofty Webb cough nervously.

'Er, what sort of girl we getting for our money, then?' He asked.

'Very pretty, Tommy, very nice French girl,' the woman answered. Snatching the money out of Collins hand she got up from her chair and walked over to the double doors. Taking out a key she unlocked the doors and motioned to them to follow her. Opening the doors she led them into a long corridor that gave access to a number of hotel rooms. The fat woman closed and locked the doors behind them. 'You do not come back through here,' she said, 'the girls will show you out when you have finished. Understand?'

Telling Collins to remain where he was she led Webb along the corridor for a short distance and then stopped outside a door. Muttering something in his ear that Collins couldn't make out she pushed the door open, shoved the Englishman through, and then closed the door behind him. Collins nerves were at breaking point as she crooked one of her fat fingers at him and beckoned him to her. He started towards her but after only going a few yards the fat woman suddenly disappeared off to his left. Collins followed her into a dimly lit room and heard a door slam behind him. It had all happened so bewilderingly fast. One moment he had been behind her and the next moment she was gone.

As he listened to her footsteps fade away along the corridor outside his nose picked up the scent of heavy perfume and the smell of stale cigarette smoke. He became aware of a rustling sound in front of him and realised he was not alone in the room. Uncertain of what to do next, he stood motionless, while his eyes became accustomed to their dimmer surroundings. In front of him was an oil lamp and by its flickering light he could just make out the shape of a figure reclining on a bed. He walked tentatively forward. The rustling sound occurred again and suddenly the lamp was turned up a fraction. Collins could now see that the person on the bed was a woman. She wore a black nightdress and was lying on her back with her knees raised and her hands resting on top of them. The lamp on the table next to her illuminated the room in such a way that, although he could see her body clearly, most of her face remained in shadow. He stopped at the foot of the bed and wiped his sweaty palms down the side of his trousers.

'Come closer, *Cherie*. You can't do much from there.'

The voice didn't sound to Collins like that of a young girl. He hesitated for a moment and then walked slowly around to the side of the bed and stopped.

'What's the matter, Tommy? Hurry, get undressed, I don't have all night.' The woman's left hand patted the grubby mattress she was lying on.

He began unbuttoning his tunic, but his curiosity to see what the woman looked like got the better of him. He moved closer to the lamp and almost immediately stepped back in revulsion. Instead of the pretty young French girl he had been expecting, a scrawny woman of mature years lay on the bed looking up at him! The woman appeared annoyed by his hesitation and swung her legs around until she was sitting on the edge of the bed facing him. Collins steeled himself and took a closer look at her. To his horror she looked even older than he had first thought. Long greasy hair fell over one side of her face and her cheeks, narrow and pinched, had a greyish tinge to the flesh. She gave him a hard look as she watched him eyeing her up.

'You are very young, non? What is your name?' she asked. Her thin bloodless lips formed themselves into a smile; but it was a smile that contained no warmth.

'Davy,' he whispered.

'Well, *Davee*, don't you like me? You should be undressed by now, you know. There are others waiting and you will get me into trouble if you don't hurry.'

'I'm sorry,' Collins stammered, 'its just that, well, er, can't we just talk for a bit first?'

'Talk, what do mean, talk?' She glared fiercely at him for a second. Then, to Collins surprise, her expression softened. She reached out and grabbed his hands in her bony fingers and began stroking them.

'Ah, I understand. You are shy. I think maybe it is the first time for you, oui?' Clutching his hands tightly she lay back down on the bed drawing him closer to her, then, to his horror, she kissed him briefly on the lips.

Collins nearly choked on her foul breath as their lips parted. She let go of his hands and reached down to the hem of her nightdress. Pulling it up over her waist she opened her legs and exposed her sex to him. But the sight of the straggly patch of pubic hair that sprouted from her groin stirred no feelings of desire in Collins. Nor did her legs; they were pitifully thin and riddled with varicose veins that ran along the surface of her skin in little blue ridges. Davy Collins wiped his lips with the back of his hand and fought back the tears of shame and embarrassment that were welling up inside him. This was not how it was supposed to be. The woman was offering herself like a piece of meat in a butchers shop. He had been expecting a girl that would treat him tenderly, a pretty girl who would feel passionate towards him. He shut his eyes to block out the sight of the repulsive creature lying on the bed. His nostrils felt clogged with the scent of her vile perfume and his head was spinning. He tried to take a step backwards but her hands closed around his wrists and she pulled him back towards the bed.

'Come on! Don't be afraid, I won't bite you!' A dry laugh came from her mouth. Her hand went into the top of his trousers and found his penis. She closed her hand around it and began to squeeze. He pulled her hand away and she looked up at him sharply

'What is wrong with you? Don't you like girls?'

'Yes, it's just that, well, you're not what I expected,' Collins blurted the words out without thinking.

'Who did you expect for four francs, Marie Antoinette?' Her voice sounded like a rasp on metal.

'I thought you'd be younger that's all,' He said naively. 'I thought you'd be nearer my age.'

'I am a woman of experience and you are a scared young boy who thinks he is a man but is not!' Her eyes flashed angrily and she waggled her little finger in front of his nose. 'You are like this finger, soft, and useless for fucking!'

Collins eyes widened in astonishment, he had never heard such crude language from a woman before, not even in the roughest pubs in Whitechapel. He knew it had been a mistake to come; he should never have listened to Lofty. He just wanted to get out of the room and leave the building as quickly as possible.

'You are running out of time, little boy. Do you want to fuck or not?'

Collins knew he couldn't make love to such a creature under any circumstances. 'Well, em…' he began, lamely.

'You won't get your money back if that's what you are thinking,' she snapped, 'it is not my fault that they send me schoolboys instead of men!'

He decided not to enrage her further. He moved away from her until he felt the comfort of the door against his back. With his hands behind him he groped frantically for the doorknob.

The woman lay on the bed, her hard narrow eyes watching him as he tried to get out of the door. Then suddenly she jumped up and spat in his direction. 'Go then, useless *Anglais!*' she yelled at him, pointing at the door, 'get back to your whore of a mother, where you belong!'

Collins finally located the doorknob and rushed out into the corridor. Behind him he could hear the woman swearing and cursing. Slamming the door shut behind him, he looked left and right hoping to see which way led to an exit. One thing was certain; he couldn't stay where he was. The irate prostitute on the other side of the door might come out at any moment. He ran back along the corridor until he reached the double doors he had come through a few minutes earlier. Ignoring the fat woman's words about not leaving the same way he had entered, he rattled the handles furiously but found the door securely locked against him. Desperate to find a way out he ran on to the end of the corridor. A pair of heavy drapes blocked his path. More in hope than in expectation, he pulled them aside. To his relief a door was revealed. The key was in the lock and he wasted no time in opening the door. A blast of cold air hit his face; in front of him was an iron stairway that led down to the street. He gave a quick glance over his shoulder, the corridor was empty. He slipped through the door and pulled it shut behind him.

Taking the stairs two at a time Collins reached the bottom. Leaning against the wall of the building he drew in a long breath of the cool night air. From around the other side of the building he could hear the sounds of men's voices as they waited in the alley for their turn to enter the brothel. It suddenly occurred to him that his friend might come out at any minute. He would almost certainly want a full and juicy account from him of his bedroom experience. What would he tell him? That he'd panicked and fled? No! He'd had enough embarrassment for one night. He had to get away from the hotel and have some time to think before meeting up with Lofty again. Buttoning up his tunic, he wandered forlornly off down the street.

In the warmth of the hotel's lounge, Renton sipped appreciatively at his whisky and soda; the evening had turned into a pretty enjoyable affair. At the next table sat some young officers from another regiment. They had recently arrived in France and Renton was revelling in the boyish respect they were according him and Beamish. In the far corner of the lounge a group of officers had formed themselves into a quartet and were singing with great enthusiasm. They were accompanied on a piano by one of the older nurses who concentrated on playing every note as if her life depended on it. Every table in the place was occupied by men and women having a good time while they had the chance. Renton closed his eyes for a brief moment and listened to the general hubbub of noise going on around him. The discomfort and danger of the trenches seemed a million miles away. For a second he felt guilty to be in the comfort of Rouville's hotel while elsewhere in France men were suffering and dying, but the feeling soon passed. He opened his eyes to find Beamish smiling at him from behind a haze of tobacco smoke.

'Not keeping you up, are we, Simon?' Beamish asked.

'Just savouring the moment, Freddie. How long have we got before we have to head back?'

Beamish looked at his watch. 'Plenty of time yet, anyway, the transport won't go without us if we're a bit late,' he tapped the three pips on his epaulette, 'adjutants perks, old boy.'

Renton raised his glass. 'Here's to all adjutants then,' he said, laughing.

'And to all padres,' Beamish replied, touching Renton's glass with his own.

Renton's laughter died in his throat as he looked over towards the bar and saw the grinning face of Ron

Watkins staring at him. The sight of the cocky Quartermaster amongst a group of officers enraged him. Curse the man! Why did he have to be here? He was spoiling his convivial evening. 'What's the QM doing here, Freddie? I thought this place was for officers only.'

'It is, but the owner of this place is a good friend of Watkins and he's the exception to the rule.'

'It's disgraceful. The man's too familiar with officers if you ask me.'

'I should be a bit careful what you say about our QM.' Beamish leant forward in his chair and lowered his voice. 'Most of the men, officers included, think a lot of Watkins.'

'But why?'

'Because, Simon, he can lay his hands on all sorts of things that men want, even in this war torn place. In your case I happen to know its whisky. Me! I like expensive cigarettes; even the colonel has the odd bottle of brandy. It's good for morale so the old man looks the other way. The way the colonel sees it, a lot of us are going to cop it over here anyway, so we might as well make the best of it before we go.'

Renton sat quietly considering the implication of Freddie's words. Watkins obviously wielded even more power than he had first supposed. He also possessed plenty of initiative and a shrewd head for business. 'Doesn't he realise what would happen to him if someone blew the whistle on him?'

'Why would anyone do that?' Beamish said. 'As far as we know Watkins is not doing anything terribly illegal, so it would be like cutting off your nose to spite your face. Besides, think how unpopular a chap would be if he stopped the supply of goodies to his mates.'

Renton nodded thoughtfully. It was a good point and he knew it.

'He doesn't always profit on his deals mind you,' Beamish continued, 'very often he'll supply goods to someone and then they go and get them selves killed before he can collect his money. It's a gamble Watkins takes.'

'With the odds heavily in his favour,' Renton added. It was no consolation to him that he was probably unlikely to be killed in action and thus avoid any debt he owed to Watkins. He glanced quickly over towards the bar but Watkins had vanished. His anger slowly began to disappear. Finishing his drink, he caught the eye of the hovering waiter and ordered another two. A few more and Watkins would be forgotten, if only for the rest of the evening. But Collins queuing in line for the services of a whore was a different matter. The boy kept intruding on his thoughts no matter how hard he tried to push him to the back of his mind. He waited impatiently for the waiter to return with the drinks.

Chapter 13

Collins gave little attention to his surroundings as he wandered aimlessly through the dark and narrow streets of Rouville. Far weightier matters occupied his mind. Back home he'd always taken notice of a pretty girl when he saw one and never had occasion to think that he was anything other than a normal red bloodied young man. Like his mates in the market, he enjoyed it when one of the girls working there ambushed him for a quick kiss behind a stack of crates in the yard. The fact that he'd never developed a lasting relationship with any of them he put down to his shyness where girls were concerned. But tonight had shaken his confidence badly and made him think perhaps he wasn't like the rest of his mates after all. Had the whore really been so unattractive, or had he just used that as a feeble excuse not to have sex? What would Lofty Webb or any of the other men have done? In all probability the other women in the brothel were just like the one he'd encountered; but he hadn't seen any other men running away. It might have been just nerves and shyness of course; but what if there was more to it than that?

He agonised in this manner for some time until, with the doubts still unresolved in his mind, he finally gave up in despair and began instead to think about where he was heading. He was unfamiliar with the town, and to make matters worse he was walking along an empty street. With no one to ask directions of he suddenly realised he hadn't the faintest idea how to get back to the main square. Walking on a short distance he came to a side street that ran off to his left. He stopped and had a look. The street appeared promising. It was wide and fairly well lit and the little houses standing on either side were all neat and well maintained. About fifty yards down on the right hand side was an illuminated sign above the door of a small café. Collins felt confident that the street would lead him back to the town square and was pretty sure that he had plenty of time to spare before catching the transport back to his lines. As he stood on the corner of the street deliberating a drop of rain fell on his forehead. The rain began to fall harder. There was only one thing to do. He ran for the café.

An appetizing concoction of cooking smells hit Collins nose as he closed the door of the café behind him. Straightening his wet uniform, he gave a quick glance around him. The café was fairly small, but looked clean and tidy with a rectangular marble counter near the entrance that served as a bar. In the dining area of the cafe a welcoming fire burnt in the fireplace. Of the six tables in the dining area only one was in use and Collins didn't bother looking closely at the occupants.

The interior of the café was definitely more inviting than the dingy place he had visited earlier. At the bar two old men were in conversation with a man behind the counter who Collins took to be the owner of the cafe. He nodded to them but they didn't acknowledge him so he went over to a table near the window. As he sat down a burst of laughter broke out behind him. He looked round and his cheeks turned bright red. Four young women were sitting at a table looking at him with amused curiosity. One of them smiled at him and he quickly looked away in embarrassment. They were all wearing nurses uniforms, something he'd failed to notice when he'd first glanced around the dining room. He was still blushing when the owner of the cafe approached him.

'I am sorry, Monsieur,' he said, 'I do not serve English soldiers here. They get drunk and give me too much trouble with the authorities.' The man had a thin, waxed moustache that twitched as he spoke.

'But I'm on my own,' Collins protested, 'and it's pouring with rain outside. Besides, I don't want any wine, I just want something hot.'

'But how do I know you are alone.' The owner pointed towards the door. 'Your friends may follow in after you at any moment. No! This is a respectable establishment and I intend to see it stays that way. Sorry but you must leave.'

'Please, I'm on me own, honest I am. I won't cause any trouble, really I won't. Let me stay for just a little while. I'm cold, and wet.' Collins could feel the eyes of everyone in the café directed towards him. He looked hopefully into the face of the owner for any sign of a change of heart but the man stood solidly in front of him with his arms crossed in front of his chest and shook his head. Collins sighed with frustration and started to rise from his seat.

'What's the matter, Emile? Is there a problem?'

The girl spoke in English with a London accent. It was the nurse that had smiled at him earlier. He hadn't noticed her arrive at his table but was glad to see her, and very relieved at hearing another English voice besides his own.

'I am trying to tell this soldier that, regretfully, I cannot serve him, Mademoiselle.' The owner smiled at the girl and it was evident that she was a regular customer.

'Oh but he looks harmless enough, Emile, and he is wet. Please let him stay for a while and dry out.' She turned to Collins, 'Emile's very protective of us girls, so you will behave if he lets you stay, won't you?'

'Yes, of course I will,' Collins said, nodding his head. A few drops of rain fell from the tip of his nose onto the table; he wiped them away with the sleeve of his tunic and the girl laughed.

The owner looked at her and shrugged his shoulders. 'All right, Mademoiselle, as you wish.' He wiped his hands on his apron. 'Can I get you a menu, Monsieur? We don't have much to offer I'm afraid.'

Collins hadn't thought about having a meal. 'I, I don't know really,' he stuttered, 'I just want something hot. Have you got a cup of tea?'

The girl start laughing again and this time the owner of the café joined in. She said, 'I'm sorry, I don't mean to be rude, but this is a French café. Nobody drinks tea here.'

Collins looked at the girl for help. 'I don't really want much cos I've already had a meal. What do you think I should have, Miss?'

'Leave it to me,' the girl said confidently.

While she was giving his order to Emile, Collins took the opportunity to take a better look at her. She looked to be about his age, possibly a bit older and was slim with a shapely figure that even a plain nurse's uniform couldn't hide. Her hair was chestnut coloured hair and framed a pretty face covered in golden freckles.

Her eyes were grey with a hint of green. His pulse quickened as his eyes lingered on the shape of her breasts under her blouse. He thought she was the most attractive girl he'd ever met in his life.

When she finished with Emile the girl turned to him. 'There, that's all settled. I've ordered you some hot onion soup with a dash of cognac in it. I hope you like it, it's my favourite.'

'Oh, I'm sure I will. Thank you. Thank you very much.' Collins desperately wanted the girl to stay with him. 'Would you care to sit down? Please! I'd really like you to.' He felt himself blushing again. He couldn't believe he'd been rash enough to ask the girl to stay. She was bound to refuse.

The girl hesitated briefly then said, 'all right, just for a little while then. I'll just go and fetch my drink, back in a jiff.' After exchanging few words with her friends she returned and sat down opposite him.

'Sorry we laughed at you when you first came in, but with the rain dripping off you, and that sorry expression on your face, you looked just like that Charlie Chaplin fellow.' She paused, and then added, 'without the moustache, of course!' She held out her hand. 'Anyway, my name's Rose, Rose Walker, what's yours?'

Collins took her hand and shook it very gently. The feel of her fingers in the palm of his hand sent a tingling sensation up his arm. 'Davy Collins, and I'm very pleased to meet you, Miss.'

'Likewise I'm sure. But please, don't call me Miss, call me Rose.'

'Rose. That's a nice name. I've never met a Rose before.'

She looked at him with her grey-green eyes. 'Well you have now, haven't you? By the way, I work at the casualty station. I'm not a proper nurse though, just an auxiliary, but Matron says when we get back home she's going to recommend me for a nurses training course because I've got what it takes to be a good nurse. I'm part of a voluntary aid detachment from London. I come from Islington by the way. You're from London as well, aren't you? What part?'

'What part?' Collin repeated blankly trying to think what the question was. He'd never met a girl that talked so much and so fast. So fast that he hadn't kept up with her and couldn't remember her question.

'Well are you going to tell me where you come from, or is it a secret?' she said, toying with the glass in her hand.

'Yes of course. Whitechapel! I come from Whitechapel,' he said. Thank goodness she'd repeated the question.

'We're practically neighbours then,' she said, 'I bet that means we'll have ever so much to talk about.'

She was right and there was no stopping her once she got going. Her parents ran a local newsagents shop in Islington and she had two younger sisters but no brothers, which was a shame she told Collins because she would have liked a brother, maybe even two. After conversation about her family was exhausted she talked about anything and everything that came into her head. Collins would have been content just to watch and listen to her talk, but he wasn't allowed to. The girl wanted to know what his parents did, how many brothers and sisters he had, what he was doing before the war. She asked him so many questions that he ended up talking almost as much as she did. To his relief, she never asked him how he had spent the earlier part of the evening or how he had found the café. When his soup arrived, he managed to consume it without spilling a drop, a minor miracle considering the distraction of Rose's presence.

He could have happily sat with all night. He loved the way her face lit up whenever anything was said that excited her. He especially loved the way she kept flicking her hair back across her face whenever she moved her head. Her conversation, the cosy warmth of the café, and no doubt the cognac in the soup, had all combined to make it an unexpectedly wonderful evening. His earlier doubts and fears had all vanished in her company. Even the experience in the brothel was forgotten. When she was preparing to leave, he wished with all his heart he were going with her. 'When will you be in here next?' he asked her.

'That depends on how many casualties we get. Things are quiet at the moment, so we come here pretty regularly. Why do you ask?'

'Because I'd like to see you again,' he said, blushing furiously. 'That is, if you'll let me, of course.'

'Yes, all right, *Davy Collins*,' she said, emphasising his name, 'I'd like that. I'd like it very much.'

She stood up and Collins helped her on with it her coat. It felt good being up close to her. It had stopped raining and the other nurses were waiting for her outside on the pavement. She said goodnight to the owner and walked towards the door. Collins walked with her and she took his arm. She gave off an aura of wholesome cleanliness that reminded him of his mother. In the doorway he felt clumsy and awkward because she was leaving and he didn't know what to say. She let go of his arm, and as if sensing his predicament, put him at his ease.

'Will you get back to the main square, all right? She asked. 'Do you remember the way I told you?'

'Yes, I think so.' He went over the directions she had given him earlier to gain a little more time with her.

'If you get another evening in town, get a message to me at the casualty station and if I'm not on duty, I'll meet you here. That's a promise, Davy.'

She leaned forward and kissed him quickly on the cheek before walking off to join her girlfriends. He watched her from the doorway as she went off, arm in arm, with her friends. After fifty yards or so she turned and waved to him. He waved back until the little group disappeared out of his sight.

It was just after 11pm by the time Collins got back to the square. He found it full of British soldiers, many of which appeared to be blind drunk, standing around in groups awaiting transport to return them back to their lines. Occasionally an ill tempered scuffle would break out amongst one of the waiting groups but it didn't last long. Military police, using pickaxe handles as batons, stood silently in the shadows, waiting in case anything more serious should develop. He wandered around looking for Lofty Webb. A couple of hours ago he had dreaded facing him; now he couldn't wait to tell him about Rose.

'Good evening, Collins! Had good time?' He was so busy looking for Webb that he hadn't noticed the padre standing with Captain Beamish at the side of the road. He stopped and saluted. 'Yes thank you sir,' he said. 'I've had a very good evening.'

'Well just remember that tomorrow is Sunday, and you'd better be in a fit state to work. Now go off and find your transport.'

Collins saluted again and went off to resume his search. Was it his imagination or did the padre seem angry with him? Suddenly he heard a collective groan emanate from the soldiers gathered in the square and guessed that the transport had arrived. A day of enjoyment was coming to a close and soon he would return to the discomfort and danger of the front. The lorry stopped but Davy noticed that only a handful of the waiting soldiers made their way towards it. The majority stayed put until the Military Police went amongst them and ordered them to start moving. A chorus of obscenities filled the air as the soldiers reluctantly obeyed.

Collins had almost given up on his search when he saw his friend in company with a group of men near the rear of the lorry. He was very drunk and arguing with a soldier who also looked the worse for drink. Collins knew the other soldier, his name was Brewer and he lived in their dugout. He also knew that Lofty Webb didn't like Brewer. They were always coming close to blows because of the way Brewer made fun of Lofty's lack of height and he had often acted as peacemaker between the two. Now they were shouting insults at each other and squaring up for a fight. A short distance away, Davy saw the Military Police watching the pair arguing. He rushed forward to stop Webb doing something stupid but before he could reach him, Webb let fly at Brewer with his fist and the fighting started. Egged on by the soldiers around them, the two protagonists flailed wildly at each other.

Few of the punches thrown connected and no damage was being done until one fateful punch landed. It was thrown by Webb and intended for Brewer but unfortunately he missed and hit one of the Military policemen who had moved in to break up the fight. It hit the Redcap in the face and sent him reeling backwards. For a few seconds there was a stunned silence and nobody moved. Collins, who had almost reached Lofty when the fateful blow was struck, looked at his friend in disbelief and shock. Then a shrill blast on a whistle sounded followed by the shouts of the Military police. They began herding everybody on to the lorry; everybody except Lofty Webb who was being held firmly in the grip of two burly Redcaps.

Collins tried to approach Webb but another Redcap, wearing a Lance Corporal's stripe on his arm, waved him away with his baton. Collins was undeterred. 'He didn't mean it,' he cried out, 'you know he didn't! It was an accident. Let him go, please!'

'He struck a Military Policeman,' the Redcap said. 'Now piss off before you're on a charge as well'

'But he's drunk! He didn't know what he was doing. I saw it all'

The Redcap prodded Collins in the chest with his baton. 'It's your last chance, soldier! Go now, or you'll end up like your mate. It's up to you.'

Collins moved back a pace, but reluctant to leave, stopped. The Redcap smiled grimly and stepped forward.

'What's happening here?' Captain Beamish's voice brought both men sharply to attention. He pointed to Webb, who, held tight by the Redcaps, was slumped forward with his head resting on his chest. 'Why are you holding that man?' he asked the Lance Corporal.

'He's drunk and was fighting, Sir. He struck a Military Policeman who was trying to break up the fight, Sir.'

Beamish turned to Collins. 'And this man?' he asked, 'I only saw him a few minutes ago, he's certainly not drunk.'

'Must be a friend of the prisoner, Sir,' the Redcap answered, 'won't get on the lorry, Sir.'

Collins tried to tell the Adjutant what had happened but he was silenced and ordered on to the transport. From the back of the lorry, he watched helplessly as his friend was dragged away by the redcaps.

Renton had been watching Beamish deal with the situation from a distance; now the excitement was over, he sauntered over to him.

'What do you think will happen to him?' he asked. He already had a pretty good idea what the answer would be.

'If it was just fighting he'd go on report and the CO could punish him fairly lightly, but striking a Military Policeman is a court-martial offence.'

'Yes, I rather thought it was. By the way, thanks for getting my man Collins out of it, very decent of you.'

'That's all right. He hadn't done anything, but he's got to learn not to argue with the Redcaps. He was on the point of being arrested back there.'

The arrival of their transport ended the conversation. Getting onboard, Renton noticed how silent the square had become; silent save for the low moan of the wind as it blew through the tall trees.

Chapter 14

Early on Sunday morning Renton did his usual stand-to round under leaden skies. He felt very tired and out of sorts. It had been well after midnight when he finally got to bed and it seemed that no sooner had he closed his eyes than he was being woken by Collins to do his tour of the trenches. It didn't help matters that he had received the usual apathetic response from the men as he trudged through the mud from one group to another. After breakfast he had lain on his bed in a foul mood until Collins brought him his robes for morning service. Collins had wanted to talk to him about his friend, Private Webb, but he was in no mood to listen to the misfortunes of some drunken soldier.

As soon as the service had finished and the last of the congregation had left the chapel, Renton took off his robes and threw them to Collins. 'See that these are washed before my next service. They're filthy! And tidy the chapel up before you leave. You're getting slack, Collins. If you can't do the job, there's plenty that can.'

Collins had a puzzled look on his face. 'But of course I was going to tidy up, I always do. Is there anything wrong, sir?'

Renton glared at his orderly. 'Is there anything wrong, sir?' he mimicked. 'After what happened last night you have the nerve to ask me if there's anything wrong.'

'But Private Webb was drunk, sir. He didn't hit that Redcap on purpose.'

'Forget Private Webb, Collins. It's nothing to do with him. It's you! You're the reason I'm so angry and upset.'

Collins looked mystified. 'Me sir, what have I done?'

'What have you done,' Renton said angrily, 'you've let me down; that's what you've done.'

'Let you down, sir! How? I wasn't doing no fighting.'

'No, you did something far worse,' Renton snapped. 'You defiled your body instead.'

'De– what, sir?'

'Whoring, Collins, that's what I'm referring to, whoring!'

'But I didn't, sir.'

'Don't make things worse by denying it!' Renton's voice grew louder as his anger increased, 'I saw you last night. Saw you queuing up in that alleyway with countless other wretches for the services of some disease ridden prostitute. I thought you had better sense than that. I had you down as someone who wanted to better himself.' A pained expression came to his face. 'You want to know something, Collins? I was actually getting fond of you. But it seems you're just like the rest, stupid and ignorant! I'm obviously wasting my time trying to help you.'

'Please, sir, please listen,' Collin's said, his face had gone bright red, 'I didn't go with no prostitute, honest, sir.'

'Are you calling me a liar, Collins? Because if you are, I've got a good mind to replace you right here and now.'

'No, sir, 'course not, sir. You did see me waiting to go with a prostitute, but I only went 'cos of me mate. Then, when I got in the brothel, I couldn't go through with it. Nothing happened. That's the truth, I swear it!'

'Do you take me for a fool, Collins? Do you think you can save your safe little job by lying to me? Don't let this dog collar fool you, Collins. I'm no soft touch.'

Collins looked beseechingly at Renton who stared unwaveringly back at him. 'Please believe me, sir. I didn't sleep with no prostitute, honest! I wouldn't lie to you sir, ever! Not even to keep me job, I wouldn't. I was going to, it's true, but when it came to it, well, I just couldn't. That's the truth, I swear on my mother's life!'

For a moment there was awkward silence between them. Renton's expression didn't change, but Collin's impassioned words had made him think that maybe the boy was telling the truth. He knew that Collins worshipped his mother and wouldn't use her name lightly. Leaning forward, he picked up a Bible from the pile that had been neatly stacked up on the floor and thrust it into his orderly's hand. 'Are you prepared to swear on your mother's life and on this Holy Bible that you did not go with a prostitute last night?' He despised himself for what he was doing, but the desire to know the truth was overwhelming, and he knew the boy would not lie on oath. To his relief, Collins didn't hesitate to pick up the Bible and do as requested.

'All right, Collins, let's say I'm inclined to believe you. What happened to make you change your mind then?'

He listened patiently as Collins told him everything that had taken place in the brothel from the moment he entered to his hasty departure into the street. It was obvious that the boy was ashamed of still being a virgin and had wanted to prove himself in front of his mates.

But what was really interesting to Renton was that, in reply to a pointed question by him of why Collins hadn't been able to perform sexually, the boy's only explanation was that the woman had held no physical appeal for him. Looking at the downcast face of his orderly, Renton felt sure he knew the real reason why, and if he was right, then his own chances looked brighter. 'You appear to have had a lucky escape, Collins,' he said eventually. Knowing the boy must be feeling ashamed to be standing in a chapel talking about brothels and prostitutes he placed his hand on the boy's shoulder and squeezed gently. 'All right then, you may carry on as my orderly. But I hope the experience has taught you a valuable lesson and that in the future you heed my advice when I give it to you.'

'Oh yes, sir. I won't be going back there, sir. That's a promise'

'I'm very glad to hear it. And by the way, I shouldn't worry too much about not being attracted to woman, not all men are.'

He left Collins tidying up the chapel and started for the officers' mess. He felt sure his domination over Collins was just a matter of time and the thought of having the boy completely in his power and at his mercy, aroused him sexually. For a fleeting moment he had an image of himself and Collins together, naked in a proper, comfortable bed but his fantasies had to take a back seat to reality as the rain started up again releasing a steady drizzle from the grey coloured skies. A light mist, mixed together with the drizzle, meant that visibility was reduced to a few yards. His attention elsewhere, he failed to notice Sergeant Watkins appear out of the gloom and fall into step with him. Watkins took him by the arm. He tried to pull away, but the burly Quartermaster had a firm grip on him.

'What's the matter, Mr Renton?' he said. 'Anyone would think you weren't glad to see me.'

'What do you think you're doing, Watkins? Take your hands off me this instant!'

'Now, now, that's not very friendly like, is it? Not when we're just about to have another cosy little chat. Your attitude won't do Mr Renton. It won't do at all. Let's walk back to the chapel, shall we?'

Renton opened his mouth to protest but Watkins increased the pressure on his arm. Not until they arrived back at the Chapel did Watkins release his grip on Renton's arm.

'After you,' he said, giving Renton a shove towards the door.

Renton hesitated before entering, afraid of what Watkins might be planning. 'My orderly is in there tidying up. Can't your talk wait?'

Watkins grinned. 'I'm afraid not. Tell Collins to come back later. I'm sure he won't mind.' His grin grew wider. 'I expect he'll do anything you ask of him, won't he, padre. Especially as you treats him so nicely.'

As the two men entered the chapel, Collins was busy sweeping the floor. He looked up as they approached and seemed surprised to see Watkins with the padre.

'Leave that for now, Collins.' Renton said, keeping his voice as normal as possible. 'You can come back and finish it later. Sgt Watkins and I need the use of the chapel for a while.'

'Run along then, lad! Look sharp about it,' Watkins said, adding unnecessary weight to Renton's order.

As Collins closed the door behind him, Watkins took a cheroot from his pocket and put it to his lips.

'I'd rather you didn't,' Renton said. 'After all, this is a chapel you know.'

Watkins smiled. 'Fair enough, padre,' he said, replacing the unlit cheroot back in his pocket, 'It's a reasonable request and I'm a reasonable man.'

'I doubt that very much, Watkins. What do want anyway? Is it money for the whisky I drank that night in your quarters? I'm not trying to avoid paying you if that's what you're worried about.'

Watkins removed his cap and ambled over to the cloth covered wooden table that Renton used for an altar. Tossing his cap down on the altar, he turned and faced Renton. 'You already paid me for the whisky, Mr Renton. But then of course you wouldn't know that would you, on account of you being so drunk. In fact I bet you can't remember anything you said or did that night, can you?'

'Look Sergeant, I admit I had too much to drink. It was very wrong of me but I was very upset that night. It won't happen again, I assure you.'

'Oh don't worry, padre. I won't tell anybody that you were pissed out of your mind. It's our little secret.' Watkins eyes narrowed and he gave Renton a crafty look. 'And that goes for what you said to me that night as well.'

Renton went pale and his pulse quickened. 'Yes, well, unfortunately I don't know what I said.'

'No, you wouldn't, would you?' Watkins said, casually inspecting his fingernails. 'I mean, how could you be expected to know? After all, you were very drunk, padre. But take it from me; you did a hell of a lot of talking that night, and very interesting it was too.'

'Get to the point, Watkins, if there is one.' Renton spoke with a bravado he didn't feel; deep down inside he felt terribly afraid of what might be coming.

'Now then! Now then!' Watkins said wagging his finger, 'no need to be so touchy! Mind you, I can quite see why one of '*your kind*' would have every reason to worry about what he might have let slip when drunk.'

Renton's mouth went dry and he felt an icy shiver run down his spine. 'What do you mean by 'one of my kind', Sergeant?'

'You know perfectly well what I mean. But I'll spell it out for you if you want. A nancy boy! A bum bandit! A shirt lifter! Whatever name you prefer. It's all the same to me. And don't bother denying it. I couldn't have stopped you talking that night even if I'd gagged you. I know all about your liking for men, and your desire for young Collins. In fact, I know all there is to know about you now, padre. You told me everything when you were pissed!'

Renton's head spun and his whole body shook as if gripped in a fever. He lurched forward and put his arms out to steady himself and would have fallen to the floor if Watkins had not stepped forward to catch him. The Quartermaster helped him over to the altar and sat down beside him. Renton sat hunched forward with his head in his hands until the dizziness had passed. At length he recovered his composure enough to speak. 'What do you want, Watkins? You obviously haven't reported me or I'd be under investigation by now. I suppose you want money for your silence, is that it?'

Watkins smiled at him but didn't answer straightaway. Reaching into his pocket he took out a cheroot and lit it. He inhaled deeply and then blew a neat little ring of tobacco smoke into the air and watched it drift slowly upwards towards the roof. He waited until it had disappeared up into the rafters before answering Renton's question.

'Don't worry, padre, it's not your money I want. Although I must admit I was very tempted in view of what I know about you. But like I said, I'm a reasonable man, and I'm also a broadminded one. It makes no odds to me if you like your meat sliced a different way from the rest of us. The trouble is, other people don't see it that way. That's why being queer like you happens to be a criminal offence. But of course you know that, don't you?'

Renton lifted his head. 'If you don't want money, what do you want? There must be some price I've got to pay for your silence.'

'Ah well, I didn't say there wasn't, did I? I just said I didn't want your money. You're right; you have got to pay a price for my silence, padre, but not in money. All I want is a little favour from you, that's all.'

'What sort of favour?'

'I'd like to store some of my things here in the chapel. I haven't any room left in my place and I know they'll be safe in here.'

Renton leapt to his feet. 'You're lying. There's plenty of room in your store. '

Watkins expression darkened. 'You should be careful who you call a liar, Renton or I might change my mind about turning you in. Anyway, storing a few boxes is a small price to pay for staying out of prison, wouldn't you say?' Watkins flicked the ash off his cheroot and waited for an answer.

Renton felt sick with fear at the thought of going to prison. After a while he said. 'All right, Watkins, you win. What's so special about these boxes, anyway? Why can't you keep them in your store?'

'That's better.' The grin was back on Watkins face. 'I knew you'd see things my way. As far as the boxes are concerned, I think the less you know about the contents the better. What you don't know can't hurt you, as the old saying goes.'

Renton was incredulous. 'Doesn't it mean anything at all to you that this is a chapel, Watkins? Have you sunk so low as to keep illicit merchandise in God's house? Think of the after life, man! Do you really want to end up burning in hell for all eternity?'

Watkins laughed and shook his head. 'It's no good appealing to my conscience, Renton, because I haven't got one. Anyway, I've never been caught, and don't intend to be. And let's not kid ourselves. This place isn't a proper chapel. Look at it! It's nothing more than an old broken down barn in the middle of nowhere.'

'It doesn't matter what it looks like,' Renton cried. 'It's still a house of God.'

'Have it your own way, padre.' Watkins picked up his cap. 'Mind you, it doesn't make any difference though, because if it is a house of God as you say, then I reckon I'm entitled to put my stuff in here and claim sanctuary for it!'

Renton was so taken aback at Watkins twisted sense of humour that he could think of nothing to say. The big man stood in the doorway and laughed until his whole body shook. Tears came to his eyes as he struggled to contain himself. Finally, he got himself under control.

'You should see your face, Renton,' he said, wiping his eyes. 'It's a proper picture. Listen, it was only a joke, all right? You and I both know this is the last place the provost would think of searching for any dodgy gear. That's why I chose it. It's only a precautionary measure anyway. Relax; you've got nothing to worry about.'

'You're an evil, corrupt man, Watkins,' Renton's voice was surprisingly calm despite his fear, 'I shall pray to God to save your soul.'

Watkins pushed the door open a fraction. 'Oh, that's good coming from you, Renton, very good! Especially as we both know it's your soul, you should be praying for, not mine; right, nancy boy?' He waited for an answer, but when Renton didn't rise to his provocation, he grinned and gave him a mocking salute. 'Sorry to end our little chat, padre, but I've got things to do. I'll bring in the stuff tonight.' He pointed to the far end of the barn where some old farm machinery and animal troughs were half hidden under lengths of tarpaulin and empty feed sacks. 'Don't worry, Renton! Nobody will see a thing once they're mixed in with that lot.'

Watkins was going through the door when Renton had a flash of inspiration. 'What about Collins? You've forgotten about him. He's in and out of here all the time tiding up for me and he's bound to stumble across anything that's hidden.'

Watkins paused in the doorway with his back to Renton. He didn't bother turning around, but Renton still heard every word clearly. 'Collins is your problem, padre, not mine! Fuck some sense into him if you have to, but find a way to deal with him.'

For a few seconds Renton stood motionless unsure of what to do. His mind was in turmoil; what if the big

Quartermaster returned to torment him further with some new threat or demand? He rushed forward and closed the chapel door. Leaning with his back against the woodwork he put his head in his hands and wept. Then he did something he hadn't done in private for a long while. Walking over to the altar he dropped to his knees and, putting his hands together, began to pray.

Chapter 15

Collins sat on his bed polishing the padre's shoes. It was a chore he normally hated doing but he needed something to do to stop himself from constantly thinking about his friend Lofty. He really missed his company; it was awfully quiet in the dugout without him around. He glanced at the neatly made up bed next to his. It was neatly made up because it hadn't been slept in it; Webb was still in the hands of the Military Police. News of his arrest had spread like wildfire through the trenches, but Collins sensed that he was the only one who felt really sorry for him; nobody else appeared to care about him much. Hearing the sound of footsteps outside, Collins looked hopefully towards the top of the stairs. He knew it couldn't be Lofty; but he looked anyway. The footsteps faded away into the distance. He rubbed his eyes with the back of his hand in an effort to help stay awake. The other men in the dugout had returned from town drunk and slept soundly in their beds until stand-to but Collins had lain awake tossing and turning in his bunk. He blamed himself for Lofty's troubles. Stick together, that's what they had both agreed. If only he had waited for Lofty outside the brothel instead of going off on his own, they would have returned together safely.

The only consolation was that he had met Rose. He thought he'd done well there, thought he'd made a good impression on her. Best of all, she'd agreed to see him again. He closed his eyes and tried to recall the image of her face, but it wasn't easy. The fine details of her features were blurred but he did remember that she looked really smashing in her nurse's uniform. He wondered what Lofty would say when he met her.

Lofty! Once again all thoughts came back to Lofty. He had to do something to try and help him. But what could he do? The padre had been no help. Wouldn't even hear what he had to say. That was at breakfast though, when the padre was mad at him. It might be worth having another try when he'd properly calmed down. Thinking of the padre made him realise just what a fool he'd been not to listen to his advice in the first place. Ever since he'd started working for him, the padre had tried to help him; and how had he repaid his kindness? By ignoring his advice and giving him grief, that's how! Collins lifted up the pair of shoes and spat on each one. Picking up a cloth he polished away furiously until he was satisfied that he could see his face clearly in each toecap.

Minutes later he heard the sound of footsteps again. This time they stopped outside. He put the shoes down and looked up expectantly. A soldier descended the steps and came towards him. But it wasn't Lofty. It was Brewer, the soldier Lofty had fought with last night. Collins looked down at the bedclothes. He had nothing to say to him.

'Got a minute, Davy?' Brewer said in a friendly tone of voice.

Collins lifted his head and looked at Brewer fiercely. 'Go away, Brewer, you've done enough harm already.'

'Look Davy, I'm sorry about Lofty, really I am. I know I was pretty sozzled last night, but then, so was Lofty.'

'You should have stayed out of his way.'

'But I was only queuing up for the bloody lorry, Davy! I didn't get in his way deliberately. Christ, we must have been out of our sodding heads to be fighting with the redcaps about. But honest to God, I'm really sorry about Lofty dropping in the shit like he has.'

Collins was surprised. He was expecting to hear Brewer say that Lofty had got it coming. 'Yeah, well, that's as maybe, but it's all right for you. It wasn't you that got nabbed, was it?'

'No, it wasn't. But Lofty was looking for trouble last night, Davy, and that's the truth. If it hadn't been me, he would have picked a fight with someone else.'

Collins knew Brewer was right. He remembered how Lofty had almost dragged him into a fight with the Scotsman in the bar. Lofty was bad enough with just a few drinks inside him. Last night in the square he'd had more than just a few. He was roaring drunk and spoiling for a fight with someone. Brewer was an obvious choice.

'I guess you're right. But you could have walked away. You saw how drunk he was.'

'Do me a favour, Davy. I told you, I was just as sozzled as he was,' Brewer paused, 'have you heard anything yet?'

Collins shook his head. 'I'll have a word with the padre at lunchtime, and if he doesn't know anything, I'll ask the Adjutant.'

'If it'll help Lofty, you can tell the Adjutant that I'll be a witness, Davy. Tell him it was me that Lofty was trying to hit, not the redcap.'

Brewer's offer of help brightened Collins up. If they both gave evidence, then perhaps the charge might be reduced, or even dropped altogether. He knew army discipline was harsh, and perhaps he was expecting too much, but he had to give it a try; he owed it to Lofty.

Collins hopes of helping Lofty were dashed at lunchtime. He was working in the officers' mess when Captain Beamish entered and told the other officers present that a soldier of the regiment had gone missing. 'Gentlemen, I'm sorry to have to tell you that Private Webb has deserted the regiment,' he announced bluntly. Sitting down, he filled in the details. Private Webb had given his military escort the slip after breakfast. Left alone in the washhouse he'd decamped through an insecure window. When the military police realised he was gone they made a limited search of the area but so far had failed to find him. Beamish concluded by saying that, earlier, Private Webb had told the redcaps guarding him that whatever happened, he was never going back in the line again. The redcaps had taken no notice; it was the sort of bravado they often heard from prisoners in their charge and they didn't think he really meant it.

Collins listened with dismay. He could have told the redcaps that Lofty meant it. But then they hadn't seen the look of terror on Lofty's face on the day the shell exploded near the cookhouse. Nor had they heard the determination in his voice when he said he would never take part in another attack again. There was a moment of silence from the officers when Beamish finished speaking followed almost immediately by an outburst of angry comments. When the hubbub died down, one of the officers addressed Beamish. His voice rang with indignation. 'This is the first desertion we've had in the regiment since we arrived in France. Private Webb has brought shame and disgrace on the good name of this unit. When he's apprehended, he should be punished as severely as military law allows.'

Collins felt very uneasy as a murmur of agreement ran through the other officers present. What was meant by severe punishment? The officer had been with the regiment long enough to know about Lofty's terrible ordeal in battle, and his nervous breakdown afterwards; why didn't he mention that instead of going on about punishment and the good name of the regiment? He wanted to hear the rest of the conversation but he had his orderly duties to carry on with.

Renton was among the officers listening to Beamish's news. The fate of Private Webb was of no concern to him. He had his own problems to think about. The business with Watkins was bad enough, but something else had come up that was far more serious. He pulled a letter from his pocket that had been delivered to him just before lunch. It was from his sister, Joanna, and he had read it several times already. He had recognised her neat handwriting on the envelope and knew, even before he opened it, that it wouldn't contain good news. Joanna never wrote unless she had bad news or something important to tell him. His worst fears were confirmed when he read the letter. His mother's health was deteriorating rapidly. She had kept the full extent of her illness from her family for as long as possible but had finally been persuaded to agree to a medical examination. The doctors had diagnosed cancer and it was in a very advanced state. Her body was now so weak that she was unable to move from her bed. Joanna had taken temporary leave from her job and was coming in daily to attend to her. Their father was shattered by the diagnosis and taking his wife's illness very badly. The worst part came near the end of the letter.

'The doctors say it could be a matter of weeks, rather than months, and I believe them,' wrote Joanna, 'I realise that the war takes precedence over everything in our lives at the moment, and that leave for you at Christmas is out of the question, but please speak to your superiors about getting back immediately after the Christmas period.'

Renton read the last paragraph over again to make sure he fully understood what his sister was telling him. Joanna was a sensible, intelligent woman and was not given to exaggeration. Besides, her husband was a doctor, and she would have discussed her mother's condition with him. The letter was almost certainly an accurate report on the gravity of his mother's illness. He had suspected for some time that his mother's health was far worse than she mentioned in her letters, but he was shocked to hear what little time was left to her. Renton let the letter fall from his fingers on to the bed. He looked down at his hands. They were shaking uncontrollably. He could feel his heart racing under his tunic and, although he was taking in rapid gulps of air, he was struggling for breath. Leaning forward, he began to slowly exhale air from his lungs. When he was breathing normally again he reached under the bed and pulled out a bottle of whisky. Half filling a tin mug, he drank the contents in one go, hardly noticing the burning sensation as it hit the back of his throat. Pouring himself a refill, he replaced the bottle back under the bed making no attempt to conceal his actions from the other occupants of the mess. Right now he couldn't care less what they thought about his drinking. It was all very well for them. If they had any personal problems they could bring them to him to sort out. He was expected to listen because he was their chaplain, the man they could tell their troubles to. But whom did he have to turn to, apart from Mr Johnny Walker? Nobody! God had never listened to him no matter how hard he prayed, so how could he be expected to stop drinking now when so many terrible things were happening in his life.

A movement on the floor caught his eye and made him freeze. It was a rat; a big one with sleek, glistening fur the colour of gunmetal and a thick black tail as long as its body. The rat was eating a piece of hard biscuit that had fallen from someone's plate and despite his fear and loathing, Renton watched fascinated, as the rat gnawed voraciously at its meal. Holding the morsel of food securely between its two front feet, the rat was making short work of the biscuit. Suddenly, as if aware of Renton's interest, the rat stopped eating and turned its head towards him. Two burning red orbs pierced the gloomy murk of the dugout and stared straight into Renton's face. It was almost as if the rat was staring him out, waiting to see who would blink first. Renton shuddered and looked away. The rat returned triumphantly to the biscuit but before it could finish it off it was spotted by a young Lieutenant who hurled a boot at it.

Renton watched the rat flee and shuddered again. Rats! His horror of them would never diminish. But watching the rodent eating had made him realise something about them that had never occurred to him before. Unlike the countless thousands of men serving at the front, the rats were here by choice. They were free to come and go as they pleased. There were no rules or regulations governing their lives. Theirs was a simple existence, based on scavenging food from the living, or feeding off the decaying flesh of the dead. When chased away, they simply disappeared into the darkness as quickly and easily as they had arrived. Renton stared at the abandoned crumb of biscuit on the floor. He wished that he too could disappear from the trenches as quickly and easily as the rat had.

A few minutes after nine o'clock in the evening all but one of the boxes had been stashed away in the chapel. Watkins held a small lamp in his hand and by its dim light he watched as Corporal Brown brought in the last one and hid it behind a pile of rusty farming machinery. Then he put the lamp down and helped Brown to collect up some old sheets of tarpaulin that lay scattered around the floor. They arranged the sheets in layers on top of the machinery so that everything was well hidden under the tarpaulin. When he was satisfied that nothing could be seen that would arouse suspicion, Watkins stepped back and admired their handiwork. 'There,' he said. 'I defy anyone to find that lot.'

Corporal Brown nodded approvingly. 'You're right. Not that the redcaps would think of searching the chapel anyway. You're a bloody genius, Sarge, thinking of this place.'

Watkins acknowledged the corporal's praise with a mock bow. Brown was a good man. Also, he was reliable and knew how to keep his mouth shut. It had been a good idea for only the two of them to hide the boxes. It had meant quite a few trips back and forth to bring all the stuff in but the less people who knew about the hiding place the better. Of course it also meant that Brown would expect to get a bigger cut for doing more work, but Watkins agreed with that. Brown had been with him a long time and had developed into a man after his own heart.

'What beats me is how you got that piss artist of a padre to let you use this place. What happened, did you threaten to stop supplying him, Sarge?'

'Something like that,' Watkins laughed, 'let us just say I didn't give him much choice in the matter.' He pulled out a hip flask from his pocket and after taking a drink himself, handed the flask to his corporal. 'You know something, Brownie,' he continued, 'if this war carries on for another year I'm going make a packet; you too, if you stick by me.'

'Don't worry on that score, Sarge. I'm with you all right. Let's just hope we both manage to stay alive to the end of it.'

Watkins ignored Brown's pessimistic remark. He never worried about the possibility of dying. In fact he was supremely confident of his chances of survival. Death in battle wasn't meant for the likes of him. His position as quartermaster ensured that he would never have to follow some glory seeking officer's suicidal orders. If anything it was the other way around where officers were concerned. They relied on him. The public thought that *'brave Officers and Gentlemen'* led the men of the British Army. Well Watkins knew they didn't! It was Non Commissioned Officers that ran the army and not a bunch of gormless, ex public, schoolboys who didn't know their arse from their elbow. They could keep their patriotism and stiff upper lip mentality,

Watkins intended to be very much alive when the war ended and have a nice little pile of money to take back to England with him. Better to be a live NCO than a dead officer. In two years time he would be eligible for a pension. If the war was over by then, he could leave the army, pick up his pension, and buy a shop, maybe two, if he could afford it. Corporal Brown gave him back his flask and Watkins raised it in a toast. 'Here's to all NCOs, Brownie,' he said, 'as for officers; well— who the fucking hell needs them?'

Corporal Brown echoed his Sergeant's words. 'Yeah, fucking officers; fuck the lot of them, Sarge, that's what I say.'

After leaving the chapel, Watkins spent the remainder of the evening in his quarters doing some paperwork. The army had a form for practically everything and Watkins knew that the best way to keep the army happy was to keep their forms in order. It didn't matter if the amount on the form didn't always represent the amount held in store. The vagaries of war meant that Watkins never even had to give explanations for a lot of the missing equipment. He picked up an invoice for a consignment of tinned food that had just arrived and put it to the bottom of a pile of forms. It was a golden rule of his 'to always make the buggers wait'. He never issued supplies to the men as soon as he received them and never returned paperwork promptly. When he finished he treated himself to a little nightcap. He was pleased with himself; it had been a good day's work. Half an hour later he turned in for the night and slept like a log.

In the officers' quarters, Renton tossed and turned fitfully in his bed. Despite finishing the bottle of whisky he could not sleep soundly. The health of his mother and the threats made by Watkins lay heavily on his mind. Furthermore, the pursuit of Collins seemed to be getting nowhere. If only he could get home his troubles might go away. That's what his mother always did for him when he was a child; made his troubles go away.

In his bunk Collins closed his eyes but much as he needed to get some sleep, thinking of Lofty Webb's fate kept him awake. The second night of his friends absence was even more miserable for him than the first. All evening he'd listened to the men in his dugout talking about what sort of punishment Lofty could get. They all agreed on one point. Fighting and hitting a redcap was one thing, it even earned a bit of admiration, but desertion was another matter entirely. Some of the army punishments that the men spoke about were so harsh that Davy found them hard to believe. Flogging over gun carriages, hard labour that involved carrying ammunition boxes until a man dropped of exhaustion—ten years in a military prison—the list of sentences seemed endless. Finally, someone mentioned the worst sentence that Lofty could receive. Collins shivered and pulled the blankets over his head.

Chapter 16

The next morning Renton decided to request compassionate leave to go and see his mother. The only person authorised to grant him such leave was the senior chaplain, Colonel Morris but when Renton contacted his office he was informed that the Colonel was very busy. The only time he would be free to see him was two days before Christmas. As Morris was based some considerable distance from the front line, the visit would mean an overnight stay.

Kerr was sympathetic to the news of his mother's illness and agreed that if he got permission he could travel home as soon after Christmas as possible but not before. 'The men must have a padre here at Christmas time,' he told Renton. 'It's when they miss home the most.'

Renton didn't need Kerr to tell him that. Ever since his arrival in France he had resigned himself to the fact that he would be spending Christmas at the front.

Collins received the news that the padre would be away for the best part of two days with mixed emotions. He knew the padre's mother was very ill and felt sad for him, but on the other hand it would give him the chance to get into town and see Rose again. He badly needed somebody to cheer him up because nothing seemed to be going right at the moment. To start with, there was no further news about Lofty Webb. He had been on the run for five days now, and each day Collins asked himself the same questions. Where could he be hiding out? Was he getting any food? Was he still alive even?

Then there was the effect that Lofty's desertion was having on the regiment. It cast a shadow over everybody. Collins knew the officers in particular, felt the disgrace badly, they took their feelings out on the men by tightening up on discipline and giving them unnecessary tasks to do. The men in turn blamed Lofty for their plight. Collins thought it better to keep his mouth shut than risk being unpopular by standing up for his friend. As he listened to them, night after night, in the dugout, grumbling about the latest stupid order they had been told to carry out, he thought once again just how lucky he was to be the padre's orderly. It got him out of so many of the dirty jobs that the infantry soldiers moaned about. He was worried about the padre also. Since the day he had received a letter about his mother, he had barely touched any of the meals that Collins had served him. He hadn't been sleeping well either, Collins could tell by the untidy state of the blankets on the bed in the mornings. The padre looked awful too, especially early on in the day. Big, red circles had formed under his eyes and he looked permanently tired and unwell. He was also drinking a lot of whisky; Collins knew because he was buying it for him now. It started the day after the padre had talked with Sergeant Watkins in the chapel. He had finished his duties in the officers' mess and was just leaving when the padre took him aside and, in a voice barely raised above a whisper, asked him if he would go to the quartermaster and buy a bottle of whisky from him.

'I don't want to deal with him myself,' he had said, 'the less I see of that man the better.' He stuffed a roll of notes into Collins hand and hurriedly shooed him out of the dugout. It had all happened so quickly that he hadn't had a chance to say no. Not that he would have done so anyway; he felt too sorry for the padre to refuse. He didn't like the idea of dealing with Sergeant Watkins after their last encounter and hoped to get his errand done as quickly as he could; but it didn't turn out to be that easy.

Sergeant Watkins had obviously lied to him when he said that he and the padre were good friends because from the moment he entered the quartermaster's dugout, Collins was left in no doubt that the big man had it in for the padre. 'What's the matter?' he sneered as he handed over the bottle, 'Mr Renton too drunk to come in person?'

'No, Sergeant,' A flush of colour came to Collins cheeks, 'it's just that he's very busy at the moment, so he sent me.'

'Busy! That's a laugh. Busy drinking more like. Don't try and kid me, lad. I supply him with the booze, remember.'

Collins found himself leaping to the padre's defence. 'He's having a bad time, Sergeant. His mother's very ill and he's trying to get permission to go home and see her.'

'My heart bleeds for him,' sneered Watkins. 'Doesn't he know there's a war on? What would happen if we all went home because someone in the family was ill?' He jabbed his finger into Collins chest. 'I'll tell you what would happen, Collins, my lad! There'd be no one left to fight this war, that's what would happen!'

Collins thought it best not to answer back. He just wanted to get away.

'Well, don't you agree? Speak up, lad. I won't bite you.'

'Yes, Sergeant,' he said, timidly. 'But the padre isn't here to fight. He's here to pray, and do other things like, like …' Collins paused, trying to think what other jobs the padre did.

'Bollocks!' Watkins said, 'he's got to take his chances just the same as everyone else. The medics aren't here to fight either, but they get killed on the battlefield all the same. Still, I suppose you're bound to stick up for him seeing as you've got a safe little number looking after him'

Collins said nothing, even though he thought the comment was a bit strong coming from someone who had one of the safest jobs in the regiment. He started to fidget and looked anxiously at the door hoping to be dismissed, but Watkins hadn't finished with him yet.

'I expect you've asked him to say a few prayers for that mate of yours, Private Webb. Not that it'll do much good, the gutless little swine.'

Collins face went red and, despite his fear of Watkins, his eyes flashed with anger.

Watkins smiled. 'That got to you, didn't it? Don't like to hear your mate called gutless do you? Well it's true. If he had any guts he'd be fighting Germans, not his mates, wouldn't he?'

Collins bit his lip and stared straight ahead.

'I said he'd be fighting Germans, wouldn't he, Collins?' Watkins stood directly in front of Collins, their faces only inches apart. 'Answer me when I ask you a question, damn you!'

'Yes, Sergeant, he would,' Collins agreed quietly. The close, menacing, presence of Watkins scared Davy. It would be best to go along with everything he said if he wanted to get away quickly.

Watkins' face was almost touching Davy's and his breath reeked of stale tobacco and beer. 'Bloody right he would,' Watkins bellowed, 'so don't you go feeling sorry for him; we don't want any prayers wasted on the likes of scum like that, do we now?'

'No, Sergeant.'

'Good, so long as that's clear then,' Watkins snapped. He looked at his watch and then, in a calmer voice, said, 'I've better things to do than stand around talking to the likes of you.' He pointed to the bottle in Collins hand. 'And don't get caught with that on you.'

Thinking he had been dismissed, Collins, turned to leave, relieved that the ordeal was over at last.

'Stop!' Sergeant Watkins barked out. He went over to a wooden box that contained a pile of sandbags. Picking one out, he threw at Collins. 'Better put the bottle in this. In case you run into anybody.'

Collins hastily stuffed the bottle in the sandbag. 'Can I go now Sergeant?' he asked, unsure as to whether Watkins was finished with him or not.

Watkins wasn't. 'Just one question and then you can go. Tell me, just out of interest, what exactly do you do for the padre in that chapel of his?'

'The chapel!' 'Well, I clean it out once a week, and after a service I collect the hymn books up; that's all.'

'I see, and you've had no other instructions about the chapel from Mr Renton lately?'

'No, Sergeant.' Collins was puzzled by the quartermaster's interest in the chapel but didn't have the courage to ask why.

'Never mind, it's of no matter my lad. Forget I ever asked you about it. You can go now.'

When he was safely outside the quartermaster's billet, Collins turned and stuck two fingers up at the closed door. Then he hurried away into the darkness as quickly as the muddy ground would allow.

On the morning of his appointment with Colonel Morris, Renton told Collins to pack a few overnight things in a bag for him. After breakfast they walked together to the rear area where transport had been arranged to take the padre to Morris's headquarters. Renton was sorry that Collins wasn't going with him; he had been a great comfort to him over the last few days. He was surprised at the amount of compassion Collins showed to him over his mother's illness. Renton hadn't expected it after refusing to listen to his orderly's plea to do something for his deserter friend, Webb. As the wheels on the army lorry slithered their way along the muddy road out of the Westhampton's lines, Renton came to the conclusion that any hopes of seducing Collins had been temporarily dashed. At present he was in no condition to make any sort of move on anyone and he knew it. All his sexual urges had been washed away in a tidal wave of alcohol, and the anticipated pleasures of Collins body would have to wait until after he'd sorted his problems out and cut down on his drinking. But it pained him to think that it would be over twenty four hours until he saw his orderly again. Since his run-in with Watkins, he didn't like being alone and liked to keep Collins close to him. He was giving Collins extra reading lessons to ensure that he stayed with him a bit longer during the day. No doubt Collins thought that the extra lessons were a reward for his whisky buying trips.

It was during the course of one of these reading lessons that Renton learnt about the disparaging remarks Watkins had made about him. He also found out that Collins detested the quartermaster almost as much as he did. When the boy told him he had spoken up for him against Watkins, Renton congratulated himself on having won him over so completely. There was nothing Collins could possibly do to help him, but it was reassuring to know he had such an obedient and loyal ally.

The journey to the rear was slow, tiresome, and uneventful. The army driver didn't volunteer much in the way conversation and Renton passed the time staring out of the window smoking endless cigarettes. Most of the French countryside he saw had a war ravaged look about it. For mile upon depressing mile, Renton the landscape was mostly devoid of trees, or greenery of any kind. The earth in the fields, presumably once rich and fertile, was now blackened and strewn with the debris of war. Some of the fields were so disfigured by the scores of water filled bomb craters that they looked like the surface of an alien planet. It wasn't until they approached the busy rear areas that Renton noticed any trees or hedges in significant numbers, and even they looked dismal without leaves hanging from their branches.

It was late afternoon when Renton finally arrived at Colonel Morris's headquarters. Stiff and tired from the long drive, he was relieved to find out from the Colonel's clerk that a room had been prepared for him in the officer's mess. Better still was the news that he could get a hot bath. He was ordered to dine with Colonel Morris in his quarters at eight o'clock. His request for leave could be put to the Colonel over dinner. The officers' mess was a pleasant surprise after being at the front. It turned out to be a large country house that had been taken over by the British Army for the duration of the war. A mess steward, immaculately dressed, took Renton's overnight bag and showed him to a room on the first floor.

Twenty minutes later Renton was lazing in a large white bath that was almost full to the brim with hot water. Soap, clean towels, bath salts, and other toiletries were lined up on a shelf on the wall. He had forgotten what it was like to have a proper bath and it made him realise just how much of a contrast there was between the living conditions of the men at the front, and the comparative luxury enjoyed by the headquarters staff. He should have been angry but he wasn't, he was envious. He was envious that some of his fellow chaplains who, because they were favourites of Morris, or had the ear of some other senior chaplain, could sit out the war in safety and comfort far behind the front line. He lingered in the bath letting the hot water take away the grime of the trenches while he ran a critical eye over his pale white body. Despite the heavy drinking, his lack of appetite for the food at the front meant that he had lost at least twenty pounds in weight. He didn't look too bad for a man of his age, he told himself, running his hands over his stomach. When he'd had enough of lazing in the bath he got out and dried his body off in soft, clean towels. He took his time getting dressed before going down to the mess lounge.

He had nearly two hours to kill before meeting Morris for dinner. Sitting down in the most comfortable looking chair he could find, he summoned a mess boy and ordered a pot of tea and biscuits. When they arrived, he noticed with approval the china cup and saucer on the tray; tin mugs obviously wouldn't do for headquarters staff. The hot tea scalded his throat and he would have preferred something stronger to drink, but knew he dare not risk it. One drink would lead to another and he needed to be sober when he saw Morris. Picking up a newspaper from the table, he settled back in his chair and nibbled on a biscuit.

In Rouville, Davy Collins sat in Emile's café waiting for Rose. It was nearly half past eight and he was on his second glass of beer. She was over an hour and a half late and he had a sinking feeling in the pit of his stomach that despite her promise to him, she wasn't going to turn up. He felt embarrassed sitting on his own. The café had half a dozen customers and they kept looking at him as if they knew that he'd been let down. He should have guessed that Rose was only having a laugh with him that night. After all, why would she want to go out with a penniless soldier like him? She probably only did it as a dare to show her friends. When he worked in the market, some of the girls often did the same thing to his mates. Thinking about it now it was obvious that it didn't make any sense for an attractive girl like her to go out with an ordinary bloke like him, but she'd been so convincing with her promise that, like an idiot, he thought she really meant it.

He heard a noise from somewhere in the street and looked out of the window but could see nobody outside. Picking up his beer glass he rolled the glass around in his hands and stared gloomily at the amber liquid as it gently lapped against the inside of the glass. The day had started so promising. After seeing the padre off for his appointment, Collins had the rare luxury of a day to himself. The first thing he did was get permission to go into town. Getting transport wouldn't be difficult; he could hitch a ride on one of the transports that regularly shuttled back and forth. He wrote a note asking Rose to meet him in the café at seven o'clock and then went in search of a medical orderly that would take the note to the casualty station where she worked. He was lucky; he found one that was just leaving to collect some medical supplies. The man was only too willing to take his note. 'Please make sure she gets it personally,' he told him. 'Its very important you give it to her and no one else.'

The medic assured him he would deliver his note safely. He would be back in a couple of hours he said and would find him and let him know if there was any reply. The time waiting for her reply dragged, but eventually the medic returned with a note from Rose saying that she would be there as requested. Collins felt pretty pleased with himself. It was just a case of making himself as presentable as possible and counting the hours until seven o'clock arrived.

'Monsieur wishes another beer?'

Emile's voice startled him. He had been so wrapped up in thought that he hadn't noticed the café owner approach his table. He looked at the clock on the wall. It was a quarter past nine. Rose wasn't coming now. 'No, no thank you,' he said, handing Emile his glass. 'Can you tell me if your clock is right, please?'

'Why yes, Monsieur, it is maybe a minute or two fast, but it is right enough for me.' The café owner smiled at him and waved his hand towards the door. 'Monsieur was expecting someone, yes; a young lady perhaps?'

'Yes, I was, but she won't come now.' Collins said. He was embarrassed. He just wanted to pay up and leave. It must be obvious to everyone in the café by now that he'd been stood up.

Emile sighed heavily. 'You have my sympathy. In wartime, things are difficult, yes! But do not despair, Môn ami. Who knows? Perhaps you will see her soon.'

He couldn't be cheered up that easily. 'I don't think that's very likely, not after tonight.'

'Pah! What is one night?' Emile said loudly. He twirled one end of his moustache between his fingers. 'You should not give up so easily, soldier.'

'Maybe you're right.' he shrugged his shoulders. 'Maybe I shouldn't.'

'Well, *Tommy*, you are welcome to visit my café anytime to look for her. You are not like the other soldiers who drink too much and make trouble. You are a good man I think.'

Collins turned down Emile's offer of a free beer and paid his bill. He'd spent over two hours sitting in the café waiting for Rose. What he needed now was some fresh air. He shook hands with Emile and left the café to begin the now familiar walk to the town square.

Chapter 17

The evening spent with Colonel Morris was a tedious experience for Renton. He had hoped that at least one other chaplain would be present to lighten the load, but on arriving found that only the two of them would be sitting down to dine. Throughout dinner, Morris dominated their conversation to such an extent that Renton was reduced to the role of listener. His host aired his views on everything from the conduct of the war to the quality of the chaplains under his command. Renton learnt that Morris had over thirty years' service as an army chaplain and was a stickler for military discipline. It was also clear that he was proud of being an Anglican Chaplain and expected those who served him to have the same religious zeal. Towards the end of the meal, Morris steered the conversation around to the subject of other faiths and religions and confided to Renton that he saw ministers of other denominations as a threat.

'We're losing our grip on the soldier in the trenches,' he told Renton. 'We don't want to suffer in comparison with the Catholics, or the Jews for that matter.' He glared at Renton in a way that suggested that he would brook no argument on the subject. 'Why only last week I had an Anglican chaplain sent back from a regiment. To make matters worse, the commanding officer of the regiment involved then suggested that a Catholic priest be sent in his place. It's not good enough, Renton, not good enough by half.'

'No. I suppose not.' Renton put his hand over his mouth to conceal a yawn. The colonel was in full flow and it was doubtful if even an artillery bombardment would stop him.

'We're not fighting this war for a lot of Papists and Jews you know,' Morris ranted on, 'and while I'm in command here I'm not going to stand idly by and let good Christian soldiers be converted over to other religions.' He went on in this vein for most of the evening. To make matters worse, Morris was a teetotaller. There was no wine on the table to dull Renton's senses and help speed the evening along. Eventually Morris stopped talking long enough for Renton to get round to the subject of his mother's illness and his request to go home on compassionate leave. Renton was half expecting a lecture on his patriotic duty and to be told he couldn't be spared, but to his amazement Morris gave his permission without hesitation. Then, to his surprise Morris told him how pleased he was with him.

'I don't mind telling you Renton, I had some reservations about sending you to a regiment at the front, but so far I've had no complaints from anybody. You've obviously buckled down to the job and got on with it as best you can. Carry on the good work for another couple of months and then come and see me again. After twelve years as an army chaplain it's about time we thought of getting you some promotion.'

Renton was flattered at being considered for a higher rank at last, but it had come too late and he knew it. In his heart he just couldn't bring the same devotion to his job that he had done twelve years ago. Then he was young, keen, and idealistic. Now he was a chaplain who drank too much and only went through the motions of being a priest. He thanked Morris, but didn't want to push his luck. He'd got the leave he came for and that was the main thing. Better to leave now, while he was ahead. Pleading tiredness after his journey, he hurriedly left.

Walking back to the officers' mess he tried to imagine Morris as a young chaplain. Although it was hard to believe now, he must surely have had some liberal views about his profession years ago. How long had it taken for Morris to undergo such a radical change? Renton wondered. He had a pretty good idea how it had come about. Morris had almost certainly spent too many nights listening to high-minded officers who still thought that the British Empire could only be run successfully by white, protestant Englishman from the aristocracy. The higher Morris had gone in his career, the more intolerant he had become to the opinions of younger men whose views differed from the old ideals. It invariably happened when men reached senior rank. And now, at last, he was being offered the first step on the rung of the promotion ladder, something he had wanted for years. But did he want promotion it if it meant ending up like Morris? He wasn't at all sure he did.

The following morning was Christmas Eve and Collins was still annoyed with Rose for letting him down. The more he thought about it, the more he convinced himself that she had done it on purpose. He was still sulking when it was time for stand-to. Hurriedly pulling on his uniform he grabbed his rifle from under his bed and stumbled out of the dugout. It was still dark as he arrived at his defence position. He saw a group of men already sitting on the fire step so he sat down alongside them. The men cursed and grumbled at being dragged from their warm beds into the cold morning air but he took no notice of them. For the life of him, he couldn't understand why they kept complaining every morning. Didn't they realise by now that all the moaning in the world wasn't going to get them out of stand-to duty.

Suddenly a corporal sitting near to Collins piped up with some news that immediately silenced the grumbling men and made him forget all about Rose. According to the corporal, who had it on good authority from his sergeant, who in turn had heard it from someone else, Lofty Webb had been captured trying to beg food from a house in a village some four miles from the front lines.

'It was bad luck really,' said the corporal, 'the house belonged to the local gendarme. He takes one look at Lofty, looking all filthy like and obviously English, and guesses he's an army deserter. He calls one of his Froggy mates and together they get hold of him and march him off. As I was told it,' the corporal continued, 'Lofty was cold, wet, and starving hungry; too weak to put up any resistance. So he was handed over to the army and now he's back in the care of them same redcaps he got away from just under a week ago.' When the corporal finished telling his story Collins joined the clamour of voices wanting to know more details, but the corporal had none to tell them. The men fell silent for a moment and then began discussing the capture.

Collins went and sat beside the corporal. 'If it's true about him being caught, what'll happen now, corporal?' he asked. His voice seemed to echo off the walls of the trench and ring loudly in his ears.

'They don't hang about with desertion cases, lad,' the corporal said. 'They've got to make an example of 'em, see. If you ask me, they'll have his court martial all over and done with by the start of the New Year. Believe it or not, the army can move quite fast when it wants to.'

Davy was horrified. The corporal must surely have made a mistake. 'But that's only about a week away. They wouldn't deal with him as quick as that, would they?'

'Oh yes they would! You see lad, a deserter's court martial is treated as priority and if he's found guilty the punishment is always carried out straight away. The idea is to deter others who might be thinking of doing the same thing.'

'Do you think that, seeing as its Christmas, they'll go a bit easier on him?' Davy asked hopefully.

'No chance,' the corporal said, shaking his head. 'He'll have some officer appointed to defend him of course, but it won't make any difference. Christmas or not, he's for the high jump all right, you can take my word on that, son.'

Collins looked up at the sky; dawn was starting to break. Normally when he watched the early morning sky grow lighter, it helped to cheer him up. It made him think that with a bit of luck, each new day might be the last day of the war. But this morning was different. Even if the war ended this very minute, it would be too late to help Lofty. He felt faint and closed his eyes until the feeling passed. When the order came along the line to stand down, Collins trudged his way wearily back to his dugout and threw himself down on his bed.

Renton had been assigned a different driver to take him back. The new man drove faster than his predecessor and at the rate they were travelling he would be back in plenty of time to take Christmas Eve service. It had been good to wallow in a bit of comfort and taste decent food again at headquarters, but even so he wasn't sorry to be heading back. The evening with Morris had been tiresome despite getting the result he had wanted, and he had drunk too much in the bar later on. His mouth was still dry from the whisky and he was looking forward to getting back and having a cup of coffee. As the miles rolled by, he had trouble keeping awake. Finally he gave in to the temptation, and slumping back in his seat, closed his eyes. Five miles from the Westhampton lines, the driver took a bend in the road too fast and lost control of the vehicle. The back wheels slewed across the muddy surface of the road and slammed the lorry up against a row of stunted trees running alongside the road. Renton was thrown from his seat and ended up lying on the floor of the driver's cab. The driver turned the steering wheel hard to the right and gunned the engine; the lorry bounced back onto the road and the vehicle was back under control again. The driver stopped the vehicle by the side of the road and attempted to get Renton back into his seat. As soon as Renton put his weight on his left ankle, he felt a terrible shooting pain.

He managed to pull himself back into his seat with the driver's assistance. The driver kept apologising to Renton, blaming the mud on the road for the crash. Renton waved him away and with trembling hands lit a cigarette to calm his nerves. His left ankle was throbbing and the slightest movement of his foot resulted in an acute stab of pain in his ankle. It was starting to swell up and Renton took off his shoe. Gingerly removing his sock he inspected his ankle. He could see no sign of a bone protruding through the flesh although the skin was already turning an ugly bluish yellow colour. The driver produced a water bottle and Renton soaked his handkerchief and bound it around his swollen ankle. It was all he could do for now; the medical officer could take a look at it when he got back.

The driver set off again but this time he drove more steadily and to Renton's relief they arrived safely back by mid afternoon. His ankle had ballooned up to an alarming size and the doctor who examined him thought that it was possible he had broken one of the smaller bones in the ankle. Either that or a very bad sprain, it was hard to tell. In any event he would need the assistance of a pair of crutches for two or three weeks and should rest his ankle as often as he could. Renton couldn't believe his bad luck and asked one of the medical auxiliaries to go and find his orderly Collins.

When Collins arrived Renton was sitting in a chair with his left leg stretched out in front of him and his foot resting on an ammunition box. Within reach, a pair of crutches leant against the wall. His trousers had been slit at the bottom and the left ankle was heavily bandaged. Not having been told about the driving accident, Collins seemed to assume that he had been the victim of a German attack.

'Crikey! Have you been wounded, sir? Did you get shot at and wounded, is that what happened? Did you see any Germans, sir, did you?'

Renton smiled at him and shook his head. 'Nothing as exciting at that I'm afraid, Collins,' he pointed to his ankle, 'I was just the victim of a stupid driver.'

During the slow walk back to the officers' mess Renton told him about the accident. Collins, carrying his overnight bag, walked at his side as he floundered his way through the mud on his crutches. At the entrance to the dugout he lost his grip on one of the crutches and slipped. He would have fallen but Collins dropped the bag he was carrying and caught him in his arms, managing to stop him from hitting the ground. For a moment their bodies were pressed together, chest to chest. His arms were wrapped around Collins neck to stop him from sliding down and his head was resting on Collins shoulder with his hair brushing against the side of the boy's face.

Renton's heart beat rapidly against his chest at the closeness of their bodies. He was genuinely having trouble recovering his balance and rested his head on Collins shoulder unable to move. After a few seconds respite, he raised his head and their bodies began to move apart. He put his left hand on Collins shoulder to help him stand upright while his right hand cupped the left side of Collins head for balance. As they separated he could not resist the impulse to trail his fingers slowly through Collins hair and down the side of his face.

Once in his quarters Renton stretched himself on his bed like a dog awakening from a nap. The day's events had exhausted him. He yawned loudly and shook his head vigorously from side to side in an effort to keep from nodding off to sleep. The pain in his ankle had settled down to a steady, but bearable throb. A glance at his watch told him he had about an hour before Davy would return and help him with the Christmas Eve service. He started to reach for his cigarettes and then stopped. Davy! Did he say, Davy? Was he thinking of Collins as Davy now? It struck him that the pursuit of his orderly had now become a painful yearning; a delicious but bitter anguish the like of which he had never experienced before. None of the young men he had known in the past had meant as much to him as this one did. He had wanted them of course; but in truth they had all been just fancies of his at the time. Some relationships had lasted longer than others, but to the best of his knowledge, when they ended nobody had been hurt emotionally. In fact there had always been a certain amount of relief on his part at the end of a relationship and if he was completely honest, most of his sexual encounters had been so brief that after a few months he couldn't even remember the boy's name.

But this boy, Davy Collins, was a different matter. His very existence tugged hard at his emotions and he felt a strange sensation in his heart just thinking about him. He had nearly given himself away earlier when he slipped in the mud and Davy had saved him from falling. Being in Collins arms, and having Davy's head nestling close to his, was a moment of pure ecstasy and it was all he could do to stop himself from kissing him.

The boy was handsome of course; anybody could see that. The profile of his face for example was simply beautiful. The contrast between the opaque whiteness of his skin and the shiny blackness of his hair was startling. His body was slender and he moved easily and gracefully for a boy from his background. He looked, thought Renton, like a youth that had just stepped out of a painting in ancient Greece or Rome. He had often wondered if he would ever fall in love and now it was dawning on him that at last he was. He had started out wanting to seduce Collins, seeing it as a challenge. The challenge had then become an infatuation and now came the realisation that he actually loved him.

He had pictured himself in love so many times in the past, but now the reality of love had arrived, it was nothing like the picture. To start with Collins might be beautiful but he was also common. His education still had a long way to go before he could be considered as truly literate. He wasn't the intelligent, sophisticated young man that Renton had previously envisaged in his picture of an ideal mate. He didn't even know if the boy had any feelings for him. After all, if he was a normal heterosexual male, why should he? But there were still enough little signs to give him hope. When he gave in to temptation earlier and stroked Davy's face and hair, the boy must have known what was happening, but he didn't seem to mind, perhaps he had even enjoyed it. Or could he really be so naive as not to know what was happening between them? Renton looked at his watch again. In a few minutes Collins would help him get ready for evening service; he looked forward to it. Maybe having a gammy ankle would have some advantages after all.

Chapter 18

Christmas Day for Collins began the same way as countless other days, with stand-to at dawn in mist and drizzling rain. Afterwards however, the daily routine changed, and except for the unlucky few on essential duties, the men had the day off from their normal chores. Collins was one of the unlucky few who had to work over Christmas but one thing he didn't have to bother about was getting breakfast ready. It was a tradition that on Christmas Day the officers of the regiment served breakfast to the men. After breakfast came the highlight of the morning, the handing out of parcels from home. His mother sent him a knitted scarf and gloves and one of her home made cakes. With typical thoughtfulness she had included an extra pair of gloves for his pal Lofty Webb. But for countless millions of soldiers at the front, the best present of all was silence. The heavy guns on both sides had ceased firing for Christmas Day.

Renton also received a package, and a letter, from his sister, Joanna. Enclosed in the package, was a brief accompanying note written in shaky, almost illegible handwriting, from his mother saying how much she loved him and wishing him a happy and peaceful Christmas. Joanna wrote that the parcel was from his mother but that she was too frail to package it up herself. There was no other mention of his mother's health and Renton detected his mother's hand at work in that. He could almost hear her pleading with Joanna not to spoil his Christmas by worrying him with her illness. The package contained a selection of food that his mother knew he liked and would be missing.

He was putting the contents of the parcel in his locker when Collins arrived to help him get ready for his Christmas Day service. On a sudden impulse he picked up a bar of chocolate from the parcel that his mother had sent him. 'Merry Christmas, Collins!' he said, placing the chocolate in Collins' hand, 'a little present for you. You do like chocolate, I hope?'

Collins eyes grew wide with incredulity as he stared at the present Renton had given him. 'Thank you, ever so much, sir,' he said. Then, in a concerned voice added, 'are you sure it's all for me, sir? I've never had a whole bar of chocolate given to me before.'

Renton smiled at Collins' naivety. 'Of course it's yours. You can eat it all yourself if you wish. I hope you enjoy it.'

Collins reached into his pocket and pulled out a small brown paper packet. He handed it to Renton, blushing as he did so. 'I got you a present as well, sir. I'm sorry it's not as grand as yours. But I thought it might come in handy, seeing as you get a lot of letters.'

Renton opened the little packet. Inside, carved out of wood, was a simple paper knife.

'I made it in me spare time,' Collins said. 'I don't know if it's any good, but carving is sort of a hobby of mine, like.'

Renton was touched. Collins' gift, unlike his, was no spur of the moment idea. He must have carved it some time ago and taken great pride in making it. The boy's kindness overwhelmed him. He made a great show of admiring the paper knife in order to gain time and collect his composure. 'Thank you Collins it's lovely, and just what I need,' he said, 'it was very clever of you to make it.'

As Collins got his robes ready for service, Renton, restricted by his injured ankle, sat and watched him. In truth he realised he was helpless now; helpless to stop himself from wanting Collins more and more with every passing day. He hadn't loved anyone like this since he was a schoolboy exploring his homosexuality with Maurice. He didn't know why he loved Collins. It was only natural to lust after his body; he'd done that since he first saw him. But why was he falling in love with him? Collins wasn't witty, or clever. He had only ever mixed with working class people, yet he had a gentleness and softness that belied his rough upbringing. There was bound to be a few little faults and defects in his nature but Renton reckoned that, given time, he could smooth them out.

'Shall I help you on with your things now, sir?' Collins said, breaking in on his thoughts.

Renton nodded. For once he was actually looking forward to taking a morning service, but he must distract himself from constantly thinking of Collins. With a busy day ahead of him, and his injury hampering his ability to move about, it was not a day to be moping around like a love struck schoolboy.

The rain had eased enabling Christmas service to be held outside. There was a larger turnout of men than usual and Renton, leaning on his crutch, waited impatiently for his congregation to assemble. By the time the service was over Renton realised just how handicapped he was going to be until his ankle mended. He was forced to rely on Collins for everything. It was Collins who collected the prayer books from the chapel and handed them out to the worshippers as they arrived. It was Collins who held the bible for him and turned the pages when requested. To his surprise, and relief, they worked well as a team and things went without a hitch. After the service, Renton was approached by Major Kerr who commiserated with him about his injured ankle.

'It's only a week until you go home on leave,' he said. He pointed to Renton's pair of crutches. 'Even when you've finished with those, you'll still need a stick for a while. It'll make it dashed difficult for you travelling home.'

'Yes, that thought had crossed my mind.' Renton said, giving his CO a wry smile.

Kerr took out his pipe and tapped the contents of the bowl into the palm of his hand. 'Look here,' he said. 'Go and see Freddie Beamish. He's bound to come up with a plan to help you. Whatever he suggests, I'll approve it; all right?'

Renton decided now was a good time to push his luck. Christmas was the time of goodwill and Kerr appeared to be in a good mood. 'I was going to ask you to let me take my orderly, Collins. He's absolutely invaluable to me while I'm like this. To be honest I don't think I'll be able to make it home without him.' Renton waited as his CO slowly and methodically thumbed fresh tobacco into his pipe. He knew Kerr well enough by now to know that he was using his pipe as an aid to gain time while he thought things over.

'Yes, all right then, Simon,' Kerr said, still fiddling with his pipe, 'officially, he isn't entitled, you understand.

But he's an orderly, and strictly speaking won't be on leave. He'll be on duty at your beck and call all the time you're in England. It's entirely up to you what time you give him off, of course.'

Renton offered up a silent prayer for his good fortune. At last something was going right for him. It wouldn't be a happy trip home, but having Collins with him was a lot better than travelling to England on his own. The rest of the day passed very agreeably. With Collins at his side helping him, he was even enjoying his religious duties for the first time in ages despite his injured ankle. The ankle pained him most when he put weight on it and he enjoyed having his orderly's arms around him helping him get to his feet. The sensation he felt as their bodies came into close contact made it worthwhile being injured. He was addressing Collins by his first name now, except when officers were present. It was more intimate and gave him the feeling that their relationship was moving along much quicker.

The last of the Christmas evening service worshippers had left and Renton's duties were finished for the day. He was alone with Davy in the chapel and waiting for him to finish tidying up before telling him that he would be going to England with him. When he did convey his news, a look of surprise and delight came to Collins face at the realisation that he was going home. But as they prepared to leave the chapel the boy's face took on a more solemn expression.

'Is it possible that we could go and see my friend, Private Webb, before we go, sir? I know it's a lot to ask, but I'd really like to know what's happening to him. It must be terrible being locked up for Christmas. Please, would you speak with the adjutant, sir? He wouldn't refuse you a visit, surely.'

Renton knew it was his duty to visit military prisoners in custody if they requested it but to his knowledge he had received no such request from Private Webb.

'Are you sure he wants to see me? He hasn't asked for me as far as I know. For that matter, has he even asked to see you?'

'No sir, but I know him. He's probably ashamed for what he did and doesn't want to face me. But he's my mate, no matter what he did. Please help me to see him, sir.'

Renton looked into the boy's anguished face and knew he wouldn't refuse. It was no hardship to go and see Webb really. It would show him in a good light with Davy and help pass the time before going home. 'All right, I'll have a word with Captain Beamish and we'll try and see him sometime after Boxing Day.' The look of gratitude on Collins face told him he'd made the right decision.

They were about to leave when they heard the noise of approaching footsteps outside. The footsteps stopped and the light from one of the oil lamps hanging from the rafters threw a large and sinister looking shadow across the open doorway.

'Merry Christmas, Mr Renton.' Sergeant Watkins said, slurring his words as he spoke. He glanced over at Davy, 'you too, Collins! Mustn't forget young Collins, must we, padre?' Watkins eyes were bloodshot and his forehead gleamed with perspiration. As he stood swaying in the doorway, his massive bulk occupying the whole space, he gave Renton a mock salute with his right arm. His left arm was hidden behind his back.

'You're too late, Sergeant. I'm afraid the service finished some time ago,' Renton said coolly. He was angry but determined not to let Watkins spoil his day.

'Oh dear! What a pity.' Watkins said, grinning. 'Still never mind, I didn't come for a prayer meeting, anyway. I'm here to give you a Christmas present.' He brought his left arm out from behind his back and in his hand was a bottle of whisky. He offered it to Renton.

'Go on padre. Take it! A little bit of festive spirit for Christmas.' He looked Renton in the face for a few seconds, the bottle held in his outstretched hand. Then he saw the crutches under Renton's arms and burst into laughter.

Renton was determined not to lose face in front of Collins. He could see by the look on his face that that the boy was worried by Watkins' unexpected appearance at the chapel. 'Wait outside for me, Davy. I'll be out in a couple of minutes.'

Davy started for the door but Watkins, still laughing, thrust out an arm and blocked his way. 'Here, you'd better take this for him. Don't drop it,' he managed to say through his laughter. He shoved the bottle into Collins hands and then wiped the tears from his eyes on the sleeve of his jacket.

Renton saw Davy hesitate and look over at him. He smiled reassuringly and nodded to him. 'It's all right, Davy. Take it. I'll be out in a moment.'

'And close the door behind you,' said Watkins roughly.

Renton waited until Davy had gone. He took a deep breath and swung himself around on his crutches facing Watkins. 'Because it's the season of goodwill to all men, I'm going to be polite and civil to you, Sergeant Watkins. Thank you for your unexpected gift and I hope you have a happy Christmas. Now, if there's nothing else, I've had a long day and I want to leave.'

'Of course, padre,' Watkins said, nodding. 'I only dropped in to give you the whisky, but Christ, what a laugh, I wasn't expecting the crutches.' He walked unsteadily over to the chapel wall and started looking under the tarpaulin covers. 'Everything still nicely stowed away and safe from prying eyes, I see! Well done, padre. You've earned your bottle.'

'I've earned nothing, Watkins. You gave me no choice in the matter. Now please go.'

'Yes, yes, I'm going. Don't be so impatient! I hear you're off on a spot of leave soon. Is that right?'

'I'm going home to see my mother,' Renton said quietly. 'She's dying, Watkins, not that it concerns you.'

'I'm sorry to hear it. How long will you be gone?'

'That depends on my mother, Watkins...and God. Why? Are you worried I might not come back?'

Watkins shook his head. 'No padre, you'll come back all right.

'You seem very sure of that.'

'Oh I am! There's two good reasons why you'll be coming back, Mr Renton and the first reason has just gone through that door there.' Watkins glanced towards the doorway. 'I think you get my drift.'

'And the second reason?'

'The second reason is because you know damn well that you'll always be looking over your shoulder for the police if you don't come back.'

'And supposing I get posted away from here after I get back, what then?'

'Don't worry; you'll be here long enough for my needs.' Watkins pointed towards the tarpaulin covers. 'I'll have one of my men keep an eye on my merchandise while you're away, so tell your boy not to bother coming in here while you're away. Goodnight, padre.' With that Watkins lurched over to the door and left.

Renton heaved a sigh of relief. The visit had been short, and not as unpleasant as it might have been.

A few seconds later, Collins entered the chapel still clutching the bottle of whisky. 'Is everything all right, padre?' he asked.

Renton could detect the anxiety in the boy's voice. 'Yes, everything's fine, thank you! Sergeant Watkins was just a bit drunk, that's all. Turn the lantern out, Davy. Let's go and enjoy the rest of Christmas Day, shall we.'

The day after Boxing Day, Renton took Collins to see Private Webb in his cell at the military police gaol. Permission for the visit had been easier to obtain than he expected. In fact Beamish had welcomed his interest in Webb.

'The consequences of his actions could be very serious,' he warned Renton before he left. 'Under the circumstances I think he'll be very glad of a visit from you, and his friend Collins.'

Renton and Collins were escorted through the gaol by a talkative Irish corporal who told them that the court martial was to be held the next day. Renton made no comment but he knew that such quick action by the army did not auger well for the unfortunate prisoner. Collins face had dropped at the corporal's news and Renton tried to avoid looking directly at him.

As they entered Webb's cell, Renton felt an uneasy sensation in the pit of his stomach.

'On your feet, Webb and stand to attention. You've got visitors,' the corporal barked.

Lofty Webb got up from his bed and rose shakily to his feet.

'When you're finished, pound on the door,' the corporal said to Renton. Then he left the three of them together, locking the cell door behind him as he went.

It was damp and gloomy in the small cell. What little natural daylight there was came filtering in through a small barred window high up on one wall. Renton was shocked at Webb's appearance. The last time he had seen the young soldier he had been fighting drunk in the main square at Rouville. He had looked fit and healthy then and been full of life, if anything too full of life on that night. Now he looked a physical wreck.

Webb's face was gaunt and the flesh had a ghostly blue pallor to it. His eyes had a frightened, cowered expression and the skin surrounding them was puffed up and covered with bruises. Webb's lower lip was split and traces of congealed blood were stuck to his chin. Before their arrival, Renton had determined that he would be merely an observer to Davy's visit. As far as he was concerned, Webb's predicament was entirely of his own making and he should be prepared to take his punishment. But seeing him like this was something he hadn't bargained on.

'Please, sit down, Webb,' he said, suddenly realising the prisoner was still standing at attention and waiting for his permission to stand at ease.

'Thank you, sir.' Webb's voice was barely audible even in the small cell. He sank back down on his mattress and looked gratefully at Renton before transferring his gaze to Collins. 'I'm sorry Davy,' he whispered. His eyes filled with tears and putting his head in his hands he began sobbing uncontrollably.

'Hey, come on, don't upset yourself, Lofty,' Collins said. He looked distressed and near to tears himself. 'It'll be all right. They'll go easy on you, mate, you'll see. They will go easy on him, won't they, sir?'

'Yes, I should think so,' Renton said with an optimism he didn't feel, 'look, would you prefer it if I left, Webb? I can call for the gaoler and leave you two together if you like.'

Webb stopped sobbing and shook his head. 'I'd like you to stay, sir, if you don't mind.'

Renton spent an uncomfortable twenty minutes in the cell listening to the two friends talking together. He contributed little to the conversation and when he did it was only to explain some point or other about army procedure.

Renton took the opportunity to observe Webb more closely. The youth was obviously terrified at what might happen to him and had clearly been severely beaten by his gaolers presumably as punishment for escaping from their custody earlier. His earlier escape would have earned them a reprimand at the very least and, judging by the state of Webb's face, they had exacted a painful revenge for their humiliation. Listening to Webb talk it was apparent that he was not very intelligent and Renton couldn't help thinking that in such a dire situation, a lack of intelligence might not be such a bad thing.

As they left, Renton told Webb he would pray for him in his evening service and he meant it. Walking out through the gates of the gaol, he noticed the miserable look on his orderly's face and knew he must be thinking the worst. It was a perfectly understandable reaction; the unfortunate Private Webb had very little chance of mercy and no amount of prayers could help him now.

Chapter 19

On New Year's Eve, after evening service, Renton began putting a few last minute items in his bag for his trip home. Collins had packed the bulkier stuff earlier and there were only a couple of things to add to the bag. To his great relief the swelling around his ankle had gone down slightly and he had decided to dispense with the unwieldy crutches and make the journey home with the aid of a walking stick that Collins had obtained for him. He was just making a final check to make sure that he had everything he needed when an orderly came and told him that the CO wanted to see him in the command post.

Major Kerr was sitting at the operations table drinking whisky in the company of Freddie Beamish when Renton arrived.

'Sit down, Simon,' Kerr said pointing towards a chair, 'care for a drink?'

A quick glance at the bottle in front of them indicated to Renton that they had already disposed of most of the contents. Still, it was New Years Eve and it was good of them to invite him to join their celebrations. He rested his walking stick against the table and sat down. Leaning forward in his chair, he picked up a spare mug from the table and poured himself a measure of whisky. 'Cheers! Happy New Year to you both,' he said, raising his mug.

The two men picked up their drinks. Only Kerr had returned his toast and his voice sounded unusually subdued. Renton looked over to Beamish who was staring at the table with a melancholy look on his face. The fact that he hadn't said a word yet struck Renton as odd. Then the penny dropped. He'd got it wrong; this was no festive celebration. A depressing thought came to him. 'What's the matter? Has my leave been cancelled? Is the regiment on the move?'

Kerr finished his drink and poured himself another. Renton had the distinct impression that his presence was making the two men nervous and that they had something unpleasant to tell him, but didn't know how to begin. Kerr took out his pipe and started to inspect its contents. Renton's heart sank. The bloody pipe routine again! He steeled himself for the bad news that he was certain Kerr was about to tell him. But it wasn't Kerr that eventually broke the awkward silence; it was Freddie Beamish.

'It's nothing to do with your leave, Simon. We've just had the verdict of Private Webb's court martial. He was found guilty on all charges, the most serious of which was desertion while on active service. He was sentenced to death by firing squad. The sentence is to be carried out tomorrow morning.'

Renton was stunned. 'But he's no more than a boy of what, eighteen or nineteen at the most? It's barbaric to shoot a boy of that age.' He put his drink down on the table and began fumbling for his cigarettes.

'He's just turned nineteen, actually,' Beamish told him. 'And speaking for myself, I agree, it does seem harsh, especially when he could be given another chance by posting him back in the line. The trouble is high command says discipline must be rigidly maintained and that, I'm afraid, means shooting deserters as an example to the rest. I'm afraid there's no appeal against the sentence, Simon.'

'But the death penalty is absolutely wrong!' Renton turned to Kerr. 'I've got no sympathy for the position that Webb's finds himself in, but to shoot him for it! You do realise we're doing the Germans work for them, don't you? What Webb did was wrong, and he should be punished, yes! But not shot! If it's God's will that he's going to be killed in this war then at least let the enemy do it, not us.'

Kerr shifted round in his chair to face him. 'I'm sorry, Simon,' he said, 'but Webb's fate was inevitable once he was caught. He's not the first soldier to be shot for desertion, and he won't be the last. But I'm afraid I didn't ask you here just to tell you that he's going to be executed.' Kerr placed his pipe on the table and picked up some sheets of paper. Without looking at them, he handed them over to Renton. 'I'm aware that you're going on leave tomorrow, but as his regimental chaplain you will have to attend the execution. The details and timings are all on one of those bits of paper you're holding. You can go straight home on leave afterwards, of course. I'm truly sorry about this, Simon. What with your mother's illness and all, it's a lousy way to start the New Year I know, but it has to be done.'

Renton began reading the top sheet of paper in his hand. It was a letter from Webb asking for him to attend the execution. The handwriting was childish, with several spelling mistakes, but the message was clear enough. Webb wanted him with him on his last day on earth. Renton's mouth went dry. Without waiting to be invited, he reached for the bottle and replenished his drink. Kerr was right in saying it was a lousy way to start the New Year, but he was telling the wrong person. Renton considered it ironic that he, of all people should have to witness the execution of Collins best friend in the regiment. Webb could so easily have been a threat to his plans where his orderley was concerned, but thanks to his drunken stupidity, that threat no longer existed. All the same, the thought of having to witness Webb's death by firing squad made his stomach feel decidedly queasy.

'Are you all right, Simon? You look quite upset,' Beamish said, cutting in on his thoughts. 'I know it's a bad show, but you've seen enough death by now to be used to it, surely?'

'Yes, of course' Renton said. 'After all, does one more death really matter one way or another in this war, Freddie?'

Beamish's face flushed. He didn't answer and looked at Kerr who started fiddling with his pipe again. Renton finished his whisky and stood up, there was no point in staying; he would only get angry. Wishing them good night, he picked up his walking stick and limped out the door.

The next morning Renton woke with a lot on his mind. His first thought was for Collins and how he was going to break the news to him that his friend would be facing a firing squad in a few hours' time. Worse still, he had to tell him that they were going to be there when it happened. He dressed hurriedly and sat on his bed. Reaching into his locker, he took out one of the pieces of paper Kerr had given him the previous evening. It only had a few lines on it and they made stark reading.

Name of prisoner: date and time of execution: place of execution: details of transport. Renton sighed heavily and took out his watch. It was still early, not yet breakfast time. He looked down at his hands. They were shaking. Pulling out a bottle from under his bed, he poured himself a whisky and waited for Collins.

At the military prison they were met at the gate by the same corporal that had greeted them on their previous visit. This time he was more subdued than on their last encounter and barely spoke a word to them. The execution was scheduled for 10am. Renton checked his watch; it was 9.25am. The corporal took them to the Provost Marshall's office and after ordering Collins to wait in the corridor, knocked on the door before ushering Renton inside. The Provost Marshall, an elderly Lieutenant Colonel, was sitting behind his desk drinking tea. He was not alone in the office. A smartly dressed Sergeant stood at ease in front of him. The Colonel rose from his seat, shook Renton by the hand and invited him to sit down.

'Good morning padre,' he said. 'I'm Colonel Lang. Sorry we have to meet under such circumstances. This is Sergeant Bartlett. He'll be in charge of the firing squad this morning. He's just reported to me that everything is ready to proceed as planned.'

Lang dismissed the Sergeant and they were left alone. Renton declined the offer of tea and, after some small talk about his injured ankle, Lang got down to the business in hand. He asked Renton if he had ever attended an execution before and when Renton shook his head, Lang explained, in a brisk manner, the execution procedure.

At the end of Lang's briefing, Renton was told that he was to have ten minutes in private with Webb in his cell. Afterwards he was to accompany Webb when the escort took him out to the firing squad. 'The main thing is to get the execution part over and done with as quickly as possible. That way it doesn't give the prisoner much time to dwell on his fate and makes it easier for the men in the firing squad. So I'd be grateful if you could keep your prayer short. Is that all right, old chap?'

Renton was thinking ahead of Lang and had already decided to do just what the colonel was proposing. He was sickened by the whole business and just wanted to get it finished with and get away on leave to England with Collins. Poor Davy! He'd forgotten that he was waiting outside in the corridor. He must be feeling absolutely wretched knowing that in a few minutes his friend was going to be taken out and shot.

Collins had taken the news of Webb's sentence better than Renton expected; a sign of the boy's growing maturity, perhaps? He had been stunned, quite naturally, on being told that Webb had been given the death penalty, but it was obvious to Renton from Collins muted reaction afterwards, that he had already contemplated that possibility. Still, it must be rotten for him to have to be so close to the scene of his friend's execution. Renton decided to ask Colonel Lang if Collins could see the prisoner before the execution took place.

'I'm afraid not, padre,' Lang said, looking at his watch. 'Only me, you and the escort allowed in the cell. Regulations, I'm afraid. Anyway, it's better for the prisoner that way, doesn't get him all upset. Shall we go, now?'

On entering the cell, Renton was immediately struck by the fact that it seemed a lot smaller than the last time he had visited Webb. Then he realised that the lack of space was due to the presence of two military policemen who were in the cell. They were sitting with Webb around a wooden table that Renton didn't recall being there on his previous visit. All three occupants of the cell held playing cards in their hands and seemed absorbed in their game. On seeing Renton and Colonel Lang, Webb's two guardians shot to their feet and stood to attention. Only Webb remained seated, a lopsided grin stretched across his face, staring at the cards in his hands as if he were in a trance.

Lang ordered the guards out of the cell and looked at Renton. 'Ten minutes, padre! We'll be outside if you need us, all right?'

Lang closed the cell door behind him and Renton walked over to the table. A strong, familiar smell hung in the air, but to his annoyance Renton couldn't place it. He sat down and took out his cigarettes. 'Would you like a smoke?' He said, holding out the opened packet to Webb.

Webb continued to stare at the cards in his hand. He gave no indication of having heard Renton's words.

'I asked you if you would like a cigarette, Webb.' Renton repeated his offer in a louder voice.

Webb slowly put down his cards and reached for a cigarette. Renton struck a match and, leaning forward, lit it for him. As he did so the familiar smell hit Renton's nostrils again, but this time it was much stronger. Suddenly it dawned on Renton what the smell was. Whisky! Why hadn't he realised it sooner. He looked closely at Webb's eyes. The pupils were dilated and from the way his eyelids kept drooping, Renton knew Webb was having great difficulty in staying awake. Then the realisation hit him. Webb was blind drunk on whisky!

Renton knew he should be shocked, but he wasn't. If anything he was relieved that Webb's guards had been humane enough to get him in such a drunken condition. It made his job that much easier and had doubtless saved Webb some unnecessary mental suffering.

Webb lifted his head and spoke to him. 'Th... Thanks for c, c...coming, padre,' he said, in a whispered, sleepy voice that Renton had to strain to hear, 'ver..ver... good of you.' The cigarette dropped from his fingers and fell to the floor but he appeared not to notice. 'Good blokes here, you know, padre, fucking good blokes, I could...' His voice trailed off and his head slumped down on to his chest.

Renton stood up and put his hand on Webb's shoulder. 'Let us join together in prayer.'

Webb began to snore softly as Renton took out his bible. 'Blessed is he whose transgression is forgiven, whose sin is covered...'

The metal studded boots of the two escorts made a solid rhythmical sound as they marched in regulation military style in to the prison courtyard. In sharp contrast, the sound of Lofty Webb's toecaps scraping along the ground as he was dragged, stupefied, in front of the firing squad by the same two escorts, made a noise that set Renton's teeth on edge.

Escort and prisoner came to a halt at a wooden post near the prison wall. Some twenty yards in front of them stood the firing squad waiting for their orders. As instructed, Renton went forward and started reciting a short prayer. While he was praying for the condemned man, the two escorts secured Webb to the post and placed a black hood over his head. Finally, Colonel

Lang stepped forward and pinned a piece of white cloth to Webb's jacket. Renton said 'Amen' softly then followed Colonel Lang and the two escorts as they marched off to a safe position behind the firing squad.

Sergeant Bartlett gave the order and there was a crash of gunfire. Two black crows that had been perching on the cellblock roof took flight in alarm, their harsh screeching cries filling the courtyard. Renton looked towards Webb. Prevented by his tethered arms from being thrown backwards by the impact of the bullets hitting his chest, Webb's body had slid down the post and fallen to his knees into a grotesque attitude of prayer. A Lieutenant, accompanied by a medical officer, walked forward. Taking out his revolver, he fired one shot into the back of Webb's neck. The medical officer removed the black hood from Webb's head and made a brief examination of the body. Satisfied there was no trace of life, he closed Webb's eyelids and nodded to Colonel Lang.

Renton looked up into a miserable, grey, January sky and closed his eyes. He began to offer up a prayer to God for granting Webb a quick death but the words stuck in his throat and he couldn't continue. The prayer was meaningless! Webb was dead and nothing could change that. A really merciful God would have deflected the bullets and saved him, but Renton knew that miracles didn't happen in real life.

'Well, that all went off rather well, I thought.' Colonel Lang said. He shook Renton's hand. 'Got time for a snifter in my office before you go, padre?'

Renton looked at Lofty Webb's lifeless body and politely declined the Colonel's offer.

Collins was sitting in the back of the lorry when he heard the gunfire. The padre had told him that whatever happened he had to keep his chin up. He had told him to pray for Lofty, to have courage and hope, and for Lofty's sake he had done as the padre asked. But when the echo of the last gunshot finally died away, Collins couldn't contain himself and he broke down and wept. Lofty was gone and with him went all the ideas and plans the two of them had made for after the war. Whatever he did, wherever he went, it wouldn't be the same without Lofty. He was the only friend he'd made in the regiment apart from the padre and there would never be another like him. He would liked to have seen him before he died, even if it had been for just a second, but when they refused to allow it he hadn't wanted to stay inside the prison and waited outside with the lorry. It had been terrible waiting for Lofty to die and he had been on the brink of tears several times.

He wiped his eyes with the back of his hand, he didn't want the padre coming out and finding him crying. He would never forget the padre for the kindness he'd showed to poor Lofty who'd had no relatives to comfort him, or write to him, in his time of need. The padre had been there for Lofty when he needed him most and had been the only source of comfort for Lofty in his last moments on earth and Collins told himself he wouldn't ever forget that. Waiting in the back of the lorry he made a solemn vow; if the padre ever called upon him for anything, no matter what, he wouldn't let him down, whatever the cost to him personally.

Chapter 20

London was bathed in early morning winter sunshine when the train drew in at Victoria Railway Station. Renton, who had been dozing in his seat in the first class carriage, sat up and peered drowsily out of the carriage window as the train came to a jerky halt. A sea of khaki uniforms met his eyes. Renton was a little disappointed at the sight of so many troops milling about the station. He had been hoping to attract some admiring attention with his walking stick. He wasn't completely reliant on it now that his ankle was mending but he thought the stick gave him the look of a front line veteran. Instead he realised he was going to be just another anonymous figure in khaki among hundreds. It was somewhat of a blow to his ego but one from which he quickly recovered; the main thing was he was home, or nearly so.

He waited until his fellow passengers got out of the carriage and then took his walking stick down from the luggage rack. As he stepped onto the platform, he looked towards the rear of the train for his orderly. He'd missed Collins company on the train from Dover but they were back in England now and mere privates like Collins didn't travel first class with officers. Collins, and the bags in his charge, had travelled third class. Looking down the platform he saw Davy walking jauntily towards him carrying their bags. The boy had a big smile on his face and his eyes looked bright and merry. Renton felt a twinge of regret at the prospect of not having him with him for the first couple of days of his leave but at Dover, in a moment of largesse, he had told Collins that he could go home on leave for two days before joining him at his father's vicarage. The look of happiness and joy that had spread over Davy's face when he realised he was going home to see his family dispelled any doubts in Renton's mind that he might have had as to whether or not he had done the right thing.

They made their way through the crowded station to the main entrance where a line of taxis was parked. Renton hailed the leading taxi and told the driver to take him to Liverpool Street Station in order to catch the train that would take him on the last leg of his journey home to Suffolk. Collins, who only had a short omnibus ride to his home in Whitechapel, insisted on going with him to the station in order to carry his bag on to the train. Before Renton could refuse his offer of help, the driver had taken both their bags and put them in his taxi. Collins got in next to Renton and they set off. Renton had half an hour to wait before his train departed so together they walked through the busy station and entered the buffet lounge. It was packed and people were waiting in queues to be served. Renton was about to walk out when a waitress, clearing away a dirty table, looked in their direction. Noticing Renton's walking stick, she beckoned them over to her table.

'Sit yourself down here, sir,' she said to Renton cheerily, 'you can't possibly be expected to wait in a queue with that poor leg of yours. I'll be finished here in a second and then I'll take your order.'

They sat down and Renton ordered tea and sandwiches. Leaving Collins at the table, Renton went in search of a telephone. He found a kiosk and telephoned his father's number. The phone rang for some time before eventually being answered by his sister, Joanna. She had been upstairs with mother, she explained to Renton. Father was not back from morning service yet and she was alone in the house apart from Mary, the housekeeper. Yes, they had received his telegram telling them that he was coming and Mary had already got his old room ready for him. In answer to his query about his mother, Joanna told him she was sinking fast. The doctor had just left and had expressed his surprise that she had made it through the night. Joanna sounded tired and Renton guessed she had sat up all night with her mother. He gave Joanna his expected time of arrival at the station and she informed him that Richard, her husband, would meet him off the train and bring him to the house. Renton finished the call and hung up.

When he returned to the buffet lounge, the tea and sandwiches were sitting, untouched, on the table. 'You didn't have to wait for me, you know,' Renton said as he sat down. 'Better pour the tea now Davy before it starts getting cold. And do get stuck into those sandwiches.'

'It hasn't bin standing long, sir,' Colins said, carefully pouring out the tea. 'The waitress said they had to wait for the water to boil. Anyway, I wouldn't dream of starting before you, sir.'

Renton ignored the sandwiches and lit up a cigarette. He wasn't hungry and was content with just a cup of tea. He watched his orderly devouring the delicate little slices of bread with a hearty youthful appetite. 'Take some more, Davy,' he said. 'I'm not going to eat any and there seems to be an awful lot there to get through.'

'The waitress said she put extra on the plate,' Collins explained. 'I think she must have taken a shine to you, sir.'

'Taken a shine to you more likely, Davy.' Renton laughed.

'I doubt it, sir.' The boy blushed and reached for more sandwiches.

Renton leant forward in his chair. 'I want you to stop calling me sir, Davy. Not in private anyway. While we're in England call me Simon, all right?

'Yes... Simon. Thank you.'

'Good! Now, do you remember what I told you to do when you come up to me in two days time?'

'Yes, I'm to get off the train and get a taxi to your father's house.'

'That's right. Don't forget to ask for the vicarage. The taxi driver will know where it is.' Renton took out a pound note from his pocket and handed it to Collins.

'Take this for the fare. Don't worry about the change.'

'Thank you, you didn't have to I could have paid meself.' Collins put down his tea and tucked the note in his jacket pocket. He looked at Renton and his face suddenly reddened. 'I do hope your mother gets better,' he said earnestly. 'I really do, honestly. I'm happy to be at home on leave, of course, but I'm sorry it's because of your mother. I know I wouldn't like it if my mum was ill. It must be rotten for you.'

Renton stubbed out his half smoked cigarette. He reached out his hand and gently squeezed Collins arm. 'Thank you very much, Davy. You've been a great source of comfort to me in the last few weeks and I appreciate it.' Renton noticed once again the look of shy embarrassment that always appeared on the boy's face when he received any thanks or praise. On a woman it might conceivably be thought artificial or coquettish even, but with Collins it was just youthful innocence. He looked at his watch. It was time to catch his train. He put some coins on the table and Collins picked up the bags. Together they left the buffet lounge and walked the short distance to where Renton's train was standing, amid great clouds of steam and smoke, ready to depart. They found an empty first-class carriage and stowed Renton's bag in the overhead luggage rack. When he was safely aboard, Colins got out and shut the door.

Renton leant out of the window. 'Goodbye, Davy! See you in two days.'

'I'll be there. You can count on me, sir.'

'Simon, the name is Simon. Remember?'

There was a great slamming of carriage doors. The train gave a jolt forward and then started off. As it began to gather pace, Renton looked back along the platform and saw Collins waving to him. He waved back out of the carriage window as the train steamed out of the station.

Richard was waiting for him in his motorcar outside the station and greeted him politely, but formally. It was what Renton expected. The two men hadn't met for a number of years and had never been particularly close. Richard never showed much emotion about anything except his favourite subject, medicine. On the drive to the house his brother in law explained, in his clipped, precise doctors' manner, the exact nature of his mother's cancer and why, despite the best efforts of the medical profession, she was losing her fight for life. It made depressing listening and Renton was glad when they finally arrived at his father's house. He left Richard to bring in his bag, and went into the house. Joanna met him in the hallway. She ran towards him with tears in her eyes and threw her arms around him. She hugged him tightly and cried softly into his shoulder.

'I'm so sorry, Simon,' she sobbed, 'Mother passed away just after Richard left to pick you up at the station.'

Renton opened the door to his mother's room and peered in. The curtains were almost fully drawn and the room was in the semi darkness. His mother was lying in bed with the covers pulled up to her chin. She looked so peaceful that Renton thought she was sleeping. James Renton sat in a chair next to the bed holding a bible in his hands. Hearing the creak of the door, he looked up.

'Is that you, Simon my boy?' he asked.

'Yes, father. It's me.' Renton said. He walked slowly towards the bed.

James Renton put aside his bible and held out his hand. 'Let me hold your hand, Simon.'

Renton gave him his hand and his father clung to it as if his very life depended on it. His father's hand was cold and clammy. Renton looked into his father's face and was shocked to see how much his father had aged since he last saw him. He had never been close to his father in the same way that he had been to his mother, but seeing him now, with his face old and lined with grief, he felt a surge of pity and compassion for him.

The old man let go of Renton's hand and turned towards his dead wife in the bed. 'Look at your mother's face, Simon,' he said in a quavering voice. 'See how peaceful it looks. God in his infinite mercy has released her from her suffering.'

His father was right. His mother's face had a look of serenity and calmness about it that gave no indication of the terrible suffering she must have undergone in the last few weeks of her life. He leant over the bed and kissed her gently on the forehead. He wanted to cry for her, but the tears wouldn't come. He felt ashamed and guilty. She had been the only person in his life that he had truly loved and he had always dreaded the thought of her passing. Now it had really happened he was taking her death with so much composure that it worried him. 'Perhaps it's because I've seen too much death,' he thought to himself, 'maybe I've grown indifferent to it.'

His father rose from his chair and they stood together at the edge of the bed.

'I'm sorry I couldn't get here sooner, father,' Renton said, finally breaking the silence.

'It's all right, Simon. She went happy in the knowledge that you were here in England, on your way home to see her.'

Renton gave his father a quizzical look. 'But Richard told me she'd been in a coma for the last few days, how could she have known?'

James Renton smiled at his son. 'She knew, Simon. Believe me, she knew.'

Renton stayed up late that evening with his father. Joanna had gone home in the afternoon exhausted and badly in need of some sleep. That left just the two of them in the house, apart from Mary, the housekeeper. Renton's parents had never been wealthy enough to afford both a maid and a housekeeper and Mary did a little of both jobs. She had been part of the house since Renton was born. After supper she cleared the dining table and the two men took their coffee into the parlour. Renton sat opposite his father in one of the big leather armchairs that were placed each side of the fireplace. They had been in the same position ever since he could remember. The two sat in silence for a while, drinking their coffee. Renton felt uneasy. He wasn't accustomed to being with his father, at least not for any length of time.

Renton's father started to talk about his wife's funeral arrangements. She was to be buried within the week. 'We have a lovely plot reserved in the churchyard cemetery,' he said. 'It's by the wall and it gets the sun most of the day in the summer. I think she will be happy resting there.' He stared into the fire for a second before turning to Renton. 'You know my boy, I shouldn't like to wait too long before joining your mother,' he said quietly.

Renton didn't answer and his father moved on to talk about his possible retirement and the question of who would succeed him. The Church Council, he told Renton, would almost certainly install anyone he recommended. The message was not lost on Renton. Then the old man made a startling confession. 'I should have been a better father to you and Joanna. I should have spent more time with you both when you were growing up, but I put my duty to my parishioners first. Fate decreed it that you two came along late in my life. By then I was too set and rigid in my ways to change. I'm sorry.'

Renton's uneasiness left him and a feeling of sadness took its place. He had never given it a thought before, but now he realised just how big a part his father's age had played in his remoteness from his children. At times during his childhood his father had been almost like an elderly stranger talking to him. Renton thought of his mother, lying upstairs. She would certainly have approved of this closer relationship with his father.

Renton had been given the large back bedroom at the vicarage when he was ten years old. The house had five bedrooms and his mother had insisted that her son must have a room with plenty of space so that he could play with his friends but Renton had seldom needed the extra space in his bedroom. He undressed and got into bed. Looking around the room his eyes wandered over the familiar objects he had known since a boy. In a corner stood the bookcase containing his collection of classic novels, travel books, and books on religion and art; they were all still there, stacked neatly on the shelves. On the walls hung his many paintings, so many that they obscured much of the pale green, striped wallpaper underneath. Most had a heroic or moral theme, such as St George slaying the Dragon, or Christ preaching to his Disciples. At the foot of the bed stood a large metal trunk, Renton knew the contents well; toys, games, and sports gear. All stowed away and treasured by a doting mother. He knew too the reason why she had kept his room just the way it was. To her, he had never grown up. He had always been 'her little boy' even when he went off to war.

It was her dearest wish that someday he would grow tired of being an army chaplain and take over his father's parish. It was what his father wanted also and he had been hinting at it, albeit rather clumsily, in the parlour earlier. Well perhaps he should fulfil his mother's dream after all and follow in his father's footsteps. The war couldn't go on much longer and maybe, after the fighting ended, it might be time to make a change. At least there would be no more people like Sergeant Watkins to contend with. With a determined effort, he might make a real go of being a country vicar, especially if he could get Davy Collins working for him in some capacity or other. Renton turned out the light and nestled down in the comfortable bed. He was asleep almost before his head touched the pillow.

The next two days were long and miserable for Renton as it finally dawned on him that his mother really was dead and he would never see her again. It was a terrible agony to endure; and not just for Renton. His father and Joanna were suffering too and the result was a melancholy, sombre atmosphere that pervaded the house from top to bottom. Conversations were conducted almost in a whisper and long mournful silences prevailed when the talking stopped. The slightest little thing that went wrong in the house brought about floods of tears from Joanna and Mary. The arrival of the undertakers to prepare his mother's body for burial was particularly harrowing, especially for Renton's father.

Renton got out of the house as much as he could during the day. He was at a loss to know how to occupy his time and didn't dare drink too heavily for fear of getting drunk and offending his father. His father rarely drank alcohol and only kept a few bottles of port and sherry in the house for social occasions. Renton had brought a bottle of whisky with him in his bag, but he had drunk over half of it already. To help stop his craving, and keep him away from the local public house, Renton took to wandering alone around the country lanes of his childhood. His ankle was giving him little trouble now and he had almost dispensed with the help of the walking stick. He longed for Davy's company on his long walks. He had only left him a couple of days ago, but he missed him desperately. Only Davy's presence, he felt, could lighten his present gloomy mood.

Chapter 21

Davy Collins got a hero's welcome when he arrived home in Whitechapel. As soon as his neighbours saw him walking through the tenement buildings in his uniform he came in for a good deal of backslapping and hand shaking that didn't stop until he reached his parent's apartment. His mother was waiting for him at the door and greeted him with hugs and tears of joy. Within five minutes of getting him inside, she had sat him down at the kitchen table and began putting food on the table. When she was satisfied that he had everything he needed, she sat down and encouraged him to tuck into the food she had prepared for him.

'Your dad's at work, and your brother, George, too. The girls and Tom are at school, though they didn't want to go when they heard you were coming. Did you have a good journey home?'

Collins, his mouth full of food, could only nod by way of answer. When he had finished eating she poured him a cup tea out of a huge brown teapot and placed a tin containing home made cakes on the table.

'Lord, but how you frightened us with that telegram saying you was coming home, Davy. Your dad and me, well, we've never had a telegram before and we thought something terrible must have happened when it arrived. Dad was all of a tremble opening it, I can tell you!'

The rest of the family came home in dribbles from mid afternoon onwards. His sisters and his brother, Tom, the baby of the family, were the first to arrive. They had run all the way home from school in their haste to see him and were out of breath by the time they arrived. Collins had to walk around the kitchen several times while they admired his uniform and fired questions at him at the same time. Next to arrive home was his younger brother, George who wanted to know how many Germans he'd killed, and why he hadn't won any medals. By the time his father came home in the evening, Collins had lost count of the times he had repeated himself in conversation.

It was wonderful all the same, and he had to pinch himself several times to make sure he wasn't dreaming. Only twenty-four hours ago he had been eating army rations and living in the mud of the trenches. Now, he was warm, safe, and well fed. Best of all, he was back at home, even if it was only for a little while. It became too much for him to take. He was welling up inside with emotion and could feel the tears coming. Rather than have his brother and sisters see him crying, he told them he had to pee and fled to the toilet.

When he returned from the toilet, his mother asked him how Lofty was getting on. 'It's a shame he couldn't have come with you, I'd really like to meet him.'

In the excitement surrounding his arrival home, nobody had mentioned Lofty's name until now. He looked at the expectant face of his mother as she waited for an answer and decided not to tell her about the true manner of Lofty's death. 'I'm afraid Lofty's dead, mum. He got shot a few days ago.'

A gasp of disbelief went around the room followed by a stunned silence. Mrs Collins leant forward in her seat and gently stroked his hand. 'Oh, Davy, that's terrible. Poor Lofty. What happened? Did he suffer?'

He hesitated, desperately thinking of something to tell them.

'Now, now, luv,' Mr Collins said quietly. 'I don't think Davy wants to talk about it now.'

Collins nodded, grateful to his father for having saved him from trying to make up some story about Lofty's death.

'You're right, Dad. I was silly to ask,' Mrs Collins said quickly. 'Anyway, I can't sit here talking, I ought to be getting the washing up done.' She looked at the clock on the mantelpiece and then turned her attention to Davy's sisters and his youngest brother. 'It's high time you three were in bed,' she said. They squealed their protests but it was no good and, after helping their mother with the washing up, they kissed their brother goodnight and were packed off to bed. Mr Collins wanted to take his son down the Red Lion to stand him a few drinks and show him off, but Mrs Collins was having none of it.

'Not on his first night back, you're not, dad. The boy's tired and needs a good hot bath,' she looked at her son's uniform suspiciously, 'and I'll need to wash and iron them clothes, my lad.'

Obeying his wife's instructions, Mr Collins added more coal to the black leaded kitchen range. When the coals were glowing red-hot, Mrs Collins put four large saucepans of water on top of the range to boil. Then she took down the zinc bath that was hanging from a nail in the kitchen door and put it on the floor in front of the fire. When the water was hot, she poured it in to the bath and then added cold water until the temperature of the water was just right for Collins to climb into.

While he soaked in the bath, his mother took charge of his clothes. First she scrubbed them on the washboard in a sink full of hot soapy water. Then, after rinsing them thoroughly, she put them through the mangle and hung them over a clothes- horse in front of the fire to dry.

After his bath he sat by the fire and watched the steam coming off his damp clothes rising up towards the ceiling. Washing drying around the fire on a Monday night was a sight he had grown up with and he had never given it a second thought before; but he did now. There was something wonderfully comforting about sitting before a roaring fire in a kitchen full of damp, steaming washing. In a strange way it summed up everything he missed about being away from home and made him wish he hadn't been so hasty in volunteering to join the army. Mr Collins produced some bottles of beer and Davy spent the rest of the evening talking to his parents about life in the trenches and the duties involved in his job with the padre. He didn't say anything about Rose because he knew his mother would be interested and ask a lot of embarrassing questions. He would have to tell her that Rose had stood him up and he knew how outraged his mother would be with any girl that had done that to him.

He managed to keep Lofty out of the conversation too, although having told his parents that he was dead, Davy knew they must be curious to know more about the way he died. When he finished speaking, Mr Collins said how lucky he was to be working for a padre instead of being just another poor infantryman stuck in the trenches.

'You want to keep in with him,' he said, 'he's your best chance of staying alive, Davy,'

Mrs Collins gave her husband a puzzled look. 'Whatever do you mean, Dad?' she said.

'Well, like it or not love, we've got to face facts. We all know about the thousands of casualties on the Somme and elsewhere in France, don't we?'

Mrs Collins nodded her head sadly. 'Oh yes, it's terrible the losses we've taken in this war.'

'And who is it that always cops' it worse?' Mr Collins continued, 'the poor old foot soldier that's who! And they'll be more losses to come as well, unless the war ends soon. So it stands to reason that our Davy's got more chance of surviving if he's working for a chaplain and not in the front line.' Having said his piece, Mr Collins picked up a bottle of beer and replenished his empty glass.

Mrs Collins looked worried. 'Now just you listen to your father and keep hold of this job, Davy! Make sure you behave yourself and do everything that this Mr Renton tells you.'

Davy Collins laughed. The advice was typical of his mother. From as far back as he could remember she had told him that he only had to behave himself and do what he was told, and he was sure to get on in life. 'Don't worry mum,' he reassured her. 'I know I'm lucky the padre picked me for his orderly, so I won't go mucking the job up. Besides, he's all right is the padre. I like him. He's done me a few good turns.'

He drained his glass and sat back, happy, but tired. He couldn't prevent a lengthy yawn escaping his mouth.

'Bed for you, I think, my lad,' his mother said. 'You must be done in with all that travelling. Off you go now! I expect you'll want to sleep in for a bit in the morning, so I won't wake you too early.'

He said goodnight to his father and kissed his mother on the cheek. He opened the bedroom door as quietly as he could so as not to disturb his brothers and sisters who were asleep. By the sliver of light coming through the open door he could just see the two beds in the room. His sisters were sleeping with their heads under the covers in the bed nearest the door. He entered the room and closed the door behind him. He stood for a moment to let his eyes get accustomed to the darkness and then tiptoed his way passed his sisters over to the bed by the window. Lifting up the blankets he slid in to the space left for him on the mattress by his younger brothers.

Time at home passed all too quickly for Collins. What with being fed huge meals by his mother and fitting in visits to close friends and neighbours, the two days sped by. On his last night home he went to the Red Lion with his father. The interior of the public bar was just the same as he remembered, dark varnished wood panels around the walls, white distemper on the ceiling that had turned brown from years of cigarette smoke, and a threadbare carpet on the floor. Nothing had changed; even the pianist in the saloon bar was still playing the same old tunes. The regulars at the bar gave him a hearty welcome and his first pint was on the house, courtesy of the landlord. Looking around the pub he was surprised to see how full it was.

'Lot of work about at the moment,' his father explained. 'Like you, most of the young lads are in the army now, so workers are in demand. Good money in most jobs, too. Why, some women are earning even more than the men in them munitions factories in Woolwich.'

After just an hour in the pub, Mr Collins was already on his fourth pint and a little bit tipsy. Davy never tried to keep up with his father when it came to drinking and was still nursing his second pint. He knew his father changed when he had a few drinks inside him. A man of few words when sober, in drink, he opened up and talked about matters he wouldn't normally discuss at home. 'I hope this war finishes soon for your mother's sake,' he said to Davy. 'It's bad enough her worrying about you, but if it drags on for years and your brother has to go, well...' He appeared to be thinking something over in his mind and the conversation stopped for a while. At length he said to Davy. 'What do you think, son. You're in the thick of it. Have the Germans had enough yet?'

Collins wanted to tell his father that Germany was taking a beating and that the British Army was winning, but he remembered what Captain Beamish had said about being in for a long war. He shrugged his shoulders. 'I don't know, Dad. I think they had some big losses after the last lot because things are very quiet at the moment in our sector, which is a good sign. But how long the war will go on for is anybody's guess.'

Mr Collins looked at his son and nodded. Raising his glass to his lips, he downed half the contents in one go and then wiped the froth off his lips with the back of his hand. 'The army's done wonders for your education, boy,' he said. 'You've matured a lot since you bin in France. I reckon that padre of yours has had a lot to do with that.'

'Well I've had some reading lessons from him, and he's helped me with me spelling as well. I also picked up a lot listening to the officers talking.'

'Officers!' Mr Collins snorted, 'you don't want to go by what they say, Davy. They live in a different world to you and me.'

'But Mr Renton is an officer dad, and I reckon he talks a lot of sense.'

'But he's a chaplain ain't he? There's no harm in taking advice from him cos' he's not like the rest of em'. What I'm saying is, don't bother asking them toffee nosed army officers for any help. The only sort of help they'll give you is the sort that'll get you killed.'

A couple of the pub regulars who were standing at the bar listening, nodded their heads in agreement of Mr Collins' remarks. 'Just you listen to your father, lad. He's giving you sound advice.'

The speaker had a red face and large mutton chop sideburns. He was wearing an old greasy brown jacket that had several medals pinned to the lapels. Seeing Davy staring at his jacket, he said: 'Got `em' in the Boer war, lad. Right fuck up by the top brass that one was, too!'

Collins joined in the chorus of laughter that followed the old soldier's remark. He was on his third pint and having a good time, the war in France almost forgotten. Almost: but not quite. Although he was doing his best to forget it, Lofty's death still troubled him. No matter how hard he tried to push it to the back of his mind, it kept coming back into his thoughts. That, and the illness of the padre's mother, made Collins feel guilty about enjoying himself.

His father put his arm around Davy's shoulder and they moved to the end of the bar where it was quieter. 'What's up, son?' he said, 'your face as gone as long as a fiddle.'

'Sorry, Dad, I don't mean to be miserable. I suddenly thought of poor Lofty.'

'I thought it might be that,' Mr Collins said. He drained his glass and put it down on the bar. 'You know we get a lot soldiers in here on leave, Davy, and I'll tell you now that a lot of em' behaved like you're doing now.'

Davy gave his father a puzzled look. 'What do mean, dad?'

'Feeling guilty `cos' you're still alive and your mate ain't! It's only natural for it to play on your mind, especially after a few pints.'

'No it's not that. Listen, Dad, about Lofty, about the way he got shot, I want to....' Collins stopped. He didn't want to tell anyone yet how Lofty died, not even his father.

'It's all right, son. I understand. You'd rather not talk about it, so don't. After all, you lost your best mate so you're bound to be cut up about it.' Mr Collins picked up his empty glass and waved it in the direction of the landlord. 'Same again, Fred and a glass of rum for my lad.'

Ten minutes after the landlord had rung the bell for closing time, a policeman popped his head around the door of the public bar and that was the end of the evening for Collins and his father. They reluctantly left the pub to make the short walk home. Collins was a little bit the worse for wear but not as bad as his father who was very drunk and having difficulty in walking in a straight line. Mr Collins had a fair singing voice and always burst into song when he was drunk; tonight was no exception and he sang all the way back home. Davy happily joined in with him even though he didn't know the words to most of the songs. As the last chorus of, 'If you were the only girl in the world,' faded away into the cold, dark night, Mr Collins suddenly stopped walking. Turning to his son, he gripped him by the shoulders and drew him close until their heads were almost touching.

'S'hoosh,' he slurred drunkenly, putting his finger to his lips, 'got to be quiet going in. Don't want to wake your mother or the kids, all right?'

Father and son looked at each other and burst into laughter then, arm in arm carried on unsteadily towards their apartment in the tenement block. There were no lights at the bottom of the stairs that led up to the landing and the night was very dark. In their happy drunken state, Collins and his father never saw the row of dustbins that stood in their usual place at the entrance to the stairs. They walked straight into them, knocking half a dozen of the bins over. Mr Collins fell to the ground taking Davy with him and both of them ended up on their backs in piles of rubbish. The noise of the dustbin lids' as they rolled around on the cobbled yard was deafening. Davy Collins heard the sound of windows being opened and saw lights appear in a few of the apartments above him. He heard voices shouting angrily at him to keep the noise down. Getting unsteadily to his feet, he looked down at his father.

Mr Collins had managed to get his foot stuck in one of the bins and was trying desperately to shake it free. But in banging the dustbin up and down on the cobbles he was only succeeding in adding to the noise. Freeing his father from the bin they eventually made it up the stairs to the landing. As they neared the front door to the apartment Mr Collins paused and turned to his son once again. 'Remember what I said before Davy boy. No noise going in, right!'

Chapter 22

Renton had very little to do with his mother's burial arrangements. His sister had taken on the task and for that he was grateful. His father spent most of the time alone in his study in the days leading up to his wife's funeral seemingly content to go along with everything his daughter suggested. Renton watched his father getting more depressed with each day that passed. He was a shadow of the man Renton knew before he left for France. Perhaps, after the funeral, he would find some way of coming to terms with his grief and carry on his ecclesiastical duties for a year or two longer, but Renton doubted it. On the day of the funeral everything went off without a hitch. The service was well attended and Renton noticed a great many people from the poorer side of town packed into the back of the small church of St Mary's. Before her illness his mother had worked tirelessly to help the less fortunate in her husband's parish and they obviously remembered her many kindnesses and wanted to pay their last respects.

Seeing the packed church reminded him that his mother had had a great knack of being at ease with people of all classes. She knew exactly how to handle people, especially the more affluent people of the town. Lecturing them on their civic responsibilities wasn't her style. Instead she would gently remind them of the favour they would find in the sight of God as a reward for their generosity. As a result she had been very successful in raising the monies she needed for her various charity ventures.

It was only after the service as he watched the coffin being slowly lowered into the ground that the full implication of his mother's death came home to him. As the oak casket come to rest in the freshly dug soil, he wondered how he was going to endure life without her. He had been passionately devoted to his mother and had never hesitated to go to her for advice and comfort. If, as he thought, she knew about his homosexuality, she had never condemned him for it, and certainly never loved him any the less for it. When he was young, she praised even his smallest achievements and when he grew to manhood she encouraged his every endeavour. It was for her sake that he had followed his father into a religious vocation. He knew it would please her and it was his way of repaying her faith in him. He had so wanted to see her before she died to tell her how much he owed her for all she had done for him, but he'd arrived too late. With all his heart he wished that she were alive again, even if it was only for a fleeting moment: just long enough to tell her how much he loved and missed her.

Renton stood alongside his father at the side of the grave as the mourners started making their way out of the cemetery. He shook the hands of family friends and strangers alike as he accepted their condolences. He was tired and needed a drink but there was still the gathering at the vicarage to get through. Joanna had invited about a dozen people to attend. Tea and sandwiches were being laid on for the guests and she had got in two extra bottles of sherry for the occasion. Renton looked at his watch; it was a few minutes before twelve thirty. Davy was coming on the afternoon train and would be here in less than three hours. Renton could hardly wait to see him.

He turned to his father and gently took his arm. The old man's shrivelled face looked lost in thought and he seemed not to notice his son's presence at his side. In silence the two men walked slowly out of the cemetery towards the vicarage.

A sharp north easterly wind blew through the garden. It was mid afternoon, and the last of the guests had gone. Renton had slipped out of the house to take in some much needed fresh air. A combination of heat and cigarette smoke had made the air in the lounge very stuffy. Joanna and her husband had gone home and his father was resting in his bedroom, the funeral proceedings having left him exhausted and upset. He was at the far end of the garden when he heard the sound of automobile tyres on the gravel drive. He knew it could only be Davy's taxi: no one living locally would visit his father on such a mournful day. He hurried round to the front of the house to greet him and arrived just as Davy was paying off the driver.

Renton's heart beat a little faster. Was it his imagination, or was the boy looking even more handsome than when he had last seen him? Or perhaps it was because he'd had a haircut and was wearing a clean, neatly pressed uniform. Whatever it was, Davy certainly looked smarter and more dashing than he did when they had parted a few days ago. Renton watched the taxi drive away leaving a nervous looking Davy standing in the drive clutching his kitbag. He walked towards him and

Collins, hearing his footsteps on the gravel drive, turned and looked in his direction. Renton waved a greeting. 'Hello, Davy! It's so good to see you again. You got here all right then, no problems finding the place?'

'Good afternoon, sir! No, no trouble at all. The taxi driver knew the house.'

The boy's eyes roamed over the front of the building. 'It's a really big place isn't it, sir?'

'Yes, I suppose it is. Now stop calling me sir, Davy. Remember what I told you in London. It's Simon while you're here.'

'Oh yes. Sorry. I forgot.' Collins glanced down at Renton's ankle.

'No walking stick! Is your ankle mended then?'

'Yes, practically, thank you.'

'And how about your mother... I mean, is she any better?'

'I'm afraid she died just before I arrived. We had the funeral this morning and held a reception here for the chief mourners. They only left a short while ago.'

'Oh, I see. I'm very sorry about your mother. Really I am,' Colins hesitated, 'can I do anything to help, Simon? I mean, clearing up, or anything like that.'

Renton smiled. It was the first time Davy had uttered his Christian name without being prompted. He liked it, and he especially liked the uncertain pause Davy made before uttering his name. 'No. It's all right, there's nothing to do. Mary, our housekeeper, has already cleaned up. Come on! Pick up your kitbag. I'll show you up to your room.'

Collins had never been in a house as large and grand as the vicarage before. The hall was massive and the stairs leading up to the landing seemed endless. He was expecting to sleep in some pokey little servants' room in the cellar somewhere, so he was taken aback when he was told he would be sleeping upstairs in one of the guest bedrooms. The room Simon showed him into was twice the size of the one he shared at home with his brothers and sisters. Simon told him it had been his sister's room before she left to get married. Telling him to come downstairs for tea when he was ready, Simon left him alone in the room to settle in.

He sat on the edge of the bed and looked around the bedroom. There was no fire lit in the grate and the room was cold, but it didn't bother him; he was used to an unheated bedroom. The room was decorated a bit on the girlish side perhaps, with its flowery bedspread and pink curtains, but it was still a nice room for all that and he wondered how long he would be using it. Now that Simon's mother had been buried there was no reason for them to stay and the thought of rushing back to France depressed him. Still, they couldn't be going back right away or Simon would surely have mentioned it. And even if they did have to leave tomorrow, well so what... he was determined to enjoy every last moment of his leave.

He had certainly enjoyed his night out drinking with his father. The throbbing in his head when he woke told him that he'd drunk more than was good for him. But it had been worth it! His father hadn't looked too good either at breakfast, but nevertheless, after wishing him all the best and telling him to take care of himself, he went off to work cheerfully enough. His mother said nothing about their noisy entrance the previous night. He knew she wouldn't say anything to him while he was at home, but after he'd gone it would be a different matter and she'd have a right little go at his Dad about his drunken behaviour when he got in from work. There had been tears from his mother when he left to catch his train, and plenty of advice on behaving himself. She held on to him for so long he didn't think he was going to get out of the door let alone make it to the station and catch his train.

He unpacked his pyjamas and put them on the bed. He was feeling a little bit tired after the late night and the train journey. His head had stopped throbbing a long time ago but he was continually thirsty, probably on account of drinking too much rum and beer the previous night. Drinking made him think of Simon. Had he stopped while staying in his father's house, he wondered? Or had the death of his mother made him drink all the more? Despite his cheery greeting in the driveway earlier, Simon was obviously very upset over his mother's death.Collins had noticed how red and sad his eyes looked, even when he smiled. Well he would just have to do his best to try and cheer him up. He looked into the little mirror on the dressing table and taking a comb from his pocket, slicked down his hair. Satisfied that he looked presentable, he went downstairs to join Simon for tea.

The afternoon passed quickly and suddenly it was evening. To Collins surprise and embarrassment, Renton insisted in treating him more like his guest than his orderly. At dinner, instead of helping the housekeeper with the meal as he had been expecting to do, he found himself sitting down to eat with Simon and his father. He was very nervous, but luckily the meal was a simple one. Collins watched Renton like a hawk throughout dinner. Every knife, fork and spoon he used, Collins copied him. It worked and he got through the meal without any problems. Old Mr Renton ate very little and spoke little. But he was polite and made him feel welcome. When the meal was finished he wished them both goodnight and took himself off to his bedroom.

After his father had left the room, Renton went to the sideboard and, producing a bottle of port and two glasses, poured out two generous measures and handed one to his orderly. 'I think a drink is in order, don't you? I certainly need one after the day I've had.' He downed his glass of port in one go and sighed. 'Ah, that's better,' he said. He gave himself a refill and looked at Collins. 'Drink up then, Davy!'

Collins took a cautious sip from his glass. He had never drunk port before and was pleasantly surprised by its taste. It had a sweetness and fruitiness that he hadn't been expecting. He took a longer sip, a good mouthful this time, enjoying the rich, spicy flavour of the port as it slipped down his throat.

'Like it, Davy?' Renton picked up the bottle and topped up the boy's glass without giving him time to answer. 'There's nothing like a glass of port on a cold winter's night, Davy! It warms the bones and cheers you up.'

'It's really delicious, Simon. I've never tasted anything like it.'

'Well, drink up! It's not a spirit like whisky, you know. Port's more like wine. You can drink bottles of this stuff and not get drunk.'

After two glasses of port Collins began to relax and enjoy himself. The padre asked him about his family and what he had done while home on leave. To try and cheer Renton up he decided to tell him about his night out in the pub with his father. Renton laughed when he heard about their trouble with the dustbins and Collins confidence grew until he felt he was really helping Renton take his mind off the death of his mother. At the end of the evening, when it was time to go up to bed, he noticed to his amazement that they had drunk a whole bottle of port between them. He felt slightly flushed but in no way drunk. He couldn't be; he'd only had a few glasses of port, after all! In the hallway, Renton's arm slipped around his waist and he insisted on helping him up the stairs. He thought it was probably the padre's way of expressing his gratitude to him for cheering him up. At the top of the stairs he said goodnight and went to his room feeling very pleased with himself.

Renton sat on the edge of his bed looking at his watch. By his reckoning Davy had been in bed about ten minutes. He wouldn't be asleep yet, not an awestruck boy in a strange house. He smiled to himself. It was the port that had done the trick. Dismissing it as nothing more than a harmless nightcap drink had disarmed the boy. As a result he had drunk quite freely and become more and more relaxed as the evening progressed. Now it was the time to find out if the port had loosened Davy's sexual inhibitions. He knew he would never have a better chance. It was now or never. He looked at his watch again; it was time to make a move. He rubbed his eyes vigorously with the back of his hands until they became red and swollen. Then, picking up a water jug from the dresser, he dipped his fingers into the cold water. Taking care not to overdo it, he wiped his wet fingers over his eyes and the bottom of his eyelashes.

The flame in the bedside lamp was still flickering when he closed the bedroom door behind him. Without uttering a word, he went and over and sat on the edge of Davy Collins bed. There was enough light from the lamp for him to see that Davy was awake and looking at him anxiously.

'What is it? Is there something wrong?' The boy asked him, sitting up.

'Oh Davy! I feel so miserable and wretched.' Renton wiped away a false tear and moved closer to Davy on the bed. 'Mother's dead, Davy, and I miss her so much. I feel so very alone without her.'

His s tearful outburst seemed to be working. Davy was looking upset and concerned. 'I'm so sorry, really I am. I understand how you feel, Simon. Honest, I do.'

Renton stared at the bedspread and a shiver went through his body. It was cold in the room and he had no dressing gown on over his pyjamas.

'You're trembling, Simon,' Davy said. 'It's cold in this room. You'll catch a chill.'

Renton turned a tear stained face towards him. 'Let me come in bed with you,' he cried. 'I'll get warm then. Please!' The boy hesitated for a second then moved to the side of the bed to make space.

'Is that enough room for you?' he asked.

'Yes, plenty thank you.' He lifted the covers and got into bed. His body pressed up against Davy and the boy gave a shiver.

'Brr! You're freezing cold, Simon.'

'I'm sorry, Davy,' he sobbed, 'you see, I've been sitting in my room thinking of mother. I guess I never felt the cold.'

'No, it's me who should be saying sorry, Simon. Come on! Move closer and we'll warm ourselves up.' Collins turned over on to his side. 'Just snuggle up to

pleasure. Suddenly the boy's body arched upwards and his whole body shook in uncontrollable spasms before sinking limply back down on the bed. He was breathing hard and didn't resist when Renton turned him on his stomach. He appeared powerless to stop Renton doing anything to him now. He had just experienced the most wonderful sensation in his life. Renton moved in behind him, kissing his shoulders and rubbing his now erect penis hard against Davy's bare buttocks. The boy looked to be beyond caring what happened to him next.

Renton, breathless from sexual enjoyment, and with his nerve ends still tingling, couldn't contain himself; what he had dreamt about so often was actually happening and it had been easier than he had dared to imagine. An almost naked Davy was underneath him. His hands were gripped tight around his orderly's waist and he wasn't about to let go. The boy had had his pleasure and now it was his turn. He was almost crazy with lust at the sight of the boy's smooth, bare buttocks. Nothing on earth could keep him from his prize now. He heard a surprised gasp followed by a cry of pain as he entered Davy from behind. The boy tried to move from under him but he tightened his grip and held him firm. Groaning with pleasure and gratification, and ignoring Davy's whimpers, he thrust into him again and again, riding him like a dog riding a bitch in heat. When his moment finally arrived, his orgasm was so powerful it shook his body from head to toe and he collapsed, panting with exhaustion, on to Collins warm back.

Chapter 23

Collins pulled the covers up around his head to keep out the early morning cold and looked at the strip of daylight entering his bedroom through a narrow gap in the curtains. He was alone in bed, Renton having returned to his own room before the housekeeper got up to begin her work. He was glad that he'd gone. With Renton lying beside him in bed sleep was impossible. What had taken place between them weighed heavily on his conscience and he needed time to think. He had been trying to come to terms with what the padre had done to him. The question he kept asking himself was why he had let him take him in the way that he had? Renton had told him afterwards that it was the normal way for men to make love, but that hadn't stopped him being angry with him. He was also angry with himself because he was at a loss to explain his own behaviour. He could have struggled harder last night if he'd really tried; but he hadn't. Instead he'd closed his eyes and let it happen even though it had hurt enough to bring him to tears; but he hadn't fought Simon off or made him to stop. Afterwards he had been so kind and considerate that Collins found it difficult to stay angry with him. 'I really thought that you wanted me to do it,' he said, 'I would never have done it otherwise. I'm sorry if I hurt you. I wouldn't do that for the world.'

Renton kept telling him that what they had done was really beautiful, that it was only painful the first time; that the soreness would quickly pass. When he said that he'd heard that sex between two men was wrong, that it wasn't natural, Renton had told him not to worry, that as a priest he would never break the law or harm anyone, especially someone he loved. It didn't completely reassure him, but he didn't think Simon would lie to him about something so serious. In his heart he knew he wasn't really mad with the padre but with himself. What really worried him however was that it wasn't a woman he'd just had sex with, but a man. He kept telling himself that he wasn't '*queer*' like Renton obviously was. He had been caught unawares and had just got carried away, that was all. It wasn't just once he had allowed himself to get carried away. Before leaving him, Renton had sucked his penis again and once more he found himself powerless to stop his body from responding. Just like before he had writhed in pleasure as Simon made him reach what he described as a 'sexual climax.' To his great relief though, this time Renton didn't try to make love to him afterwards, but slipped quietly out of bed and returned to his own room. His troubled thoughts were brought to an abrupt end by a knock on his bedroom door. He called out that he was awake and waited nervously, expecting Simon to enter, but it was the housekeeper's voice that came to him through the door; breakfast would be in ten minutes.

Renton and his father were already eating breakfast when Collins came down. The padre greeted him cheerily and acted as if nothing unusual had taken place between them. Mr Renton was as quiet over breakfast as he'd been at dinner. He didn't stay at the table long and returned to his study leaving most of his bacon and eggs on his plate. Collins felt unusually hungry. Although he was in some pain and discomfort, the night with Simon hadn't spoiled his appetite, and he ate a hearty breakfast. He didn't feel uneasy while they were eating because the food gave him something to concentrate on but when he'd finished breakfast he could think of nothing to say. Being in a dining room with Renton in the morning was different to being alone in a dimly lit bedroom with him at night.

To his amazement Renton didn't say a word about what had taken place between them during the night and showed no signs of embarrassment, or shame, whatsoever. He didn't even seem to notice his unease and chatted away breezily. The sadness of the previous night had completely disappeared and considering the fact that he had just lost his mother, Collins thought Renton was looking remarkably well and talking very cheerfully.

At length Renton finished his breakfast and pushed his chair back. 'I suggest you have a stroll round the garden, or down the lane,' he said. 'Walk off your breakfast. I've got to make some phone calls to see if we've got to start back right away or not.'

They walked into the hallway and Collins was about to open the door when the padre suddenly leant forward and kissed him on the cheek. 'Wrap up warm, Davy,' he said,' 'it's a bit chilly out there.'

A lock of hair fell across Collin's forehead and Renton gently brushed it back in place with his hand. 'I'll see you at lunch, all right?'

Collins reddened and opened the door. 'Yes... yes, fine Simon. I'll see you later.'

Collins walked around country lanes for two hours wracking his brain trying to figure out how to deal with Renton. From the way that he'd behaved towards him after breakfast it seemed that he really was in love with him and if that was the case, then presumably he loved him in the same way that a man loves a woman. Collins was certain that he couldn't handle that sort of love. He was fond of Renton and was grateful to him for taking him on as his orderly and for being kind to Lofty when he needed someone; but for all that he knew he couldn't love him in the way he wanted. He had also been thinking about what his parents would do if they ever found out he had been with another man. His mother wouldn't even have the subject of sex mentioned in the house; his father saved such talk for the pub. The idea of their son having sex with another man would be completely beyond them. They would think it filthy and disgusting and probably disown him and he would never see them again. No, he told himself, they must never know. He would sooner die than they ever find out that he'd slept with a man. As he started back towards the house he realised that his biggest problem at the moment was the coming evening. Would Renton be expecting to come to his room again, and if so, how could he put him off? He mustn't dare weaken, he'd got to forget the sexual enjoyment of the night before and be strong with Simon. If he came to his room he would refuse to let him in.

Collins was determined to tell the padre of his decision; but as things turned out, he didn't get the chance. He found Renton and his father talking together in the hall and he could see from the expressions on both their faces that something was up. As he approached the pair Renton turned to him. 'Start packing,' he said, brusquely. 'Now the funeral is over the powers that be have decided that there's no point to me remaining here. We're to go straight back to France.'

He could hear the bitterness and disappointment in Renton's voice, but for him it was the answer to his problem. At least rushing back to France meant he would not have to spend another night in the house. 'What? Are we to leave right away, right now?' he asked.

'After lunch,' Renton said. 'We'll catch the first train after lunch.'

Renton leant over the guardrails of the ship and watched the lights of the French harbour getting closer. His body swayed as he moved away from the guardrail but it wasn't because of the movement of the ship. He had been drinking whiskey steadily since first coming aboard. He flicked the lighted end of his cigarette in to the sea with an angry gesture. His mood was as dark and sullen as the waters below him. Only twenty-four hours previously, and despite the death of his mother, he had been a happy man. Not only had he been safe at home but he had also achieved his dream and made love to Davy. But a single telephone call had spoilt it all. Not only had it taken him away from his home, but now it looked as if it might have taken Davy away from him as well. He hit the guardrail with his clenched fist in frustration. How on earth could he have been so stupid? Why hadn't he waited another couple of days before making the telephone call? Another day or two at home; that's all it would have taken to make Davy his lover. At home he would have had the time and the privacy to make love to him properly and he was sure Collins would have responded willingly, the boy was that naive. But it was different now they were heading back to France. Davy's behaviour towards him had changed.

The first real indication that Collins was unhappy came after they boarded the ship. He had been allocated a cabin for the short channel crossing and he was surprised when Davy said he didn't want to share it with him; that he wanted to stay on deck with the ordinary passengers. At first he'd pleaded with him to stay, but when Davy still insisted on leaving, he'd got annoyed with him and pulled rank by ordering him to remain in the cabin. When he tried to make advances towards him, the boy said he didn't want to, that he was still sore. The excuse sounded reasonable, after all, he had been a virgin up until last night and was bound to be in a bit of pain. But he had the answer; he would let Davy make love to him this time. As soon as he suggested it he knew he had made a great mistake. Collins looked horrified at the idea and backed away from him. Renton had picked up his bottle of whisky and stormed out of the cabin in anger and frustration.

The ship was inside the harbour now and Renton could make out the shapes of warehouses and other buildings on the dockside. By morning he would be back in the line with the Westhampton Regiment. He pulled the bottle from his pocket, finished the contents in one swallow, and then threw the empty bottle into the sea. He watched the bottle bobbling along in the water behind the ship until it disappeared from his view.

By the time he returned to the cabin to pick up his things for disembarking, he had worked himself up into a foul mood. He was determined to make it clear that everything that had happened between them had been his orderly's fault. 'What is wrong with you?' he shouted angrily, 'are you deliberately trying to play hard to get or something? It's no good acting coy with me now, you know. Have you forgotten last night? Forgotten how much you enjoyed me sucking your dick for you, have you forgotten that, hey?'

He glared at Davy and thought he detected a guilty look on the boy's face.

'I'm very sorry, Simon. It's not that I didn't like it... It's just that, well...we're back in France now and, and... it's different somehow.'

Renton sneered. 'What's being in France got to do with it. It doesn't mean to say I've got to stop fucking you, does it?'

Collins looked as if he was about to burst into tears. Renton knew he had gone too far and was about to apologise when the ship suddenly rocked from side to side as it came alongside the harbour wall. Before he could say another word there was a knock on the cabin door. It was the steward informing them it was time to go ashore.

There was no time for further discussion. Any apologies would have to wait until the morning when they got back to the regiment. Then he would remind Collins just what a soft job he had as the padre's orderly. He was confident that once Davy realised he could lose his job, his attitude towards him would soon change. 'Pick up the bags, Collins,' he said sharply. 'Let's get ashore and find some transport.'

The journey from the coast to the front line was torturously slow and they arrived back just after dawn. As he climbed down from the lorry, Renton looked about him. Things hadn't changed since he'd been away; he would have been surprised if they had. The mud was still as thick on the ground and the early morning sky still as leaden and grey as ever. The usual threat of mist and rain hung in the air. His nostrils took in the familiar cocktail of smells; rifle oil, cordite, urine, unwashed bodies, cooking, and above all, all the odours of war that had been absent from his life for the last few days. It was all a far cry from his father's vicarage in Suffolk and it made Renton feel even more depressed and angry than he already was.

At breakfast, Renton sat next to Freddie Beamish. After expressing his condolences over the death of his mother and enquiring about conditions in England, Beamish brought him up to date with the latest news. Nothing much had occurred while he had been away, he told him. There had been hardly any enemy activity and few casualties. There was however, an interesting rumour doing the rounds.

'There's a buzz that we're being taken out of the line for a rest, old boy,' Beamish said, grinning widely. 'Haven't heard anything official yet, mind you, but the regiment is well overdue for a break.'

Renton didn't see why Freddie was getting so excited. New rumours were started every day and few of them ever turned out to be correct. 'Do you believe it?' he asked Beamish. 'If it's only a rumour, what makes you think it will actually happen?'

Beamish drew his chair closer. 'Because,' he said confidentially, 'I have a contact at HQ who told me as much the other day. End of the month is a likely date to move to a rear area.'

'But that's only a week away,' Renton said angrily. 'If that's the case why did I have to get back so urgently?'

Beamish shrugged his shoulders 'You know how the army works well enough by now, Simon. Anyway, that's what my contact says, and he's pretty certain he's got the right date.'

Renton's heart sank as he listened to Beamish. The very irony of the situation made him want to weep. Ever since he'd been in France he had wanted to get home or at least have a posting to a more comfortable rear area. Now, just when he needed the dangers of life in the front line to use as a lever to keep Davy near him, it looked as if the regiment was moving back to a safe area. After the scene on the boat he had to make it up with Davy quickly or he might lose him. That didn't even bear thinking about. It wasn't just because of the sex, either; he really loved Davy.

Collins had travelled in the rear of the lorry during the journey back to the lines, glad of the fact that there wasn't enough room in the driver's cab for him and the padre.

He hadn't meant to get Renton upset on the boat and set him off drinking. It was just that once onboard he wanted to be on his own for a while. When Simon ordered him stay and suggested that they make love, he just knew he couldn't. Before, in the house, it had been different, it hadn't been planned, it had just happened. They had got carried away, perhaps done things in drink that they shouldn't have. He didn't know whether he would let Simon do those things to him again, probably not, but he wanted time to think about it. He'd tried to tell him that in the cabin but Simon had got angry and stormed off to get drunk. The language he'd used afterwards shocked him. He didn't think a priest would ever use such words even when drunk. Since then Simon hadn't said a word to him apart from barking the occasional order to him.

But there was good news for him when he got back and returned to his quarters. He found an envelope addressed to him lying on his bed. He opened it and inside was a note from Rose. It read:

Dear Davy,

I'm really sorry I couldn't meet you as you asked. I was all ready to come and see you but we had a load of wounded soldiers arrive that needed urgent attention and I had to work through the night dealing with them and there was no way to let you know in time. I would like to meet you again if you still want to and will be in the same cafe at 8pm Saturday. It would be lovely to see you again.

Collins lay on his bed reading the note over and over again. So he'd been wrong, she hadn't stood him up after all. He should have realised at the time that being a nurse, Rose wouldn't always be able to get away from her job easily. Why hadn't he thought about that instead of being hasty and jumping to conclusions? Suddenly a thought struck him that made him sit bolt upright on the bed; Saturday was tomorrow! It gave him very little time to think about whether he wanted to see Rose again. Not only that but, if he decided that he did want to see her, could he get permission to go into town after just arriving back in the lines? It seemed a tall order to Davy Collins unless he took the risk of going into town without permission. The question was: was Rose worth it?

Chapter 24

Quartermaster Sergeant Ron Watkins shoved the last bit of paperwork into his correspondence tray and picked out a cheroot from a box in front of him. He put the cheroot in his mouth, lit up, and inhaled deeply on the rich tobacco. He'd smoked a lot in the past twenty-four hours. Smoking helped calm his nerves when he was worried, and something had happened that had made him very worried indeed; something that not only threatened his business empire, but might even put him behind bars or even bring him a worse fate.

The threat came from a new Provost Sergeant named Griggs who had just been posted to the area. Watkins knew Griggs well. The two of them had clashed on several occasions back in England; but for all his efforts, Griggs had never caught Watkins doing anything illegal. On the last occasion they had met, just before Watkins sailed for France, Griggs told him that if he ever ran into him again, he would make it his personal duty to nail him. Watkins had laughed; threats never bothered him, especially threats made by someone he wasn't likely to see again. But now Griggs had been posted to France. Worse still, he was attached to the provost unit that covered the Westhampton's area, and unfortunately for Watkins, Griggs had got lucky.

It all started with Private Morley who worked for Watkins in his store. He was a good worker and a reasonable enough soldier when sober, but bit of a loose cannon when he'd had a drink too many. Lots of the Westhampton soldiers got into scraps after drinking too much; but Morley was different. When drunk he went looking for violence and had a sadistic streak in him that enjoyed hurting people, especially people weaker than him. He had come close to being picked up by the provost on several occasions, but had always been lucky and managed to escape their clutches. Two nights ago his luck finally ran out and he'd got himself arrested for assaulting one of the whores that worked in the Rouville Hotel. In one of his violent rages he had beaten her severely about the face and then passed out drunk in her room. The whore run out into the street screaming hysterically and straight into the path of Provost Sergeant Griggs, who took Morley into custody. When Morley sobered up it didn't take Griggs long to find out that he worked for Watkins. Through an informant in the Military Police, Watkins learned everything that had happened. Griggs had offered Morley a deal; give him everything he knew about Watkins and his rackets, and a possible charge of attempted murder would be reduced to assault, or even a simple drunk and disorderly. Morley had a wife and kids to think about back in England and, not surprisingly, agreed to cooperate.

Watkins knew it was only a matter of time now before he could expect a visit from Griggs and moved swiftly to counter the danger. His first step was to pay his informant handsomely to warn him when Griggs was coming to search his store. Then he called in Cpl Brown and together they went through the storeroom with a fine toothcomb to ensure that every item of stores was scrupulously accounted for. Anything that appeared on paper to be in the stores but had since gone missing was covered with a legitimate explanation for its disappearance that would be acceptable to the Quartermaster General's Office. He was leaving nothing to chance with Griggs. Cpl Brown and the rest of his staff would of course corroborate every explanation he gave, but as an extra precaution each man on his staff was given an extra sum of money to ensure their loyalty and to keep their mouths shut. Naturally Cpl Brown got a bigger payment than the others. Watkins needed his silence most of all because he was the only besides himself and the padre to know about the chapel.

It had been a wise move to only use Brown's help in hiding the stuff in the chapel. Absolute secrecy was vital. It wasn't just smuggled brandy, whisky and cigarettes hidden under the tarpaulins. There were far more incriminating things hidden there; things that had been bought off the soldiers who worked on burial details. Watches looted from the wrists of officers who had fallen in action, gold rings taken from dead men's fingers, silver cigarette cases and lighters; all the property of men who had perished in battle. They were small, but valuable articles that he intended selling back in England after the war. They were also articles that might conceivably earn him a spell in prison or even the death penalty if they were ever discovered in his possession. The British army didn't look kindly on people who brought items that were stolen from their own dead. But Watkins was confident the stuff in the chapel would never be found. He had checked on it regularly while the padre was away and he was satisfied that it was in the best possible place to avoid detection.

It suddenly occurred to him that to be on the safe side he should have another go at the padre. He knew he was back from leave because he had seen him and his lover boy Collins arrive that morning. He decided to call on Renton in the near future and welcome him back. That only left his stake in the brothel in Rouville to worry about and he was pretty sure that he had covered his tracks well enough in that direction. He knew old Pierre Chaval wasn't going to spoil a good thing by opening his mouth to Griggs. The old man hated the Military Police because they were always threatening to close down his brothel every time there was a fight or a bit of bother over the girls. Watkins knew Chaval treated such threats lightly because he had friends among the officers who used his hotel and he wouldn't hesitate to complain to them if Griggs started to give him a hard time.

Watkins drew deeply on his cheroot appreciating the flavour of the fine tobacco. He was enjoying it more now that he was sure he had blocked every possible road that might lead to him. In fact he might just go into town tonight and get drunk to celebrate putting one over on Griggs. Let them come and search his store; they were going to be in for a big disappointment. It didn't matter what Morley had told Griggs, if they searched and couldn't find anything, then that was the end of the matter. He had to admit that it had been a bit of a scare for a while, though. In fact the biggest scare he'd had since arriving in France and with Griggs posted to the area, things would definitely have to be run a bit tighter in the future. He had already told his men to watch what they said about him from now on, especially when in town drinking. Even so, he was pretty sure it wouldn't be long before it was 'business as usual' on all fronts. It was a shame that Griggs wasn't the type that could be bought off, or even added to the payroll; it would make life a lot easier. Still, a war zone was a dangerous place, even for a provost sergeant, and anything could happen. He pulled open the bottom drawer of his desk and took out his prized souvenir of the war. It was a German Luger pistol, complete with leather holster and spare clip of ammunition. It had been taken from the body of a dead German officer by a soldier who sold it on to Watkins for the ridiculously cheap price of a few packets of decent smokes and a bottle of rough French brandy. Now it was Watkins most treasured possession and he cleaned and oiled it with meticulous regularity every day. He had only fired a couple of rounds for practice, but that was enough to make him to fall in love with the weapon. He loved the feel of the gun in his hand and the sense of power he felt knowing it was so close at hand. He was just itching for a reason to fire it at somebody, and if someday someone like Griggs pushed him too far, well then, look out... He slid the Luger out of its holster and removed the magazine. Aiming the pistol at an imaginary enemy coming through the door, he slowly squeezed the trigger.

When Collins awoke the next morning his mind was already made up; he was going to see Rose that evening no matter what. He had read her note again last night while lying in bed and found himself repeating the same part over and over again.

'*It would be lovely to see you again*' she had written him. His heart beat faster reading the words and he knew he had to see her. It was really important to him now, he had to get his true feelings sorted out and he was sure that seeing Rose again would do that for him.

He bitterly regretted now what had happened between him and the padre in England. He couldn't change the past; what was done couldn't be undone, but it must never happen again. It had all been such a terrible mistake; he had been confused and tipsy that night and certainly hadn't meant to lead Renton on as he was now suggesting. He liked him, but only as a friend, and he had to tell him that even if it meant losing his job as orderly and being sent back into the trenches. He was sorry if Renton loved him because he didn't love him back and could never love him. But he had to be honest and tell him that, and the sooner the better.

The first priority however was to see Rose. Getting a lift into town and back on a Saturday evening wouldn't be a problem, but he had to have permission from his superior first, and that meant asking Renton. If he refused, he was prepared to take the risk and see Rose without his permission. One thing was for certain, he couldn't tell Renton the real reason for wanting to go into Rouville. He would have to make up a good excuse.

After the morning service, when the last of the worshippers had left, Collins and Renton were alone in the chapel. Collins could tell by the way that the padre had spoken to him at breakfast that his anger towards him was cooling off. He was more like his normal polite self now, unrecognisable from the ranting, swearing person in the cabin on board the ship. He decided it was best to get it over and done with quickly and ask him straight out if he could go in to town.

'May I talk to you please, Simon?'

'Funny, I was going to say the same thing to you.'

Renton's voice sounded friendly which was encouraging. He took a deep breath. 'I've got a favour to ask you. I'd like your permission to go into Rouville tonight.'

A look of astonishment came over Renton's face. 'What! Haven't you had enough travelling for a while? Why do you have to go rushing off into town tonight?'

'It's because of Lofty Webb.' Collins looked Renton in the eye and hoped the lie he was about to tell sounded convincing. 'I got a message from one of the provost lads that Lofty wanted me to have his personal things after his death. He had no relatives, you see, so he wanted me to have them. The redcap is on duty tonight in town and he's going to have them with him for me to pick up. If I don't get them tonight, I may not get another chance.'

'Oh, I see. Well, can't he get them to you any other way? Do you have to collect his things personally?'

Collins was expecting the question. 'They'll get lost or thrown away if they don't get rid of them soon. Besides, I have to sign for them, you see.'

Renton sighed heavily.

'Well, you'd better go then, hadn't you? After all, the army must have its signature, mustn't it?'

'Thank you, Simon, it means a lot to me.'

'*Thank you, Simon, it means a lot to me!* My, my, we are on good terms with the padre aren't we, Collins?'

Watkins jeering voice, coming from the chapel door startled them both and Collins looked across to the padre. His face had gone deathly pale as the big Quartermaster entered. 'What do you want here?' Renton cried, 'we're having a private conversation.' There was anger in his voice and he was trembling with rage.

'Is that right, padre?' Watkins said grinning. He took a pace forward. 'You're right, it is a private conversation; but as from now, it's between you and me, not him.'

Watkins turned to Collins and pointed to the door. 'You, out, now!

Collins started walking but the padre's voice stopped him before he had got halfway to the door. 'Wait!' He came over and put his hands on his orderly's shoulders. 'It seems our talk will have to be postponed yet again, Davy,' he said quietly, 'tomorrow. Before morning service, all right?'

Watkins went to the chapel door and held it open 'That's enough! Get out Collins.'

Collins stepped outside and the door slammed shut behind him. He started to walk away but had only gone a few paces when he stopped. Something inside his head told him to stay and find out what Sergeant Watkins wanted with the padre. He tiptoed back to the chapel door. Hardly daring to breathe for fear of discovery, he put his ear to the gap that ran down the side of the door. He could hear the two men inside talking quite clearly. Their conversation was an angry one with Sergeant Watkins doing most of the talking and Renton only occasionally getting a word in. After listening for about five minutes, he had heard all he wanted to know and crept away.

The little café was crowded, but Collins saw Rose as soon as he entered. She was at the same table he'd seen her sitting at the very first time he'd entered the café. She was in company with two other nurses but when she saw him, she stood up and waved him over. He waved back and made his way through the crowded tables over to her.

‘I’m so glad you could make it, Davy,’ she said. She was even prettier than he remembered from their first meeting. The other two girls were looking at him with curiosity and he blushed furiously. ‘Take no notice of them,’ Rose laughed, ‘they’re just going, aren’t you girls?’

The two nurses finished their drinks and stood up to leave. ‘All right, we can take a hint,’ one of her girl friends said, ‘we’ll leave you two lovebirds together and try to find ourselves a couple of handsome officers down at the hotel.’ ‘Don’t do anything we wouldn’t,’ her friend added, winking at Rose.

Laughing, the two girls picked up their coats and left them together. She apologised to him for not turning up for their date and he couldn’t believe he’d been such an idiot as to think so badly of her. Why he had got so worked up about a missed date in the first place, he just didn’t know. In the end they ended up laughing about it and agreeing that the best thing to do was to forget that it ever happened.

An hour later and he knew why he had been so taken with Rose the first time they’d met. Besides being very pretty, Rose had an easygoing, happy nature that helped him to relax and overcome the shyness he normally felt in female company. Here was a girl who he could look in the face, a girl who didn’t make him avert his eyes and start blushing, like he usually did with the few other girls he’d met. He adored the way she cupped her chin in her hands and looked at him with her beautiful grey eyes when he spoke to her; it made him feel that he’d said something really interesting. He loved the golden freckles on her cheeks and nose. In fact he loved everything she said or did. Even the simplest of things like picking up a glass and putting it back down he found fascinating. He thought himself the luckiest man in the world to have a girl like her all to himself on a Saturday night.

During their conversation, he told her about going to England with Simon, and how he had spent some time with his family in London, but he didn't mention his overnight stay at the vicarage. As the evening wore on, the café became hot and stuffy as great clouds of cigarette smoke drifted over the tables. Collins was delighted when Rose suggested they take a walk and get some fresh air. They left the café and he thought he would burst with happiness when Rose slipped her arm through his. It was a clear, cold January evening with almost a full moon showing against a rare cloudless sky. They made their way through almost deserted streets until they came to a park near the outskirts of town. At length they stopped and sat on a wooden bench near a little statuette of a water nymph.

'It's a water fountain really,' Rose explained, 'but it doesn't work now. I found this little park on one of my days off. It's quite pretty in daylight, and very peaceful too. I don't think any soldiers ever come here.'

Collins thought it very clever of Rose to find somewhere in France that hadn't been touched by the war. 'It's a great place, Rose, really it is. You wouldn't think there was a war going on a few miles from here.'

'That's what I always think. This is my secret place, Davy. You're the only person I've bought here. You should be honoured.'

'Oh, I am, and I wouldn't dream of telling anyone else about it.'

Rose smiled at him and took hold of his hand. 'Well then, I suppose you deserve a reward for keeping my secret. What do you think, Davy, would a kiss be enough?'

He was so taken aback by her directness that didn't reply. Rose laughed and squeezed his hand. 'Don't look so shocked, Davy. It's just that you're a bit shy, so I thought I'd make it easy for you. Do I seem a bit forward to you?'

'No, of course not,' he blurted out, 'I think you're lovely, Rose, really I do.'

'Then kiss me, Davy Collins!'

Davy Collins leant forward and taking her in his arms, tentatively kissed her lips. They were soft and warm and tasted ever so faintly of the wine that she'd been drinking earlier. When their lips parted she smiled at him and her eyes had a mischievous glint in them.

'Hmm, not bad,' she said teasingly, 'but I think you can do better than that.'

He kissed her again, only harder and longer than the first time. It was the first lingering kiss he'd ever had in his life and it was even better than he had imaged it in his dreams. He held Rose tight and didn't want the kiss to end and he could tell by the way Rose clung to him that she didn't want it to end either. When, reluctantly they parted for air, it was only for a brief moment and then they began all over again. He could feel her body pressing against his and he grew bolder as he became more passionate. Putting his hands under her coat he felt the warmth of her body coming through her jumper. Rose made no protest as he ran his hands over the twin woollen peaks hidden underneath her coat. She didn't object either, when he slipped his hand under her jumper and cupped one of her breasts in his hand. Even through her brassiere he could feel her nipple hardening against the palm of his hand. He felt his manhood stiffening and a tingling sensation in his groin. It was similar to his experience with Simon, but this time it was better; this time there were no feelings of guilt attached. This was the real thing, the romance he'd been seeking for so long and thought he'd never ever find. He wanted to stay on the park bench forever kissing Rose's lips and exploring her body but after a while she gently pushed him away.

'I think that's enough for one night, Davy Collins. I don't want you getting too excited.'

'I'm sorry, Rose. I didn't mean to go so far. It's just that I ...'

Rose put her finger to his lips. 'It's all right Davy. I enjoyed it so there's nothing to be sorry about.'

'Can I see you again then, Rose, please.'

'I'd be disappointed if you didn't want to, Davy.'

As they stood up they heard the town clock chiming in the distance. He kissed her once more and then, holding hands tightly, they started off back to town. Rose thought it best to say goodnight to him before they reached the town square to avoid any coarse remarks from drunken soldiers. Collins reluctantly agreed and they parted, but not before they had arranged another meeting.

He was in seventh heaven as the transport dropped him off back in the Westhampton lines. Even the drunken presence of Sgt Watkins in the lorry on the journey back couldn't affect his happiness. Not that Watkins bothered him. The Quartermaster was so drunk he had slept all the way back and even now was having to be helped to his quarters by two of his men. He'd had a smashing evening and it was all because of Rose. He loved her of course; he was sure of it now. He was so happy and excited. He felt full of energy and wide-awake, and it was all down to Rose. She was a wonderful girl and she made him feel wonderful too. He felt so confident tonight, he was sure he could do anything he wanted to. Suddenly, an idea came rushing in to his head; an idea that was bold and dangerous and meant taking risks. But it might just help the padre to overcome the disappointment he was bound to feel after their talk tomorrow.

Chapter 25

'Come on, sir, *please*! It's Sunday morning; time for stand-to.' Collins waited patiently for some signs of life from Renton but he seemed dead to the world this morning. It was the second time he'd tried to wake him and received no response. He was about to place his hand on the padre's shoulder and give it a good shake when Renton's eyes slowly begin to open. 'Here's your tea, sir, it's time to get up and go round the trenches.'

Renton shook his head sleepily from side to side and pulled himself up into a sitting position in bed. It was too dark to see his face clearly, but judging by the smell of stale tobacco and alcohol that hit Collins nostrils, it was obvious that he'd had a night of heavy drinking. Was he still angry and upset with him, he wondered? Or perhaps he'd just had a boozy night in the officer's mess. Renton swung his legs out from under the blankets and sat on the edge of his bed, Collins handed him his mug of tea and took a better look at him. The padre's face looked pale and bloated and his eyes were bloodshot; he looked like a man with a good hangover. He gulped down his tea and handed back the empty mug. Not a word had escaped his lips since he woke up but Collins was used to that; Renton rarely said much to him until after breakfast. Normally Collins would remain in the officers' dugout as long as he could in order to stay warm, but not this morning. He was tired and if he didn't hurry up he would be late for stand-to. Leaving Renton to get dressed on his own, he hurried away to his quarters to pick up his rifle and get to his stand-to position.

Sitting on the fire-step, Collins eyes began to close. He started to doze off but luckily for him a sharp dig in the ribs from the soldier sitting next to him woke him before any of the NCOs had a chance to spot him sleeping on duty. To help stay awake he started to think about what he was going to say to Renton later in the morning. It wasn't going to be an easy conversation that was for sure. Despite what had occurred in England, and what had been said to him on the boat, he knew he had a lot to thank Simon Renton for. He had saved him from returning to a fighting unit. Who knows what might have happened to him if he had gone back to his old section? He might be dead by now; he knew for a fact that one of his former section mates had been killed on a recce patrol recently. Of course Renton knew it too, and was bound to remind him of that fact. Well he had done Renton a favour now and that evened things up.

Funny to think it was only just over two months ago that he had first started working for the padre. Only two months! With so much having happened between them, it seemed like a lifetime now. But it was some comfort to know that at last the regiment might be moving out of their present position. There were strong rumours flying about that the regiment was being pulled out of the line for a while. Who knows, if the worst came to the worst and Renton did get rid of him, the war might be over soon and the regiment might never have to come back. All sorts of thoughts raced through his mind at the prospect of the war ending quickly. Going home and getting demobbed for a start. Then back to the market and being greeted as a war hero with the prospect of getting a better job than he'd had before. He would see more of Rose of course; she would easily get a job nursing in an East London hospital. He wanted to court Rose properly and introduce her to his parents. After a while, when they'd saved up enough, they would get married and have a little place of their own; start a family probably. His mind was far away from the trenches now, lost in a dream world somewhere with Rose. A place where there were houses to look at, new furniture to buy, bright curtains to hang at windows, and pretty pictures to put on walls.

'Come on, Collins! Do you want to spend all morning here! Didn't you hear what I said? Stand-to is ended; you can get back to your normal duties.'

The Corporal's words bought him sharply back to reality. Dreams of Civvie Street would have to wait a while longer.

Renton trudged wearily around doing his hated Sunday rounds. He stumbled through the muddy trenches uttering a few words of encouragement here, or saying a suitable prayer there. He knew it was a waste of time and that he was speaking to tired, lethargic soldiers who neither wanted, nor cared about religion, but he went through the motions all the same. It didn't help that he was having a hard time trying to think about religion himself this morning. The truth of the matter was that he couldn't think of anything apart from his impending talk with Davy Collins. He had been thinking so much about what he was going to say that he'd had to be reminded twice to keep his head down below the sandbagged parapet, but with Davy uppermost in his mind, German snipers were the least of his worries at the moment. It was vital to his future happiness to deal with the boy properly. He had got to handle him in the right way this time and be patient with him. Much as he wanted to make love to him again, he couldn't afford to rush in clumsily and antagonise him like he'd done on the boat. He had to convince him that he wanted a truly loving relationship with him. Davy was still a boy really, and obviously inexperienced in the ways of the world. It was only natural of him to lack confidence and be full of self-doubt about the two of them becoming lovers. So it was vital he regain his trust and admiration again, just as he had done before the trip to England. After all, he was a boy of only limited intelligence and, although his knowledge had improved in the last couple of months, his education was still only quite basic. Davy was no match for him in a discussion on morals or sex, and his resolve wouldn't be as strong as his if a battle of wills broke out between them. What had happened on the boat had been stupid and careless. He had taken him for granted and when he rejected him, he'd acted badly and scared him off. It was a setback, but not necessarily a disaster. He knew Davy liked him; it wasn't beyond the bounds of possibilities that he loved him without really being aware of it. What the boy needed was a little more time, time to accept the fact that he wasn't like other boys. As soon as Davy accepted the fact that he had homosexual tendencies, everything would be fine between them.

He would start by apologising for his behaviour on the boat. He would not go as far as to grovel, but it would do no harm to show Davy that he had a humble, contrite side to his nature. He had already shown his generous side by allowing him to go into town, a decision that had caused him to spend most of the night wondering if the boy was being led astray again. On top of his worries about Davy, there was Watkins to think about. His latest visit had been a very scary one. For some reason he appeared very worried about his property in the chapel being discovered and had renewed his threats of old, only with more menace than before.

At last the message came down the line that stand-to had finished. Renton put away his bible and thrust his cold hands deep into his coat pockets. It was time to head back to the relative warmth of the officers' mess. Figuring out how to deal with his problems had resulted in drinking more than he'd intended last night but thankfully the hammering in his head was beginning to ease now. He wasn't bothered about breakfast. He wasn't hungry and the food would be lousy as usual, but he looked forward to having Davy waiting on him. As he began his long walk back to the mess Renton started to smile, but it wasn't a smile of happiness. It was a grim, humourless smile, an involuntary action of the facial muscles that resulted in a sad, downcast look to his face like that of a child that has been hurt or upset. He paused briefly to wipe his eyes on the sleeve of his jacket and then carried on walking.

Like Renton, Ron Watkins head also ached this morning. Worse still, his mouth felt like the inside of a Turkish wrestler's jock strap. Still, it had been a good night, or at least what he could remember of it, so it was worth a little pain. He poured himself another mug of coffee and looked at his watch. It was five minutes to ten, almost time for Cpl Brown to put in an appearance. Brown wouldn't want to miss the big show; wouldn't want to miss the humiliation of Griggs and his men after they'd searched the store and found bugger all. Ten o'clock on Sunday morning Watkins had been told by his informant, the raid would definitely be at ten o'clock sharp. A throaty chuckle escaped Watkins mouth in anticipation of the fun ahead. This was one Sunday morning that wasn't going to be dull. A knock on the door interrupted his thoughts. Without waiting for an invitation, Cpl Brown rushed in and closed the door hastily behind him.

'They're here Sarge! Griggs and four redcaps are heading this way. Be here in a couple of minutes at the most, I reckon.' Brown's voice was loud with excitement and he was grinning from ear to ear.

'Right then, let's give them all the cooperation we can, shall we.' Watkins pulled a bunch of keys from his pocket and tossed them Cpl Brown. 'Right then, open up the store, let the dog see the rabbit as they say.'

As Cpl Brown entered the storeroom Watkins picked up his mug of coffee. He was just about to put it to his lips when he heard a loud gasp from the storeroom. After a couple of seconds, Cpl Brown's ashen face suddenly appeared in the open doorway.

'Jesus Christ! Oh fucking Jesus Christ! We're fucked Ron, we've had it!'

'What the hell's the matter with you, Brownie? You look as if you've seen a ghost.'

'It's all the stuff from the chapel, Ron, it's in the fucking store, laid out on the floor.'

'*WHAT*!' The mug dropped from Watkins fingers. Pushing Cpl Brown roughly aside he rushed into the storeroom. What he saw stopped him dead in his tracks. Neatly laid out in rows on the floor of his storeroom was everything that he had hidden in the chapel! It wasn't hard to see how the stuff had got there. A hole in the storeroom wall and a heap of broken sandbags told their own story. If only he hadn't got so dammed pissed last night he would surely have heard the noise of the break in. He stood hypnotised, unable to tear his eyes away from the damming evidence lying on the floor in front of him.

Cpl Brown's hysterical voice brought him out of his trancelike state. 'Christ Ron, we'll do time for sure when they find this little lot, what the hell we gonna do?'

'Do,' Watkins snarled at his subordinate, 'there's nothing we can do you fool! Griggs will be here any second.' Picking up a bottle of brandy from the floor he threw it with all his might at the wall and watched it smash into small pieces. 'That filthy double crossing little arse bandit Renton! He's the one that's done this to me. So help me I'll kill the fucker for this, padre or no padre.' A red mist descended in front of his eyes. He ran to his desk and opened the bottom drawer. Pulling out his Luger pistol, he rammed home the ammunition clip and cocked the weapon ready for firing.

Cpl Brown looked at him in horror. 'For fucks sake Ron, don't do anything stupid.'

'Shut your mouth! Nobody makes a fool of me, Brownie, *nobody*! Mark my words; that fucking queer padre's given his last sermon on this earth. Now open that fucking door and let's get out before we're caught here like rats in a trap.'

As they piled out the door Watkins glanced over his shoulder and saw Griggs and his redcaps approaching. They were less than a fifty yards away and closing in fast. Ignoring the shouts for him to stay where he was, Watkins ran from the store as fast as his legs would carry him.

Chapter 26

Renton and his orderly stood facing each other on a patch of ground outside the chapel. They had walked from the officers' mess together and Collins believed that the earlier bad mood between them had disappeared. The padre had even been talkative as they walked along asking him how many he thought would turn out for the Sunday service. But now they'd arrived at the chapel, Collins knew the serious talking was about to start and he felt nervous again. He felt so tense he forgot what he'd planned to say but to his relief it was Renton that spoke first.

'I owe you an apology for my behaviour on the boat, Davy. I'm sorry, truly I am. Please forgive me, it won't ever happen again, I assure you.'

Collins didn't want to be reminded about what had happened on the boat, but all the same, it was good of Renton to apologise to him. After all, he was an officer, he didn't *have* to apologise to a mere private.

'It's all right, Simon. I've forgotten all about it, really I have.'

'No, it's not all right, Davy. I don't blame you for being cold towards me since we got back. I behaved badly and used foul language and I shouldn't have done. It was the drink talking, not me. I wouldn't normally say such horrible things to you Davy because I love and respect you too much.'

‘I respect you too, Simon.’ Collins said. He was thinking of the right words to use to let Simon down gently. ‘I always have respected you. It’s just that I can’t....’

‘Love me?’ Simon interrupted. ‘Is that what you were going to say, Davy? Listen, I realise it’s all been a bit much for you to take in, but all you need is a little time to think things through.’ Simon placed his hands on the boy’s shoulders and smiled at him. ‘After all, you do like me, don’t you?’

‘Yes, of course I do, and I’ll always be grateful to you for letting me work for you.’ He had to tell Simon about Rose and make him understand how he felt about her, but he didn’t get the chance.

‘Well then,’ Simon continued, ‘let’s just see how we get on for a while, shall we? You obviously need more time to come to terms with what’s happening so I promise not to rush you into anything, all right?’

Collins knew he couldn’t let things go on like this any longer, he had to tell Renton the truth, whatever the consequences might be. Taking a deep breath, he plunged in. ‘Before you say anything more Simon, there’s something I have to tell you. You’ve been good to me and I wouldn’t hurt you for the world, but there’s something you must know, I...’

The sound of pounding footsteps distracted him from completing his sentence. He turned around and to his amazement saw Sergeant Watkins running straight towards them holding something in his right hand. Collins couldn’t make out what it was at first but as Watkins drew closer, he saw with alarm that it was a gun that the Quartermaster was brandishing. Collins glanced across at the padre who had moved closer to him. Simon's face had gone a deathly shade of white; he too must have seen the gun in Watkins hand.

The Quartermaster stopped a few yards away from them. He was breathing heavy from the exertion of running and his dishevelled hair flopped down over his bright red face. Sweat was running off his forehead and into his eyes; eyes that were glaring at Renton with pure hatred. Collins was scared. He had never seen such an expression of evil on anybody's face as that on Sergeant Watkins. The Quartermaster raised his arm and pointed the gun at Renton.

'You lousy, queer bastard, Renton! You've got this coming in spades, you fucker! You fucked with the wrong person this time. I'll teach you to play God Almighty with me!'

Collins saw a look of bewilderment come to Simon's face. 'What are you talking about, Watkins? Have you taken leave of your senses? You must be mad waving a gun around like that.'

Collins heard shouting close by. Looking past Watkins, he saw a group of Military Policemen a few yards away. They were heading for them and were carrying their rifles at the ready. With a bit of luck they would arrive in time to take the gun off Watkins.

Watkins gave a quick glance over his shoulder in the direction of the approaching redcaps and then turned his attention back to Renton. 'They're too late to save you padre. They may get me, but I'm gonna kill you first.'

Collins saw Watkins take fresh aim at Simon and knew he had to do something to gain a few vital seconds of time. 'NO, stop! It wasn't him,' he cried out. 'It wasn't Simon. It was me who put the stuff back in your storeroom. The padre knows nothing about it.'

Watkins half turned and levelled the gun at Davy's head. 'You!' he hissed. 'Of course, I should have guessed nancy boy here wouldn't have the guts to do something like that. Well you're going pay for it now, kid. A fucking nobody like you ain't gonna get the better of me.'

Collins eyes were riveted to the gun in Watkins hand. The little black hole at the end of the barrel was staring straight at his head and he could see Watkins finger tighten on the trigger; he knew for certain he was going to die but was too paralysed with fear to move a muscle. Suddenly he heard an anguished cry of *'NO!'* as Simon jumped in front of him a fraction of a second before Watkins pulled the trigger. He heard a roar of gunshots and his head exploded with pain. He fell to the ground and everything went black.

He was a prisoner in the inky darkness of a deep pit. He wanted to climb out but his limbs felt heavy as lead and an overwhelming desire to sleep kept coming over him. Struggling to open his eyes he could see light coming from above him and beyond the light he could hear muffled voices; but they were too far away for him to make out what was being said. He desperately wanted to see who and what was beyond the light. Thrusting his body upwards, he made one final effort to climb out of the darkness and into the light beyond.

'He's opened his eyes, he's coming round.'

'Yes, give him a minute to get his bearings, he'll be all right.'

The voices were real. It must all have been a dream. He blinked as his eyes became accustomed to the bright light. The left side of his head ached terribly and the inside of his mouth felt incredibly dry and swollen. As his eyes started to focus properly he realised that he was lying on his back looking up at a high ceiling. Slowly, and with the pain in his head increasing as he moved, he leant forward a fraction and tried to make out his whereabouts. To his surprise he was lying in a bed between clean sheets and blankets.

'Well done, Collins! You had us all worried there for a moment I can tell you.'

He recognised the voice. Turning his head to the side, he saw Captain Beamish looking down at him. Standing next to him was a man wearing a long white coat.

'Wh...what happened? Where am I?' It took an effort to get the words out. His throat hurt and his lips felt as dry as dust. The man in the white coat picked up a glass of water and gently supporting the back of Collins head with his hand, held the glass to his lips. After a few sips of water, his throat felt much better.

'I'm Dr Rennie,' the man said, 'and you're in a ward at the casualty clearing station. You were hit on the side of the head by a bullet and knocked unconscious.'

Putting down the glass of water, the doctor pulled out a watch from his pocket with one hand and took hold of Collins wrist with his other hand. 'You've had a lucky escape my lad, if that bullet had gone a bit more to the left, you'd be dead. As it is you'll have a nasty headache for a week or two but otherwise you'll be all right.

The doctor paused and looked at his watch. 'Fine, your pulse is fairly steady. I'll leave you with the Captain here while I go and get a nurse to make you more comfortable.'

Captain Beamish pulled up a chair and sat next to Collin's bed. 'Looks like I picked a good time to visit you, Collins. The doctor was just telling me he didn't know when you'd regain consciousness and then, lo and behold, you suddenly wake up! Do you remember what happened to you?'

The words of Captain Beamish brought a vivid image to Collins mind. An image of Sergeant Watkins waving a gun at him! Yes, that was it! He remembered now. Watkins had a gun and was shooting at him, trying to kill him. Simon was there too. Oh God, Simon! What had happened to Simon? 'Simon… I mean the padre, sir. Is he all right? Is he here too?'

'I'm afraid not, Collins.' Captain Beamish paused for a second. 'I'm sorry to have to tell you this, but the padre is dead. Sergeant Watkins killed him. He would have finished you off too if the Military Police hadn't shot him down.'

He stared at Captain Beamish in disbelief. 'Simon. Dead! Oh no, sir, it can't be true, it can't be! He jumped out in front of me. He saved my life. He can't be dead!'

'I'm very sorry, Collins, 'Captain Beamish said quietly, 'but it's true. It's tragic I know, but he is dead. According to the Military Police, Chaplain Renton died very bravely. They've told me that you and Mr Renton were in the way of Sergeant Watkins as he was fleeing from them and that he panicked and shot at you but Mr Renton intervened and got killed. Is that what you recall? Was it just like that? Or is there anything else you want to add, Collins?'

'No.' He whispered. He was fighting back the tears that were starting to well up in his eyes. 'No, there's nothing else to add, sir.'

'Good, I thought not. I know the padre was fond of you Collins, and I expect you liked him very much as well. I'm sad that he's dead too, but you must remember that terrible things happen in wartime. War does things to people like Sergeant Watkins and makes them act in horrible ways. Mr Renton was just as much a casualty of this war as any soldier that died on the battlefield. He may not have been killed in action, but he died bravely all the same, which I suspect was something he never would have envisaged. The best way you can repay him for saving your life is to try and forget what happened and look to the future. I think that's what Mr Renton would want you to do.' Captain Beamish stood up and patted him gently on the shoulder. 'Well, I'd best get going and leave you to recover in peace. Goodbye Private Collins.'

He waited until Captain Beamish had left and then buried his face in his pillow and wept. The tears ran freely down his face and soaked into the clean white pillowslip. Suddenly he was aware of a nurse's uniform leaning over him. The wearer of the uniform produced a handkerchief and gently wiped away his tears.

'Don't cry, Davy. You're safe now. I'm here to look after you.'

He looked up and saw Rose smiling down at him. 'Oh, Rose,' he whispered. 'I've got so much to tell you.'

She put her fingers over his lips and kissed him lightly on the forehead. 'Not now, Davy,' she said gently. 'You must get some rest. Tomorrow maybe, if you really want to. Go to sleep now. I promise to be here for you when you wake up.'

Collins lay there in silence looking up at Rose, looking into her bright young face.

He knew then that whatever else had gone before was forgettable. He had hope. He went back to sleep.

THE END

Lightning Source UK Ltd.
Milton Keynes UK
UKHW04f1330260918
329561UK00001B/3/P

9 781786 233301